LOVE & PEACE

HOLIDAYS IN HALLBROOK, BOOK 3

ELSIE DAVIS

Sweet Promise Press
PO Box 72
Brighton, MI 48116

What's our Sweet Promise? It's to deliver the heart-warming, entertaining, clean, and wholesome reads you love with every single book.

From contemporary to historical romances to suspense and even cozy mysteries, all of our books are guaranteed to put a song in your heart and a smile on your face. That's our promise to you, and we can't wait to deliver upon it...

We release one new book per week, which means the flow of sweet, relatable reads coming your way never ends. Make sure to save some space on your eReader!

Check out our books in Kindle Unlimited at sweetpromisepress.com/Unlimited

♡

Download our free app to keep up with the latest releases and unlock cool bonus content at
sweetpromisepress.com/App

♡

Join our reader discussion group, meet our authors, and make new friends at
sweetpromisepress.com/Group

♡

Sign up for our weekly newsletter at
sweetpromisepress.com/Subscribe

♡

And don't forget to like us on Facebook at
sweetpromisepress.com/FB

CHAPTER ONE

"Turn left onto Christmas Tree Lane. Continue for two point two miles. Your destination will be on the right." The level tones of the woman's British accent didn't vary as she repeated the directions.

Megan maneuvered her way down the back road, grateful they would arrive at the log cabin before it got pitch black outside. The snowflakes were getting bigger and falling with splats against the windshield, reducing her visibility. The wipers tried to keep up as they pushed the wet snow to the sides of the glass, the white hard mass causing the blade to *thunk* against it with every swish.

Having never been to the cabin before, she peered at each mailbox they passed, trying to make out a number. The last thing she wanted to do was show up at the wrong house, or worse still, get stuck somewhere. The realtor said it was the last driveway on the road, but they didn't exactly tell her when the road ended.

The cabin had been her mother's favorite place to visit, and she'd invited Megan on several occasions, but life was always too busy and had managed to get in the way every time. Being a single parent meant having almost zero time to relax, much less vacation. Her mother's death six months ago from breast cancer had left a great void in Megan's heart, although it was her husband Andy's death years ago that had started her emotional shutdown. It was her daughter and her sister who managed to keep her grounded and moving forward.

Her mother had described the place as magical, which was exactly what they all needed this Christmas. Her sister Rachael's suggestion to come here for their first Christmas without their mom had been perfect. When they'd discovered the place available for rent, it was as if their mom was smiling down upon them from heaven.

Megan had packed all her mother's Christmas decorations and loaded them in the SUV with one simple plan in mind—honor their mother in her favorite place for her favorite holiday of the year.

These past few months had been difficult without her mom around. The bond they'd shared had been deeper than a normal mother-daughter relationship. Susan Milner had been her best friend, confidante, and second parent to Rebecca after Andy's skiing accident.

Her mother loved her daughters, but her granddaughter had become the center of her world. It had been hard for Becca to understand why her daddy was never coming home, while at the same time trying to understand why her mommy's job kept her from returning home right away. Without either parent available, Becca had turned to her grandmother for comfort, a bond forming between the two that left them inseparable.

It hadn't taken Megan long to get a hardship discharge from the Air Force, but nothing took away the guilt she felt for not being there when her daughter needed her the most. It had taken her everything she possessed to pick up the pieces of her shattered heart and life and move on. She couldn't have done it without the help of her mother.

Glancing in the rearview mirror, she drew in a deep breath and then exhaled. It was hard to believe three years had passed since Andy's fatal accident, but Becca was seven now, and the difference from preschooler to second-grader was nothing short of amazing. Megan was looking forward to spending some quality time with her daughter. Lately, her work hours had been grueling, something she vowed to change in the future. But for now, this trip would have to make up for all her absences at school events.

"Mom, are we there yet?" Becca covered her mouth as she yawned.

"Yes, honey. The GPS says it's another couple of miles. We just need to go slow because the snow is starting to cover the roads, and I'm trying to be super careful."

Her daughter had been patient for the last four hours in the car, mostly because she was listening to her own music or playing games on her tablet. But apparently, her electronics had a limited hold on her attention. Becca preferred more active things, just like her father. This trip would do her good and give her a chance to play outdoors and embrace her free-spirited side. Living inside the city limits of Boston and having a mother tied on a short leash to the hospital with long hours didn't give a kid much chance to get out and play.

"Look. A deer." Becca sat up straighter, her face pressed to the window.

"The snow makes it easier to spot them. If you keep a close look-out, you might see more, especially if they look our way and our headlights are reflected in their eyes."

The snow was getting thicker on the road, the lines now completely gone.

She hoped Rachael was already at the cabin because it wouldn't be long before the roads were impassable. The road crews would be far more concerned with keeping the streets in Hallbrook plowed for the local town residents than the few homes located on the back-country roads just outside the town limits.

"The snow is pretty, and I can't wait to play in it tomorrow. Can we make snow cream, Mom? Did you bring the evaporated milk and vanilla?" Megan caught Becca's hopeful expression in the rearview mirror.

"Of course, honey. All this fresh snow will make terrific snow cream. I'm sure your Aunt Rachael will be on board to try our special treat." She *had* forgotten it, and the extra trip back to the store had put them on the road later than she'd intended. But she'd also known her daughter wouldn't forget the delicious concoction they made every year, and the last thing she wanted to do was disappoint her. Megan was trying to do the job of both parents, which sometimes meant going out of her way even when she was exhausted at the end of a long workday.

5

"Yay!" Her daughter's smile made it all worthwhile.

They passed several farmhouses lit up against the darkened sky. Megan wished they had time to stop and take a picture, although she knew from experience it wouldn't come out first-rate because the flash would reflect off the snow and white out the photo. But there was something magical about trying to capture the perfect shot that always kept her trying. This picturesque country Christmas setting would need to remain etched in her memory, at least for the time being.

The tracks in the road had dwindled to one set, and they were partially covered in snow.

"You have arrived at your destination." Megan flipped the GPS off and turned into the driveway of the well-lit log cabin home. Warm and welcoming and theirs for the week. *Nice place, Mom.*

"Look at the pretty tree." Becca spotted the decorated flagpole in the center of the yard, the colored lights twinkling brightly against the snowy backdrop in the shape of a Christmas tree. Her voice held a note of renewed excitement now that they'd arrived.

The vehicle tracks led right up to the house, disappearing into the garage. Megan breathed a sigh of relief, knowing her sister had already arrived. "It looks like Aunt Rachael is already here. Hopefully, she's got the house all warmed up. The bad news is she got the garage, and we're stuck unloading our luggage in the snow." Megan chuckled, shutting off the engine.

"Can I come back outside after we unpack?"

"Not tonight, sweetie. The thermometer says it's eighteen degrees outside, cold enough for us to freeze between the car and the house if we're not bundled up. Zip up your jacket and make sure your hood is on. Hopefully, it will warm up tomorrow, and we can play outside then. The snow isn't going anywhere anytime soon." Not to mention, Megan was tired. After an eight-hour day at the hospital, followed by a five-hour drive, it had been a long day.

"Okay, Mom." She loved Becca's sweet spirit. It was rare for her to argue about anything, a trait Megan considered a total blessing after she'd returned home to care for her daughter full-time.

Becca gathered up her belongings and stuffed them in her duffle bag.

Megan grabbed her phone, slid it in her purse, and hooked the straps over her shoulder to free up her hands. Her motto had always been to carry everything in one trip, if possible. And on a cold, snowy night, one trip sounded like the perfect plan.

Becca bounded out of the car and started dancing

in the driveway as she tried to catch the falling flakes.

Megan smiled as she popped open the trunk. "I know you're excited, and we will have plenty of time to play, I promise. Use the shoulder strap on your bag and put it over your head, and then you can carry our bag of snacks and toiletries for me. Time for teamwork."

"I'm coming. I can't believe we're finally here." Becca took hold of the two beach bags and headed for the front door. "Hurry, Mom. I just saw two eyes glowing in the dark. It looked like a wild animal." Her daughter pointed toward the side of the garage and ran for the porch and safety.

"I'm sure it's more afraid of you than you are of it." Megan glanced in the direction she'd pointed but didn't see a thing. She would check for tracks in the morning to err on the side of caution, but she wasn't too concerned at this point. "I don't see anything. It's probably long gone. I'll be right there."

Megan grabbed the rest of their belongings, leaving the boxes of Christmas decorations for another trip in the morning. She made her way up the snow-covered path to the front porch. After hoisting the largest of the cases onto the Adirondack chair, she tried to open the door.

Locked. *Of course.* Rachael was always sensible,

but this was one time Megan wished her sister had put sensibility aside.

Knock. Knock. Knock.

Brrrr. After coming from the heat of the car, the cold quickly replaced the warmth, seeping past the warm layer of her coat. They both tried to keep moving while they waited for Rachael to answer.

"Hurry, Mom. It's freezing out here." Becca's teeth started to chatter.

"I'm sorry, honey. She must not be able to hear our knock. Hang on, and I'll be right back. I left the letter with the code for the front door in the center console."

Megan slid her purse and the other bags off her shoulders and set them down. She carefully made her way back to the SUV, large snowflakes plastering to her hair and face. Thankfully, the confirmation letter was right where she'd put it, and it wasn't long before she was back under cover on the porch. A lantern light illuminating the entire area made it easy to read the code, and she punched in the numbers on the keypad.

The sound of the bolt sliding open on the first try was like a touch of Christmas magic answering their prayers. She pushed the door open and let Becca enter first. Megan picked up her luggage and followed her inside, using her foot to close the door behind her. She dropped everything in the tiled foyer area. It would be easier to wipe up any water tracks they left behind. Happy to be inside and out of the cold, she shrugged out of her jacket. She looked around the room, the cozy cabin as pleasing on the inside as it looked outside.

A large window in the living room framed out by curtains embellished with bear and deer images overlooked the front yard. The matching brown leather sofa and armchair were plush and inviting, an old red and white patchwork quilt thrown across the back. The furniture all looked handmade, with a classic rustic charm of their own. The huge ceiling beams added to the appeal, giving her an appreciation for the solidly built structure.

"Aunt Rachael started a fire." Becca dropped her bags on the couch and moved closer to the crackling fire, holding her hands out to warm them.

"Just be careful. No horsing around near the fireplace. This place is still cold, so she couldn't have been here long." Megan rubbed her arms vigorously, trying to warm up. The room smelled of fresh pine and cinnamon, two of her favorite Christmas scents.

She moved her suitcase and the other stuff into the room. "Rachael?" she hollered. Megan turned to Becca when Rachael didn't answer. "We need to haul our things to the bedroom and to the kitchen."

"Can't we warm up first? Please?" The slight whine in Becca's voice was to be expected, the effects of a long drive having taken a toll.

"I guess it won't hurt." Stopping to relax for a few minutes sounded heavenly and wouldn't change a thing. They had the entire night to unpack.

Becca slipped off her jacket and dropped it on top of her duffle bag.

They stood side by side, holding out their hands to the fire, trying to draw the heat toward their bodies as the flames danced and licked at the barely burned logs. Megan let out a deep breath. "Aunt Rachael must be out back getting more firewood. It was a great idea to warm up, and the fire is just getting toasty." Megan laughed, turning her backside to the flames.

"It's pretty here. And I love the flagpole out front. It's so Christmassy. But there are no decorations inside, so I'm glad we brought all of Grandma's stuff."

"Yes. It will be wonderful. I'll get the boxes of decorations out of the backseat of the car tomorrow when I can see better." And when it wasn't so cold outside.

"We have a flagpole at school. Charlie dared me to stick my tongue on it, but Jessie told me not to do it, that my tongue would stay stuck to the pole. She said Charlie was trying to trick me. He even double-dared me. I was afraid to try, but I don't like being called chicken. I try not to be afraid of anything."

Megan couldn't help but laugh, remembering another little girl who didn't believe it was true. Must be part of some ritual passed from generation to generation. Dare. Double-dare. Double-dog-dare. She knew the routine all too well.

"It's absolutely true. Unfortunately, when I was your age, I didn't believe it, and I did it anyway, even though I was warned. Worst thing ever. My tongue stayed stuck for almost ten minutes before the other kids stopped laughing long enough to get help. They had to use hot water and a washcloth to get my tongue off the pole. It hurt for days, and it was hard to eat. I can laugh about it now, but trust me, I wasn't laughing then."

Becca giggled. "I'm glad I didn't do it."

"You were smart. Always remember that even if you're dared to do something, you always have the right to say no. Being dared is never a reason to do anything, especially not something you're unsure of or don't want to do. Sometimes it's better to ask a grown-up first, just to be on the safe side. You should ask yourself if it's such a terrific idea, why do you have to be dared in the first place?"

"I hadn't thought of that." Becca was deep in

thought as Megan wrapped an arm around her shoulder and pulled her close. Her daughter was a smart girl, and Megan was proud of her for making the right choice all on her own.

A loud crashing noise startled them, sending a rush of adrenaline coursing through Megan. Her daughter screamed, the sound sending chills down Megan's spine. Instinctively, Megan pushed Becca behind her, going into defense mode to shield her daughter from danger.

Megan turned to discover the source of the sound and was stunned to see a man; his gaze shooting daggers at her. The logs at his feet explained the crashing sound, but not the man himself.

"I don't know who you think you are, or why you're here, but you don't belong and need to leave." The man's steely voice grated on her nerves. If looks were anything to go by, the man wasn't an ogre, nor did he set off any alarm bells in her internal radar, something she'd learned to trust over the years. But the haunted expression on his face, as well as his words, had managed to catch her off guard.

Her sister hadn't mentioned anything about bringing a friend, which left the question, just who was this guy? "There must be some mistake. I'm Megan Langley. My sister and I rented this place for the week. I assume you're the property manager." He looked the part, dressed in jeans and a leather bomber jacket, clean-cut, and delivering wood.

"Impossible." He ran a hand through his sandy-blond hair, his brow furrowed.

"Not impossible." His attitude and presence strained her good mood, keeping her on the defensive. "Look, mister, I'm not sure what you're doing here, but if you're not the property manager, then you're the one who needs to leave."

Megan took a few steps toward the couch and retrieved her jacket to fish the confirmation letter out of the pocket where she'd stuffed it after unlocking the door. "Becca, stay put." She shot her daughter a warning glance, letting her know she expected her to listen.

Unfolding the letter, Megan walked directly up to the man, who still hadn't moved an inch from the doorway of what she presumed led to the kitchen. She held up the document in her hand for his inspection. "*I* have a confirmation letter."

If anything, the strained look on his face intensified. "Impossible."

"You keep saying that, but this is proof." Megan wasn't backing down.

The man walked over to the front door where a coat tree stood, one she hadn't noticed on her way into the house. He retrieved a paper from the pocket of the suit coat hanging there. Without a word, he unfolded it and walked back toward her.

Megan had a bad feeling. The man seemed so assured of himself.

He handed her the letter. "My letter. Notice the date."

"Impossible." The word slipped out, echoing the man's own sentiment. "There must be some mix-up, some explanation. This much I do know, *we* are not leaving."

CHAPTER TWO

Sam had been outside no more than five minutes when he returned with an armload of wood. Coming through the doorway of the kitchen, the last thing he'd expected was to find a woman and a young girl warming their hands by the fire. Their heads bent together as they laughed, reminded him of another time he'd seen a similar picture. Time he could never recapture. A time that would forever leave his heart a broken shell and his soul in darkness. People were wrong. Time didn't heal all wounds.

The sight had been a sucker punch to the gut, but he'd forced the haunting image of his wife and daughter away, his sole thought getting rid of the unexpected and unwanted guests.

He hadn't counted on the flash of fire in her blue

eyes as she dug in and took a stand against leaving. *Gumption.* It was the best way to describe her not-backing-down attitude. He respected people who stood up for what they believed, just not when it got in his way. It didn't matter that she had a confirmation letter. His own was dated almost a year ago and hers only weeks old. It was obvious the rental company had made a mistake, and it was their mistake to fix.

A twinge of guilt flashed through him when he glanced at the daughter and thought of the Christmas holiday, but it was only a twinge. Not enough for him to step aside. "I'll call the property manager to settle this because we can't both stay." As he dialed the phone, a tiny shred of doubt began to form in his mind.

Cancel my trip to the cabin. Words he'd spoken almost three weeks ago to his secretary after second-guessing his intentions to return to the cabin this year. It was his way to be close to Laura and Lydia, although nothing would bring them back. It had taken hours for the insanity to pass and before he sent his secretary a new message changing his request. Megan Langley's presence and the date of her letter were too coincidental for his liking.

"It doesn't matter what the realtor says, I have a confirmation, and we're staying. This place holds a special meaning for us, and it's Christmas. I won't let you ruin the holiday for my daughter, my sister, or me." The woman stood protectively in front of the girl; her arms crossed in defiance.

She didn't understand. *They had to leave.* He rubbed the corded muscles in the back of his neck, hoping to ease his growing frustration and anger. Frustration at the situation, and anger with himself for his moment of indecision. He prayed it was all a mistake, and that Megan and her daughter would leave him in peace with his misery.

The girl peeked around her mother's back to watch him, her blonde curls and wide eyes all too much like Lydia. Sam closed his eyes, trying to block out the image. The pain in the region of his heart intensified. It felt like a surgeon's knife cutting open his heart without anesthesia. With precision, the knife split his heart in two, letting it bleed into his soul, completely overpowering his ability to think and breathe.

"Hallbrook Rentals. This is Jack Harper. How can I help you?"

Sam took a deep breath and tried to focus on the voice at the other end of the line. He shook his head to clear his mind. "This is Sam Wyatt. I'm at the cabin at fifteen Christmas Tree Lane, and there seems to be some mistake. I arrived a couple of hours ago, but a woman by the name of Megan Langley has also shown up with her daughter, claiming she rented the cabin. We both have confirmation letters."

"Hmmm, let me pull this up on the computer. There must be some mistake. I've never double-booked a rental before."

Sam knew the answer deep in his heart before Jack came back on the line. But how could he leave? The deep-seated guilt he felt for not being here the day his family died was no more than he deserved. It was all his fault and being here was his cross to bear.

"Ah, here it is. I found my notes. Your secretary canceled a few weeks ago, and Mrs. Langley book the following day. I'm sorry if that's not what you planned. I assumed she had the authority to cancel."

He'd hoped for a sliver of a chance he was mistaken about the cancellation, but the sliver had become a stick of truth. Unless he could find a way to entice Mrs. Langley to leave, he was at fault, and he would be the one doing the leaving.

Sam picked up on the Mrs. tag from the property manager, but Megan hadn't mentioned her husband coming up. He just needed to figure out Megan's weakness and capitalize on it. Everyone had a price. He just had to figure out hers.

"My secretary was acting on my behalf, but I

asked her to cancel the cancellation a few short hours later. She must not have gotten the message. Do you have anything else available?" If he was going to try and bribe Megan to leave, it would be better if he could offer her alternative accommodations. She mentioned the place was special to her, but it could be no more special to her than it was to him, and he was determined to win this battle.

"I've checked everything, and all of our rentals are completely full. It's Christmas, and places are usually booked almost a year in advance. I'm sorry. You could try the local motel here in Hallbrook. It's probably booked as well, but it's worth a shot. Other than that, the best option would be to head toward Lancaster."

Not the news he wanted to hear. It would be much harder to convince her to leave if there was nowhere for her to stay. She didn't seem like the kind of woman who would opt for a small-town motel for Christmas. After hanging up the phone, he turned back to Megan. There had to be something.

"Seems my secretary missed an important memo. I'm terribly sorry for the confusion. It would mean a lot to me to be able to stay. Perhaps there's a certain amount of money that might make it more agreeable for you to vacate the premises, let's say double the rent of the place?" Money wasn't an issue for him, but having the cabin was crucial. She could name her price, and he'd pay.

Deep lines formed across her forehead as she frowned, his comment falling on deaf ears. "I've already told you once, we are *not* leaving. I'm sorry your secretary made a mistake, but our confirmation is valid. Now, if you don't mind, my daughter and I need to unpack, and I need to check on my sister. I thought she'd be here by now." Her message was clear—she wanted him out. Now.

"Triple?" It was worth a shot, and he didn't know what else to do.

The grim set of her mouth as she shook her head brooked no opposition. Not even a flicker of doubt had shadowed her eyes. Money was not her Achilles' heel, at least not when it came to this cabin for Christmas.

Her decision left him no choice but to leave, the defeat like drinking vinegar—bitter and hard to swallow. He managed his life by demanding control and setting high expectations from all who worked for him, and he was used to people doing his bidding. Sam wasn't sure whether to be upset with Megan or applaud her backbone.

"I need to gather my things from the bedroom. I'll be out of here in five minutes. My apologies." He knew when he was beaten, even though it didn't happen often.

"Thank you. And I'm sorry, for what it's worth." Megan spoke from behind him just as he reached the hallway. Her sincerity was genuine, another surprise to a man who dealt in a cutthroat business world.

"Why can't he stay here, Mom? Maybe he has no place to go." The innocence of the child's sweet concern stopped him in his tracks.

Unable to resist, he turned back to stare at the girl, as if drawn to her by some unspeakable force. Sam gently smiled at the girl, momentarily forgetting everything he disliked about her, which at this point only amounted to the way she looked. "That's not the way things work in a grown-up world, but don't worry about me."

"Unfortunately, Becca, we can't all stay here." Megan's words brought him back to the current reality of the situation.

"No truer words could be spoken." Sam shook his head. There was no way he could stay with two glaring reminders of everything he'd lost.

He walked down the hall and into the master bedroom. Haphazardly tossing his clothes and toiletries back into his suitcase, he didn't care if they wrinkled. Leaving quickly was more important than the normal detailed order he liked for his life. It sounded as though he had no choice but to go to Lancaster and hope he'd find a place to stay. In the morning, he'd head for the airport, turn in the rental vehicle, and return home. Back to where he should have stayed in the first place.

He carried his suitcase down the hall. Megan and her daughter looked up like twin bobbleheads as he entered the living room.

"I've moved my SUV to the side to make it easy for you to get out." Megan had the good graces to look apologetic. It wasn't her fault, and he couldn't blame her for not wanting to spoil her daughter's Christmas. If the tables were turned, Sam would have insisted she leave.

"Thanks. The code is 5454 to get in the garage and you can close the door by the push button on the wall just outside the connecting kitchen door." He lifted his hand in farewell and headed for the garage. After pushing the button, the chains of the door engaged, pulling it up slowly and steadily. The motor noise strained against the weight of the door, echoing the strain on his own nerves. It had been considerate of her to move her vehicle to make things easy, even if her ulterior motive was simply to get rid of him faster.

Backing out far enough to let Megan pull in, he couldn't help but see the flagpole in the center of the front yard. He stopped, putting the SUV in park. After the garage door had closed, he climbed out and took a few steps toward the pole, his gaze automatically drawn to the spot where his daughter had made her last angel imprint in the snow. Every second of the video he kept on his phone replayed in his head. His vision blurred, and with a heavy heart, he turned and walked back to the vehicle. A movement in the front window of the cabin caught his attention.

Megan and her daughter stood there. Raw with emotion, Sam felt naked under their watchful gazes. He slid into the vehicle, put it in four-wheel drive, and backed down the driveway and out onto the street. The roads had gotten considerably worse since he arrived. He took it slowly, using the tracks visible in the snow to help him maneuver the winding road without finding one of the ditches on either side. It would seem folks around here knew enough to stay home in the storm, and that it was only visitors to town who were crazy enough to be out on a night like tonight.

Not that it had been his plan.

He tested the brakes to make sure the roads weren't icy beneath the snow. Satisfied, he turned onto Blue Spruce Road and started to make his way slowly down the mountain. The weather crew had originally thought they would get a few inches, but they'd missed the mark by quite a bit. There was already close to six inches blanketing the ground.

Visibility was reduced to about twenty feet in front of the SUV. The wipers clacked from side to side, shoving snow off the main part of the windshield and into a heap. The shoulders of the road blended with the road itself into a blanket of white with only the snow-covered guardrails and an occasional sign to help guide him.

A thunderous roar reverberated across the night sky. He'd heard of this phenomenon a few times but couldn't ever remember experiencing it. Thundersnow. He glanced at the dark sky to see if he could spot the lightning. The vehicle shook more like he was in the middle of an earthquake than a snowstorm.

The SUV started into a slide. Sam pumped the brakes, fighting for control as he muscled the vehicle back to the center of the road. Ten miles per hour felt like fifty in these conditions.

Seconds passed, and the thunderous roar grew louder, but he didn't see any lightning. Pieces of snow and ice fell across the road in chunks. Sam kept his eyes glued to the road, trying to avoid the obstacles and watch for oncoming traffic. He ventured a glance up the side of the mountain but couldn't see a thing except for the black of the night and the haze of snow blowing like a blizzard in his headlights. Stretching his head from one side and then to the other, he tried to release the ever-growing tension in his neck.

The size of the snow chunks falling in the road grew larger, the continuous roar growing louder as seconds passed. Adrenaline shrieked through his body, fear of the unknown gripping him. He came around a bend in the road and slammed on his breaks as he came face-to-face with a mountain of snow cascading across the road, the white blanket marred by dark patches of trees glinting in his head-lights. Seconds felt like minutes as the vehicle finally came to a stop.

Avalanche. Sam shoved the SUV into reverse, trying to escape the fury of the snow barreling down the mountainside and the possibility of being buried alive. The vehicle slid to the side of the road, the back tires landing in a bank of snow. His heart pounded in his chest, threatening to explode.

He slammed the gearshift into drive and tried to pull forward, desperate to turn the vehicle around and get as far away as possible. The high-pitched whir from the tires as they spun out against the slick snow wasn't a good sign. He was stuck.

Chunks of snow and debris were still tumbling down the slope, some falling off to the sides and onto the vehicle. It sounded like someone taking a hammer to the metal roof.

And then there was silence.

He looked up the slope of the mountain and back at the wall of snow across Tinsel Pass, the only way back to Hallbrook and White Mountain Highway. It had come to a stop, except for a few small chunks still finding their final resting place.

Sam laid his head on the steering wheel, his hands wrapped around the cold, hard leather in a tight grip. He let out a deep breath, trying to calm the pounding in his chest. He needed to pull it together and get out of here just in case there were any smaller, secondary avalanches triggered by the first one.

He put the gearshift in drive and then in reverse. He did this repeatedly, trying to rock the vehicle back and forth to gain the leverage needed for the tires to get traction. The third try almost worked. *Come on, baby.*

He tried again. *Bingo.* The tires grabbed and pulled him forward, propelling him back onto the road. Sam turned the vehicle away from the mountain of snow lying on the road and drove back to safety around the bend.

Pulling over to call 9-1-1, he brushed his hand back through his hair and rubbed his neck. He took several deep breaths as he waited for them to answer. If he hadn't stopped in the driveway to remember Lydia and her angel, he would've been buried alive. Lydia's angel had saved his life, but the question remained, was he worth saving?

Two years ago, he'd been late getting to the cabin because of a business meeting. It should have been him driving the car the night his family died. Maybe he could've saved them from going over the cliff into the ravine. He'd put business ahead of his family and paid a heavy price for the mistake. One he'd never be able to fix, unlike those of his father.

His father's mistakes had driven every decision, every deal, every everything for so many years that Sam had lost sight of what was most important—his family. Soon he would be free of his father's debts and could live for himself, something he wasn't even sure he knew how to do anymore. Besides, what was the point? He'd already lost everything truly important.

"9-1-1 dispatch. How may I help you?" The woman's voice snapped his attention back to the present.

"My name is Sam Wyatt. I need to report an avalanche out at Tinsel Pass. I'm on the Christmas Cove side."

"Thank you for calling in. Is there anyone else

with you, and are you okay?" Her calm voice was reassuring.

"It's just me, and I'm okay." There were several degrees of okay, but he knew what the dispatcher was asking. "I don't know if anyone was coming from the other direction, but based on the tracks, no one else was on the road headed toward town. There is at least one woman I know of that was expected out this way sometime soon, but I don't know much else about her, just what her sister told me."

"Well, at least we know one direction was clear of traffic. Let's just pray no one else is trapped. I've sent a message and notified the authorities, and they are on their way. Can you be reached at this number once we know more information, Mr. Wyatt? Do you have a place to stay while you wait?"

"Yes, you can call me on this number. And, no, I don't have a place to stay. The sooner someone lets me know how long it will take to clear out this mess, the better." The idea of sitting in the cold and dark for hours held little appeal. At least he had a full tank of gas.

"Will do. Try to stay warm, and I'll notify you once we know more."

Sam sat in the quiet confines of his car, the heater and running engine the only sounds intruding on his thoughts. Alone in the dark, he let himself remember another snowy night two years ago. The snow had turned to an icy mix, making the roads more dangerous. Images of what Laura must have experienced the night the accident claimed their lives haunted his nights but sitting here in the dark on the side of the road, the images in his head were more real. It was as though he could feel their terror.

Sam wiped the sweat from his forehead and gripped the wheel. *Why? Why?*

He knew why. Jacob Miller. His father.

Respected man of the community, loving husband, and father, at least he had been until he destroyed his legacy when he got into financial trouble and became embroiled in a Ponzi scheme. His legacy now was that of an incarcerated thief, something that almost destroyed Sam's mother and something Sam bore like a red-letter T on his forehead. *Thief.*

Sam's friends had abandoned and ridiculed him. He wasn't to be trusted. The apple doesn't fall far from the tree. He'd heard it all. And it was the reason Sam had changed his name, preferring the anonymity of his mother's maiden name as he tried to establish some credibility in the business world, vowing to restore honor to his mother by repaying every single client his father had swindled.

To Samuel Wyatt Miller, son of Jacob Miller,

business doors were closed. But to Sam Wyatt, son of nobody infamous, doors opened based on his knowledge, then on his experience, and then finally, on his reputation when it came time to negotiate multi-million-dollar investment deals. His father's failures had controlled his entire life, and it was the reason Sam hadn't been there for Laura and Lydia. Even now, if anyone ever found out who he was, it would all come crashing down around him.

Within ten minutes, his phone rang, jolting him out of the dark place he'd gone.

"Mr. Wyatt?"

"This is him." Instantly alert and focused, Sam longed to hear the words that would allow him to escape from the mountain and head back to New York City, his desire to leave now greater than his desire to stick around.

"This is Mary, from the 9-1-1 service. I've spoken with the local authorities, and there's nothing they can do until morning. It appears the avalanche could be wide enough that it might take them a couple of days to get a plow all the way through. They don't know for sure but want you to be prepared. Is there any chance you can get us some information from your friend about the woman you thought might be out on the roads? It might help us to locate her and ascertain one way or the other if anyone is trapped."

Friend. Not a likely word Megan would use to describe him.

She wouldn't be happy to see him again, but there was no choice but to return, tell her what happened, and get the necessary information. "I can talk to the sister and let you know."

"Perfect. And thanks. Can you stay with her tonight? It's supposed to drop into the single digits."

"Easier said than done. I won't exactly be a welcome guest, but I guess I don't have much of a choice. Thanks for calling me back."

Sam prayed Megan's sister wasn't trapped under the mountain of snow. But while they waited to find out, he would offer his support and strength. It was the least he could do if it meant he wouldn't be sleeping in the car all night.

CHAPTER THREE

Megan had felt bad for making Sam leave, but not bad enough to stop him. After she came back inside, his headlights shining through the front window had caught her attention. She'd been surprised to see him standing in the middle of the front yard, the Christmas lights giving her just enough glow to see a look of twisted torment on his face.

The temptation to change her mind and call him back inside had warred within her as he'd pulled out of the driveway, his tail lights disappearing into the snowy darkness. The roads had to be treacherous, but she had to think about her daughter's safety first. They didn't know a thing about the man, and there was no way she was letting a stranger hang around any longer than necessary—even if the stranger did appear to be a normal, nice guy, just one who seemed to have the weight of the world on his shoulders.

It was an expression Megan knew all too well, having seen it in the mirror many times over the past few years, and more so since her mother's death. She turned away from the window, hoping to ease the guilt filling her. She checked her phone, hoping for some word from Rachael. But if her sister was driving, it was better she wasn't on the phone, especially in this weather. The snow was coming down heavier, and Megan googled for weather updates. Eight to twelve inches? Whatever happened to two to four? This couldn't be good.

She forced a smile for Becca's sake, not wanting to worry her daughter. "I'll put our stuff in the master bedroom since it's the two of us. Aunt Rachael can have the other room. Why don't you come along and put on your pj's, and I'll see what we have for snacks to hold us until she gets here. Unfortunately, she was the one tasked with bringing the food for the first couple of days. Maybe that's what's keeping her. You know how she is, last-minute at everything."

"Okay, Mom. I get dibs on the cheese and peanut butter crackers."

"Sure. But you're going to turn orange if you keep eating those things."

"That's silly. You're just saying that because you want them. We could share."

Megan laughed. "Thanks. That's mighty generous since I think our choices are limited to crackers, chips, and chocolate."

"Sounds like my kind of dinner." Her daughter's laughter soothed some of the tension building in her neck and shoulders. She just needed to focus on Becca, and all would be well. It had to be.

"Maybe to you, but it's not exactly healthy."

Becca shrugged, and they headed down the hall with their luggage. After hanging up a few items, Megan left Becca to unpack and returned to the living room. She was grateful Sam had started the fire, and she tossed in another log, not wanting to take any chances on letting it go out.

What if they got snowed in or the power went out? The pile of wood Sam had brought in might not be enough to get them through the night and keep them warm. Maybe after Rachael got here, she should bring in more. Just in case. Megan found a couple of waters and a surprise bag of beef jerky she'd tossed in the snack bag at the last minute. It was better than just crackers. She laid a blanket down on the floor in front of the fire and spread out their dinner, trying to make it like a picnic, and therefore more fun for Becca.

Her daughter had an amazing way of simplifying life, but after she left the room, Megan couldn't shake the dread that filled her with each passing minute with no word from her sister. Rachael and Sam were both out in this mess—one coming here and one going, but both out in the blizzard because of her. With Rachael, it was by mutual agreement, but in Sam's case, it was entirely her fault. She should have stilled the doubt in her mind and trusted her instincts, something she'd learned to do quite well in the Air Force.

It didn't take Becca long to change, and the two of them settled down in front of the fire to share their so-called *dinner* and a game of Hearts. It was her daughter's favorite card game, and it helped keep Megan's mind from dwelling on the fact Rachael still hadn't shown up. Two more phone calls with no answer later, she laid the phone on the floor, determined not to call again for at least five minutes.

Four calls and twenty minutes later, a set of headlights flashed across the wall as a vehicle pulled into the driveway. Megan breathed a sigh of relief and moved to the window to watch her sister's arrival. Becca came to stand next to her.

"That doesn't look like Aunt Rachael's car. Who is it, Mom? It looks like that man's truck."

Becca was right. It did appear to be Sam's vehicle,

but he'd left almost an hour ago. "I think you're right." Megan frowned, wondering why he would have come back. It was great to know he was okay, but his return brought up a new set of worries.

"But you said he left to go home." Becca didn't forget a thing, her question echoing Megan's own.

"I thought so, too. I guess we're about to find out why he's back." Megan pulled her phone from her back pocket to see if Rachael had tried to reach her. Nothing.

"Can I let him in? He must be freezing."

Megan confirmed the approaching figure was, in fact, Sam. "That's fine, honey."

Becca ran for the door and pulled it open.

Sam stood on the porch; his hand raised as if to knock.

"Mr. Sam. You're back!" Becca's enthusiastic greeting didn't have an ounce of effect on Sam. His stoic demeanor was enhanced by lines of tension that rippled across his face.

"I'm sorry to bother you again. But there's been an avalanche, and no one's getting through the pass or leaving the area. They won't know until morning how long it will take to clear. Have you heard from your sister?"

Avalanche? She shook her head, his words beginning to sink in.

Rachael.

His gaze held hers, unyielding, as if trying to give her strength. "No," she croaked. *Please, Lord. Not again. Not Rachael.* Megan wrapped an arm around her midsection while she dialed Rachael's number again. She rocked as she waited, praying her sister would answer this time. The call rolled automatically to voice mail.

"I'm sorry. I'm sure she'll be fine. Come sit by the fire, and we can wait together. I'm sure she'll be in touch soon." Sam led her toward the couch. She was grateful for his support because her legs had turned to jelly.

"Mom, what's an avalanche?" Her daughter's voice broke through, shattering the fear gripping her with a chokehold.

"It's when the snow slides down the side of a mountain. Sometimes it crosses a road, blocking it so people can't get through." That was more than enough detail for a seven-year-old.

"So, where's Aunt Rachael?" Her face scrunched up in confusion as she tried to understand. Thankfully, she wasn't quite old enough yet to understand the reasons for Megan's deep-seated fear.

"She probably stopped for food like we talked about, and now she won't be able to get here until they clear the pass. Hopefully tomorrow." Megan had to stay strong for Becca.

"I hate to ask," he said, glancing nervously at Becca, "but the authorities have asked me to call back with details. About your sister. I'm sorry." He put his hand on her shoulder—the human connection was the strength she needed to remain grounded.

She took a deep breath. "Becca, can you run and get Mommy's pink sweater from our suitcase."

"Okay." Becca glanced back and forth between her and Sam and then left to do as she was told.

Megan could do this. She had to. "Her name is Rachael Milner. She's twenty-nine and drives a red Toyota Tundra pickup truck."

"When's the last time you heard from her?"

"Not since I got on the road to head this way. Hours ago. We were supposed to meet here." Megan shook her head. It was totally against her personality to sit and do nothing in a time of need. "I have to get to the pass. Maybe she's stuck on the side of the road. I've got to do something."

Sam's hand stopped her just as she reached for her jacket.

"You need to let the authorities do their job. There's nothing you can do, and there were no tracks on this side of the pass. You need to stay here, close to a phone and safe. You won't do anyone any favors if you end up in a ditch and there's no one who can help you. Think of your daughter." Megan didn't like it much, but he was right.

"Fine," she snapped. It wasn't his fault, but she couldn't fight the waves of tension knotting her up until she couldn't think straight.

Rachael had better be okay. And after she hugged her sister with love and gratitude, she would kill her for the gut-twisting fear she'd put Megan through.

"Were you expecting anyone else? A husband, maybe?"

"There is no husband." Andy wasn't a subject area she planned on venturing into. But other than the loneliness and lost dreams they'd shared, she'd learned to deal with his absence. "He died in a skiing accident three years ago." There, she'd said it.

"I'm sorry to hear that. It must've been a difficult time for you." Sam's voice held a note of compassion, as though he spoke from experience. And judging by the expression she'd seen on his face earlier when he thought no one was watching, she'd venture to guess it was grief he wasn't over yet. Or grief he'd never dealt with in the first place.

"Yes. It was. But nothing can bring him back, so I stay strong for my daughter."

"You're lucky to have her," he said, his voice breaking as he spoke.

Megan wanted to ask him more, but she knew how much she hated it when people pried into her life looking for details, forcing her to relive memories better left locked away. She remained quiet.

"Okay. Let me call this in." Sam stepped out of the room to make the call, and she was grateful for his sensitivity and concern. It was a discussion neither she nor her daughter needed to hear.

Glancing at her phone sitting on the couch, Megan willed it to ring.

Becca entered the living room and held out Megan's sweater. "If Aunt Rachael can't get here tonight, does that mean Mr. Sam has to stay here?" Megan hadn't thought that far. Her concern for her sister took top priority, but Sam was something else she needed to consider. He had nowhere to go, and Megan was left with no choice but to put him up for the night.

"Thanks, honey." She pulled on the sweater, adding a layer of warmth and protection. Megan pulled it tight. "I would think so. I doubt he has any other option."

Sam returned moments later. "They took the information and are looking for your sister. They'll let us know as soon as they find anything out.

Unfortunately, I hope you understand that considering the avalanche, I have no place to stay. I'd like to stay on the couch for the night. As soon as the pass is cleared in the morning, I'll be out of your way."

Based on the tone of his voice, staying here wasn't his first choice either—another reminder he was a man with a past. But his concern for her and Rachael was touching, which made him an admirable man with issues. He was more like her than she cared to admit.

"You're more than welcome to stay. I should've thought about it before I let you travel out into the snowstorm. I can't offer you anything more than a little beef jerky, chips, and what's left of our chocolate, but I hope you'll consider it a peace offering. When it's gone, I have no idea what we'll eat if Rachael doesn't arrive with food supplies, but we'll figure out something."

His lips twitched, the first hint of a smile appearing. "Apparently, you haven't been in the kitchen. I'm back because I didn't want to freeze to death sleeping in my car, but I also didn't want to starve. I left all my food here, thinking I wouldn't need it."

"You're kidding!" Megan was pleasantly shocked.

"I'm still hungry, Mom. Can we see what there is?"

Megan couldn't eat a thing, not with her sister

unaccounted for. She glanced at the door, wishing Rachael would walk through it.

"Why don't I fix something for everyone? Sam asked. "Then, whoever's hungry can eat."

Sam cooks. Imagine that. Megan wasn't about to refuse his generous offer on her daughter's behalf. Not to mention, it would give her time to regroup. The last thing she wanted was for her daughter to see her fall apart while she waited to hear from Rachael. "Thanks. I'd appreciate it."

Sam and Becca moved off toward the kitchen.

"Oh, and Sam—" she stopped him before they disappeared through the door, "—you don't have to sleep on the couch. You can stay in the spare bedroom where Rachael was going to sleep. No sense having a bed not slept in." It was the least she could do in return for his help and the food.

"That would be great. Thanks." He paused, their gazes locked, and a silent understanding passed between them. He understood her fear.

On the verge of tears, she broke the connection. "Becca, are you okay to hang with Sam for a bit? I'll be right back."

"Sure thing, Mom."

That was all she needed to hear. Megan turned and fled down the hall, seeking the solitude of her bedroom.

SAM'S GROCERY list for the cabin had included easy-to-fix meals. Apparently, his cooking repertoire ran parallel to a seven-year-old's dream menu. Macaroni and cheese. Spaghetti. Peanut butter and jelly. Bacon and eggs. Sam's sous chef wasn't much help beyond opening the blue box of mac and cheese and reading the directions, but she'd been adamant about what they would eat.

Laura had been the cook of the family. Since her death, he'd pretty much left it up to local restaurants and the beauty of to-go dinners, or an occasional meal prepared by his housekeeper. Not to mention, with workaholic lifestyle there wasn't time to cook.

Megan was having a hard time dealing with the uncertainty of her sister's welfare and helping with Becca was the least he could do, even though it was hard. He shoved the images and sounds of Lydia out of his head, a feat made almost impossible by Becca's likeness to his beloved daughter. Earlier, he'd been caught off guard. This time, he was managing to control those emotions, putting them on lockdown where they belonged.

"Should we fix Mom a bowl? It's not her favorite, even if it is one of mine." Becca rolled her eyes as if to suggest anyone was crazy if mac and cheese weren't their favorite.

"Let's take her some in case she changes her mind." He pulled three bowls from the cupboard and divided up the creamy orange noodles. It wasn't the most appetizing meal if one judged by its appearance, but he remembered having the stuff when he was growing up. It was passable then, and he doubted anything about it had changed.

Becca grabbed the forks. The lights flickered a few times, luckily finishing in the on mode. "Uh, oh. I don't like it when the power goes out." The girl edged closer to him until she was within an arm's length.

"It'll be okay. We should eat, and then I need to check on a few things. I need to get us more firewood just in case the power goes out."

They returned to the living room, and Sam was pleased to find Megan had returned, even if she was wearing a path in front of the fireplace.

"We brought you some food, Mom, in case you changed your mind."

"Thanks, honey, but I can't." Megan shook her head. "Did you notice the power? Judging by the snow still coming down, we need to be prepared. I'm going in search of flashlights or candles. And maybe extra blankets. You mentioned the wood—we definitely need more. I can help. And we should find matches. Oh, and we should fill some containers with water."

A Nervous Nellie for sure, but activity was good for Megan. It would help take her mind off Rachael —not to mention she was right. "Give me a second to finish eating, and I'll help you search. And then I'll grab the wood."

"Thanks." She shot him a look of gratitude.

"Be careful when you go outside, Mr. Sam. I saw a wild animal or something when we got here. You don't want to get eaten by a bear or attacked by a wolf." Becca's worry frown matched her mother's pained expression to a tee.

"Thanks. I'll be sure to keep a lookout. In the morning, we can search around for tracks." Sam took a few more bites and set his bowl down. "I'm ready. I can tell you're antsy and won't rest until we have everything in order." He shot Megan a look that dared her to deny the truth.

She shrugged. "Becca, you can eat my share of macaroni. We'll be right back."

"But, Mom, what if the power goes out?" Sam noticed the fear in Becca's eyes had returned.

He knelt beside her. "It'll be okay. With the fire, it won't be dark. And if the power goes out, I promise I'll be right back. Is that a deal?"

"Deal, Mr. Sam." Becca slid her hand in his to shake on it. It was small and fragile and totally trusting. He only sought to reassure her, but in return, he'd gained her trust. He might not deserve it, but he did appreciate it.

"He's right, honey. And I'll be here, too. I have an important job for you to do while we are out there. I need you to answer the phone if Aunt Rachael calls. Okay?" Megan dropped a kiss on her daughter's head.

"Okay. Can I play a video game while I wait?

Megan smiled. "Of course, but don't download any new ones without my permission. Oh, and plug it into a charger, so we have a full charge if the power goes out."

"We should probably check for supplies in the garage first." Sam led the way to the kitchen.

"Excellent idea."

He opened the garage door and let her pass.

She flipped the light switch and began to glance around. Her quiet demeanor was understandable given the circumstances, but it made him want to draw her out. Letting her create all the horrible 'what-if' scenarios in her head would serve no purpose. In his case, the worst scenario had played out, and in the aftermath, there was plenty of time to deal with the reality. No sense dealing with it

47

beforehand. It was a state of mind he wouldn't wish on anyone—not even his father. And that was saying a lot.

"Check those cabinets, and I'll check the shelves over there." He pointed toward the rear of the garage. "I'm sure they have extra lights. We should search for batteries while we're at it. The blankets will probably be in the hall closet. I saw matches in the kitchen drawer, so we're okay there."

"Okay." Megan opened the cabinet door. She stopped to stare at him, her tightly pressed lips echoing the pensive expression on her face. "Do you think she'll be okay?" Sam knew what she was asking, but he couldn't make any promises.

"I don't know, but there's always hope. Believe until you can't." It came across as philosophical, but he knew it was personal experience.

The lights flickered again. Sam remembered his promise to Becca and darted toward the kitchen door. He held it open partway and leaned inside. "You okay, Becca?" he hollered. She trusted him, and he didn't want to let her down.

"Yup. You were right, the fire's nice and bright. And the lights are still on," Becca appeared at the doorway between the kitchen and dining room.

"We're almost finished, and we'll be back inside in a minute."

"I am being brave, aren't I?" She stood there waiting for confirmation.

"You sure are." Cute kid. Sam shook his head and smiled as Becca turned and walked away, satisfied with his answer.

"Thanks. That was sweet of you." Megan had stopped searching to watch him. "You're good with kids." *Was good, not anymore.*

"Thanks." He turned away. The last thing he wanted was for her to start asking questions.

"Here's two flashlights." She flipped the switch on each one of them. "The batteries are strong. I'll grab some extra blankets and stack them on the couch. And I'll take care of getting water in a few containers as backup while you get the firewood. We should also charge our phones."

"Good thinking. Were you a girl scout or something?"

"Or something." It was her turn to be mysterious.

He shot her a tell-me-more look, his curiosity piqued.

"Air Force. *Former* Air Force to be exact."

"Surprising, but it definitely explains a few things." More than a few things, truth be told.

"What's that supposed to mean?"

"The control you seem to have. Nothing wrong with it. I find it admirable."

She laughed, but it wasn't a laugh born of humor. "External control is easier than what's going on inside a person. We should head back in."

"Are you going to be all right? Is there anything I can do?"

"I'm okay. Thanks." Megan turned and went back into the house.

Sam shut off the lights and followed. The lights in the house flickered off and on. Then off. This time, they stayed off. Sam hurried to the living room to check on Becca. "You okay?" he asked.

"I guess. Can you stay with me, please?"

"Of course." Sam sat down next to Becca and pulled a blanket over her. A white ball of light bouncing around like a firefly as it moved down the hall toward them, alerted him to Megan's presence.

"Everything okay in here?" She pointed the flashlight in their general direction.

"Yup. Mr. Sam's here." Becca turned to look at him. "You do play Hearts, right? Mom and I were playing before you came back. We still have enough light with the fire to play." The hope in her voice was unmistakable. Little by little, Sam found himself relaxing around Becca. Something he never would have expected. Her trust made him feel wanted. *Needed*. Something he hadn't felt in years.

"I don't know how to play, but if you're willing to

teach me, we can play. How about you shuffle the cards and deal while I get us more firewood?"

"Okay." She smiled, but then her eyes grew wide like saucers. "Don't forget to be careful of the wild animal."

"Thanks, kiddo." It'd been a long time since anyone had worried about him, other than his state of mind, that is.

He headed out the back door, returning a few minutes later with another armload of firewood and stacking them on top of the existing pile. "Coast was clear outside. I'm betting whatever you saw is long gone." Sam ruffled the top of her head and then sat down by the fire to join the party.

Megan clearly wasn't into the game, but he had to give her credit for sticking through it and playing. Two quick games later, Becca yawned and lay down across her mother's lap, curling her legs up like a baby. Megan absently stroked her daughter's hair as she gazed at the fire. Within minutes, Becca was fast asleep.

Megan kept checking her phone every few minutes.

"Turning it on and off won't make it ring. It's only been a little over an hour." Sam felt helpless. He didn't know what to do or say.

She fixated her sea-blue eyes on him, the color

reminding him of his favorite place in Grand Turk, just off Pillory Beach. He'd taken Laura there on their honeymoon on one of the few times he'd let his personal life overrule his never-ending quest for financial freedom.

"You don't understand. Besides Becca, Rachael is all I have left."

"Nothing's happened to her that we know of, and you'll drive yourself crazy with worry if you imagine the worst."

"It's not as if there's anything else to do." She shrugged.

"We could talk. Tell me about yourself for starters. I should know more about you since I'll be sleeping under your roof." He got a weak smile out of her.

"Or maybe I should know more about you, considering our original meeting. Do I have anything to worry about? You're not just pretending to be likable but then going to make away with all our valuables, are you?" Her attempt at humor was an excellent sign, even if it was delivered in a questioning tone that made him wonder if the thought had crossed her mind.

"My getaway would stop at the pass, and I'd freeze. Probably not advisable." Sam smiled, hoping she'd know he was teasing. It was one thing to try and help her relax, quite another to give her more reason to worry.

"So, tell me about Sam Wyatt."

"I'm an investment negotiator, and I have my own business in New York. So, yes, your valuables are safe with me; I've plenty of my own money." He gave away most of it, but there was no way he'd mention that fact. No one understood his drive to rectify the past, and it was pointless to even try and explain it to a stranger.

"Wow. I guess you don't need the thirty-three dollars I have in my purse." Megan's smile made the invasion of his privacy worth answering the questions. "Investment negotiator—like for houses and such?"

"Large companies and such."

"What does it mean to be an investment negotiator?"

"It means when one large company has money to invest, I do the research and negotiate the contracts." He couldn't keep the slight derision out of his voice. It was always like this when he talked about his job.

"Sounds complicated. You must be one of those smart guys; Valedictorian in your class, perhaps? And by large do you mean large, or large-large?"

Sam couldn't help but smile at the question. "I

guess you would say large-large. In the billions large."

"Wow. I'm impressed. What else can you tell me about Sam Wyatt?"

"There's not much else to tell. I live alone, and my work is my life." He frowned, unsure why he would say such a thing. It wasn't a subject he voluntarily talked about—with anyone.

"So, single by choice?" The question was like a dart to the heart.

He shook his head. "No. Not by choice." Exactly why he should have kept his mouth shut.

"Explain. I can't believe you're in love with someone, and they haven't scooped you up like ice cream." Her smile was a nice change from the worry frown, and he hated to wipe it away, but there was no answer he could give other than the truth.

He took a deep breath. "My wife and daughter died in a car accident two years ago, two days before Christmas."

The shock on her face was genuine, as well as the remorse. "Oh, my. I'm so sorry. I didn't mean to pry. I'm such an idiot for saying anything. Please, forgive me." The tension in the air was thick, and he appreciated that she didn't keep pushing him for more details the way most people did.

Aside from the tragedy itself, people were the

second biggest reason he'd withdrawn from the world, throwing himself into his job even more than he had before. And maybe because she didn't pry, he found himself wanting to tell her and wanting to share the piece of himself he'd long since locked away.

After all, as soon as the pass was cleared, he'd be on his way. Two strangers passing through each other's lives. Everyone he knew told him he needed to open his heart and talk about what had happened, but he'd never listened. Until now. What could it hurt?

He took a deep breath, trying to decide how to begin and how much to reveal. "We were staying here two years ago, and it's why I keep coming back. But it's also why I canceled at the last minute. A rash moment in which I thought I could stay away and that it would help me. Clearly, I was wrong. When I saw you and Becca standing by the fireplace, I thought you were them. That they had returned. And when I realized it was all in my head, I snapped at you. I'm sorry." He shook his head, not happy with himself as he recalled the moment. Or the attempt to bribe her to leave when he was in the wrong.

"I didn't know. I'm sorry. I regretted making you leave seconds after you left if it's any consolation."

"It didn't matter. At the time, one of us had to

leave. Staying with you was impossible, or so I thought."

"What do you mean?" The lights flickered and then came back on, illuminating Megan's face, the question in her eyes unmistakable.

"Because of Becca. My daughter would have been seven this year, and Becca reminds me of her, making it all that much harder to handle." Sam rose, moving to the fireplace to toss another log on the fire, preferring to avoid her gaze. "The lights seem like they are going to stay on for now. We should make sure to charge our phones in case the power goes out again." He'd already said more than he normally told anyone and a change in subject sounded like a great idea.

"But it's been two years. Surely, you're not going through life avoiding all children. That can't be healthy. What about friends' kids? Relatives?"

She wasn't letting him off the hook that easy. "Not all kids. Kids like Becca. There's a difference. And the opportunity to be around kids doesn't arise often anyway. I like it that way."

"What do you mean kids like Becca?"

Sam pulled out his wallet and flipped it open to one of his last pictures of Lydia. He handed the wallet to Megan. "That's Lydia."

"But…but…she's the spitting image of Becca.

That's insane." She looked up at him and then back at the picture. Stunned was an understatement.

"I know. Trust me, I know." It felt good to share. And best of all, Megan seemed to understand.

"You were wonderful with Becca tonight. Apparently, you can handle it better than you thought."

"Becca's not Lydia. Spending even a little time with her made me realize that, and it's pretty hard to ignore a determined but darling child." It was true. Becca made him smile more than he had in two years. Her trust had cracked open his heart, and her zest for life and sweetness were slowly replacing some of the chunks of bitterness weighing him down.

"She's a good kid. Thanks. And I'm glad you're okay with her now, since we are stuck together, at least for the night." She handed him back his wallet, their hands touching. Soft and warm. Their gazes locked, and neither one of them moved.

Music shattered the silence, and Megan grabbed her phone, her sister's ring tone the sound she'd been praying to hear for hours.

CHAPTER FOUR

"Oh, my gosh. Thank goodness you finally called me. Where are you?" A flood of relief swept through every inch of Megan's body, leaving her almost breathless. She moved Becca off her lap carefully so as not to wake her, and then pointed at her phone for Sam's benefit. "*It's her,*" she mouthed silently.

"Slow down. I'm in Hallbrook. I didn't have time to get groceries, so I stopped in town to get food and gas. I was worried we might get snowed in, so I stocked up. And then I lost my phone and spent almost an hour looking for it. But you'll never believe what just happened here."

Megan paced the room, taking in deep breaths. Her sister was alive and well if her voice was anything to go by. "Of all the cockamamie times to lose your phone. Do you know how much I've worried about you?" Megan shook her head. It was times like these she felt more like the older sister, the worrywart.

"I'm okay, so don't freak out, but I need to tell you something. There's been an avalanche on the pass."

"I was freaked out because I already know about it. It's crazy. Are you sure you're okay?" She needed to hear her sister's voice to keep reassuring herself she was okay.

"I'm still shaken up. If I hadn't stopped at the diner to get us a to-go order for dinner, I might've been caught in the middle. There are fire trucks, police cars, and ambulances everywhere."

Megan's stomach unfurled another notch. The nausea she'd barely managed to hold at bay, relented. "Thank goodness you're okay."

"Totally. My cell service has been spotty, but when I finally got a signal, I saw you'd called like a hundred times. Sorry. But wait a minute. How did you hear about it?" Trust her sister not to miss that tidbit of information.

"That's an entirely different story." One best left for when the two of them got together, and for when the person in question who delivered the news wasn't sitting in the same room.

"I hate that I'm not there, but better here than in

the avalanche. So, what's the story? How do you know?" Rachael wasn't about to let the subject drop.

"Well, because there's someone here. A man. He was trapped on this side of the avalanche and came back to tell me about it."

"Came back? Tell me more. Don't leave me hanging." Rachael's voice was full of curiosity.

She glanced at Sam, only to find him watching her. Megan walked down the hall and into the bedroom.

"It's a long story. He's going to sleep in your room tonight since you can't make it. Becca will be so disappointed you're not here when she wakes up. She fell asleep almost an hour ago. We lost power for a while, but luckily it came back on, so it won't get too cold in here."

"I've been here talking to some of the rescue team. Nice people. Hang on a minute."

Megan could hear her sister talking to someone but couldn't make out what she was saying.

"They want me to turn around and head back to town, so I'm going to have to get off the phone as soon as they clear the way. I was told I need to get a motel room for the night but that there's only one in town. There's no way they can even begin to assess the situation until morning." For someone in a pickle, her sister didn't seem overly distraught.

"Is there anything even available there?"

"I'll let you know when I get checked in. I might end up sleeping in my car if there's no vacancy. Christmas week is a bad time to find a motel at the last minute."

"You can't sleep in your car! That's crazy."

"I'm kidding. Don't worry, I'll figure something out. But quit trying to change the subject. What's going on there? I'm not the one with a strange man sleeping under the same roof as me." Her sister had a point.

"It's not like that, and you know it. He wouldn't be here if he had any choice in the matter. Trust me."

"What's he like? Is he at least good-looking? Nice?" She should have known Rachael would take the conversation in this direction. She'd been after Megan to start dating again for the past year.

Megan's focus was on Becca, and she didn't have the time nor the inclination to pursue a relationship, something her sister refused to understand. "He's quiet, in a brooding sort of way. And, yes, good-looking. Nice? Definitely. He is letting us eat his food, and he cooked dinner for Becca tonight, and he practically held my hand while we waited to hear from you. So, yeah, he's nice."

She didn't bother to mention Sam's earlier grumpiness or his demands for her to vacate the property, and she most definitely left out the part where he tried to bribe her to leave. None of that would be construed as nice, and she didn't want Rachael to worry about her.

"He cooked your dinner and held your hand?"

"If mac and cheese are considered cooking, then, yes, he cooked. And I didn't say he held my hand, so don't even go down that road. I said he *practically* held my hand. It's an expression saying he helped me to stay calm while I was scared out of my mind with worry for you."

"I know what you meant, but by teasing you, I can learn a lot more than you're telling. You like him. So how did he end up at the cabin?" Rachael's attorney brain wanted details.

"He was here when I arrived, and I thought he was you."

"You thought I was a man?" Rachael sounded more confused than ever.

"At first, anyway." Megan told her sister about the auspicious arrival and Sam's part in the not-so-amiable beginnings they'd shared. "My confirmation was valid; his was not. He left, but he came back because of the avalanche."

"And that's it?" She sounded slightly disappointed.

"What more do you expect? It's not as if it's been

a fairytale here waiting to hear from you. And then the power went out. And there's Becca to consider."

"So, you're interested in him at least a little bit?"

"Why would you say that?" Rachael's determination to explore her interest in Sam as more than it was, made Megan glad the two wouldn't meet.

"Because this is the first time in a few years you've even noticed a man as being attractive. I'd say this is major progress." The laughter in her sister's voice was a joy to hear even if it was directed at her.

"Big deal. I think you pay too much attention to my love life and not enough on your own. You don't pay attention to men, either. Want to tell me what that's all about?" Silence met her on the other end of the phone, exactly as she'd expected. Rachael didn't enjoy it when the tables got turned, but it was only fair. One day, she'd find out what had happened when her sister moved to Portland, but until then, she'd use Rachael's anti-man stance to her advantage.

"That's what I thought. Please let me know as soon as you find a place to stay."

"Since I know you won't let the matter drop until you know I'm safely tucked into a warm bed and not in my car, I should let you know, I already have a place."

It was Megan's turn to be confused. "Where? You said you had to look around?"

"Well...they are pretty sure the motel here in Hallbrook is fully booked. Glen Haven is probably no different. However, another option was suggested. I wasn't going to say anything, but I'm not sure I have any choice."

"What's going on, Rachael?"

"I'm going to be staying at one of the rescue worker's houses."

"Well, that's not such a big deal. She must be likable for you to agree so easily."

"He. And, yes."

Wait a minute. He? She couldn't have possibly heard her sister correct. "I beg your pardon?"

"He. The rescue worker. His name is Brandon Stewart if knowing his name makes you feel any better. If you don't hear from me tomorrow, you can call his boss. At the police station." Rachael laughed at her own joke. "I need to run. They've cleared the way for me and he's waiting for me to follow him home."

"Wait."

"Goodnight, Megan." The phone beeped as it disconnected the call.

CHAPTER FIVE

Small orange embers glowed in the fireplace as the sole source of light in the living room. Dawn was still at least forty-five minutes away. Sam pushed the pieces together with the poker and tossed in a few more logs, trying to reignite the fire, hoping to take the chill out of the air before Megan and Becca woke up.

He'd been grateful for a bed last night, as opposed to his SUV and the bitter cold, but the quality of his sleep was the price he'd paid. Hanging around Becca had clearly messed with his sanity because dreams of Lydia had surfaced over and over, moments of her life haunting him.

Sam sat on the couch and pulled out his phone. He pulled up his last video of Lydia, needing to see her face and hear her laughter. At times, the video was the one thing that could pull him out of the darkness he'd created, her smiling face enough to pump warmth into his hardened heart. A tear slid down his face. He closed his eyes and fought against the familiar ache in his chest.

As soon as the officials were able to clear the pass, he had to leave. It wasn't that he didn't enjoy Megan and Becca's company, for what was there not to appreciate? But he wasn't a Merry Christmas kind of guy anymore, and if he couldn't be here alone with his memories, he needed to be back in his office, doing what he did best. Making money.

Becca was the first one to wander into the living room. Sam couldn't help but smile at her messy hair, the teddy bear in her arms, and the princess slippers. Lydia used to carry her favorite stuffed puppy around with her everywhere.

"Good morning, Mr. Sam." Becca covered her mouth to hide a yawn.

"Good morning. Did you sleep well?"

"Yup. Look, it stopped snowing." She pointed out the window. "Does this mean we can play? Are you going to stay and play, too? When's Aunt Rachael coming?" A good night's sleep made a child fresh and ready for action. There was no easing into the day the way adults tried to do.

"Whoa. Slow down. I'm sure you can play later—

after breakfast, but you'll have to ask your mother. I'm waiting on a call to hear when the pass will open, and when it does, I need to leave, but then your Aunt Rachael can come here."

"But when will that be?"

"I don't know." *Not soon enough.*

Megan glanced his way as she entered the room. "Any updates on the pass?"

"Not yet, but I expect we'll hear something soon."

"Mom, if they open the pass, then Mr. Sam is going to leave. Isn't there any way to get Aunt Rachael here and make him stay?" Becca moved to stand next to him and slid her hand into his.

"Mr. Sam's a busy man. Maybe if we build an igloo and your Aunt Rachael gets here by lunchtime, Mr. Sam will share one of our famous igloo lunches with you before he leaves." Megan shot him an apologetic look.

It was all well and good for Megan to suggest it, but he was the one who would come out looking bad if he left anyway.

"You'll love it, Mr. Sam. It's tomato soup and grilled cheese sandwiches." She beamed up at him, her eyes twinkling with wonder as if him staying would be an amazing gift.

Mother and daughter were both hard to resist, and Sam didn't have the heart to say no. At least it wasn't something connected with a Lydia memory. "Sounds like a plan."

Megan's questioning look of disbelief disappeared right before she silently mouthed a big thank you in his direction. "Perfect. I'll send Rachael a text to make sure she gets what we need before she comes."

"I can't wait for Aunt Rachael to get here. This will be the best igloo lunch ever." Becca skipped off down the hall. It was as though she had some special gift to know how to wedge her way behind the shield he'd erected around his heart because it hadn't taken her long at all.

Sam's phone rang an hour later, and he let out a sigh of relief. *Finally, they would get some answers.* "Sam Wyatt," he answered.

"This is Captain James. We've got a problem. Mr. O'Malley, one of the neighbors who live at seven Christmas Tree Lane, took a fall on the ice a little bit ago. His wife doesn't have the strength to pull him back inside, and he can't walk. We aren't sure the extent of his injuries, but his wife mentioned a possible break or sprain. We can't get to him, but you can. We've been calling around to see if anyone has any medical background and can get there to help us out."

"I don't have any medical experience, but I can

definitely get to him. Hang on a sec." He stood, prepared to go find Megan, only to discover her standing in the doorway of the kitchen.

"Mr. O'Malley, a local resident just down the street, took a fall on his driveway. It sounds as if it might be a possible break or sprain. They're looking for someone to help get him inside the house and assess him. Any chance you have a medical background?"

Megan shot him a lop-sided grin. "Absolutely. Tell them I'm a nurse, and we're on our way. I just need to put a few things together that might help us out."

"Gotcha." Sam watched her hurry away as he held the phone up to his ear again. Mr. O'Malley was one lucky guy. "You're in luck. There's a nurse staying here. She's putting together some things and then we'll head that way in a few minutes."

"Thanks. Sorry it's taking so long to assess the pass and get started working on it, but it takes time to make sure we put everyone's safety first."

The last thing Sam wanted was for anyone to rush and get hurt on his behalf. Patience was a virtue in his professional career, he just needed to draw upon that quality in his personal life. "I understand. You've got a lot to deal with. We'll let you know what we find out about Mr. O'Malley."

Sam hung up the phone just as Megan reappeared, a bag in hand, and Becca close on her heels.

"We need something to brace his leg. Any ideas?" Megan asked as she put on her jacket.

"Let me check in the shed."

"Thanks. I'll search for towels or rags we can use as straps. And, Becca, see if you can find a pair of scissors, and then get your coat on. You need to come with us."

"Let me guess, Air Force nurse?" He knew she'd been enlisted but seeing her in action drove home the methodical efficiency that came with military training.

Megan shot him a smile. "Ten points for a good guess. Let's get moving before the poor man gets frostbite."

"I'll find something to stabilize his leg and meet you out front by the Navigator."

"Sounds like a plan." Megan turned and headed down the hall.

Sam made his way to the shed, trekking through the foot of snow that had accumulated overnight. He glanced around the large building, surprised at the wide array of junk filling the place. It looked as though everything and anything had been stored here over the years, including a couple of old sleds that might come in handy for Becca.

He spotted a pile of wood in one corner and grabbed a two by four that was almost perfect in size for what they needed. Sam made his way around the cabin and headed for the SUV. He tossed the board in the back and then cranked up the engine, flipping on the heat to warm up the vehicle. While he waited for Megan and Becca, he shoveled the walkway to the front porch, clearing last night's snow accumulation.

Once they were loaded inside and seatbelts fastened, Sam put the vehicle in reverse and backed down the driveway. He breathed a sigh of relief as the tires caught and held, propelling them back into the street. Four-wheel drive wasn't much good on ice, but it worked wonders in the snow. His tracks from the night before were barely visible, but they gave him a general idea of what to aim for on the road to stay out of trouble. "It shouldn't be far down the road. He said number seven."

They drove past two houses and didn't see any sign of activity in the driveways. They came to the third house on the right, but because of the trees, they couldn't get a decent view down the driveway.

"Pull up to the mailbox, and I'll check." Megan rolled her window down, some of the snow around the window falling into her lap.

"Good idea." Sam edged close, leaving a few inches so as not to scrape his vehicle.

She reached out and brushed off the mailbox. "It's number seven. I hope your vehicle won't have any problems. This house looks like it could be a long way back."

"We're about to find out. Cross your fingers, everyone." Sam slipped the shifter into reverse, backing up a few feet before putting the SUV into drive, and headed up the road.

"I hope the man is okay. It's scary to think about him out in the cold and with a broken leg. That must be awful and hurt." Becca's voice trembled, her concern for their unknown neighbor more proof she was a sweet girl, inside and out.

Sam glanced in the rearview mirror. "He'll be fine, I promise. We don't know it's broken, so let's hope for the best." He didn't know for sure, but he would do everything in his power to make it right. Becca's Christmas was already in danger of being ruined because of the avalanche, and Sam would do what he could to keep it from falling completely apart. Just as he would have done for Lydia.

They came around a curve in the driveway, and suddenly there was a petite woman frantically waving her arms, and a man lying in the snow in front of them. They were quite some distance from the house. Sam stopped and jumped out of the SUV.

"Thank goodness you're here. He's freezing. I've put as many blankets as I could around him, and I've tried so hard to move him, but I can't." The woman's voice was frantic with fear, and tears ran down her face unchecked.

Megan came around from the other side of the vehicle and briefly hugged Mrs. O'Malley to reassure her. "It'll be okay, we're here to help. This is my daughter, Becca." Becca had followed her mother, an anxious expression on her face. "Why don't the two of you wait in the SUV where it's warm, and I'll see what we can do to help your husband."

Mrs. O'Malley nodded, a look of relief on her face as she brushed away her tears with the back of her gloves.

He made his way to Mr. O'Malley and knelt beside him. "Name's Sam Wyatt. And this is Megan Langley." He glanced up at her as she joined them.

"I'm Frank. Thanks for coming." He spoke between clenched teeth, his face scrunched up in obvious pain.

"We understand you think the leg is broken. Can you move it at all? Megan lifted his hand, pushed aside the collar of his glove, and took his pulse.

"It hurts like crazy. The pain seems to radiate

from my knee to my foot every time I try to move it. Not to mention, I'm freezing. Glad it's not as chilly as it was yesterday. But sitting here in the snow sure doesn't help." Frank's weak smile was reassuring.

"Here's what I'm thinking. I'd like to stabilize your leg and wrap it up. Then the two of us can support you, one on each side, and we can get you into the back of the Navigator and drive you up to the house." Megan was a take-charge kind of woman, and Sam admired her ability to jump right in and take control.

"The house doesn't have any power. I think the snow took down our electrical line. It's why I was shoveling out the driveway and trying to get over to the Parker place. Didn't want the missus freezing to death." His teeth chattered as he spoke.

"We lost power last night also, but it's back on now. I'll have a look later, after we get you settled. But if there's no power in the house, there's no reason for us to take you there. We can head to the cabin." He looked at Megan to confirm what he was thinking.

"Good idea." She nodded. "If you turn the vehicle around, I'll get him wrapped up."

"If you're sure it won't be no trouble. We could still stay with the Parkers'." Frank's suggestion would work, but it wasn't the best option.

"It's fine. It'll be easier for Megan to keep an eye on you and report back to the doctor in charge at the hospital."

"Okay. Right now, heat and something for the pain are sounding pretty good." Frank grimaced.

Megan took the blanket loosely draped around Mr. O'Malley's shoulders and pulled it higher around the back of his head, trying to trap in some warmth. "Go on. I'll take care of him."

Sam drove to the end of the driveway, turned around, and backed up carefully, trying to get as close as he could. Megan stood and directed him until he got close.

"Becca, you and Mrs. O'Malley sit tight while we get Mr. O'Malley into the back. We'll be back to the cabin before you know it, and everyone can get warmed up." He was doing his best to keep Becca calm, not wanting her to be afraid.

Sam popped open the tailgate and pushed a couple of things out of the way to make room. Megan had tied the two by four to Frank's leg, and the man looked as if he was about to pass out. "On the count of three, we are going to lift you up under your arms. Put as much weight as you can on your good leg to help us out. And no sudden moves." Frank was a big guy, and the ice beneath them was slippery. Sam hoped they didn't make things worse in the process.

Megan unwrapped the blankets from Frank and handed them to Becca through the back of the vehicle. "Hold these, honey."

Sam leaned down to hook an arm beneath Frank's arm and waited for Megan to do the same on the other side.

She nodded when she was ready.

"One. Two. Three. Go." He used every ounce of muscle he had to bear as much of the weight as he could as he lifted Frank upright, the process made more difficult because of the board tied to the man's leg.

"Jiminy Cricket!" Frank hissed.

Sam was grateful Megan was on the other side to keep them all from toppling over. "That's the hardest part."

"You okay, Frank?" Megan asked.

"Yeah," he said, his voice tight with pain.

"You're doing amazing. Just breathe through it." Megan spoke to him softly, encouraging him.

When his breathing slowed down a bit, Sam knew it was time for the next step.

"Time to get you into the back of the vehicle. We need to get you closer to the bumper to where you can sit down. Megan, I can hold him up now, if you can back the SUV up another six inches, that would help. Just nice and easy. Keep your foot on the brake for the most part. I can talk you down to inches with the back opened up."

"No problem. I've got this." She moved to take her place in the driver's seat, put the SUV in gear, and inched her way backward.

"Whoa," he called out when she was a couple of inches away.

Megan put the vehicle in park and rejoined him.

"Frank, I need you to trust me to hold you as you sit down as far back as you can. Use your arms for support and propel yourself backward."

Frank did as he was instructed, holding his leg straight out the best he could with Megan supporting it from underneath. He managed to slide back two feet, giving Sam enough leverage to come from inside the vehicle to pull him in the rest of the way.

"I think this is good, don't you?" Sam glanced at Megan, making sure they were on the same page.

"Yes. Let's do this." She smiled and nodded. "Becca can sit upfront with me, on my lap. Mrs. O'Malley, you stay where you are, and Frank will be just fine. We're just up the street, in the cabin at the end of the road."

"Honey, you can call me Agnes. I can't thank you

enough for coming to help us. I don't know what we would have done." Agnes half turned, placing her hand on Frank's shoulder.

"Everything worked out, so try not to worry. I'm a nurse, and I'll do whatever I can to help." Megan's soft voice was working wonders to reassure the woman.

Sam drove down the road slowly, trying not to jostle Frank's leg any more than necessary. Luckily, he'd shoveled the walkway this morning as it would make it easier to get Frank inside. Back at the cabin, both he and Megan supported Frank, working together as a team as they maneuvered him down the hall to Sam's bedroom and lowered him onto the bed.

Megan cut Frank's pant leg open to the knee while Agnes paced from across the room, nervously watching but staying out of the way. Sam collected his belongings and threw them in his suitcase. He'd let Agnes and Frank share the privacy of the room until help could arrive or the pass opened.

"Sam, can you get me some ice, and there's a bottle of pain reliever in my purse which is on the couch. I'll need those and some water." Megan took charge of the patient, and Sam was more than happy to help.

"I'm on it." He dropped his suitcase off in the

laundry room and then went to find Megan's purse, finding it right where she said. If the pass wasn't cleared today, the couch would be his new bed. Hopefully, it wouldn't come to that and he'd be long gone. He grabbed everything Megan asked for and headed back down the hall.

When he walked into the room, Megan held up her hand to silence him. It sounded as though she was on the phone with the doctor based on the conversation. It wasn't long before she hung up, took the bag of ice from him, and placed it across Frank's knee.

Sam handed her the pills and water.

"Here, take these. It'll help with the pain and the swelling," she advised, handing the tablets to Frank. "From what I can tell without the benefit of X-rays, I'm thinking you might be a lucky man, Frank. The swelling appears to be centered on your knee, and there's no indication of a fracture unless it's a hair-line one, which is a lot less problematic. I'm thinking more along the lines of a sprained knee joint. Maybe you twisted wrong when you fell, and it hyperex-tended the muscle protecting the inside of your knee. The doctor wants X-rays, of course, but he agrees with my assessment based on the feedback I've given him."

"Thank you. Thank you. You have been such a

blessing." Agnes crossed the room to her husband's side and held his hand.

"I hope you're right, but I'm also hoping these pain relievers kick in soon. I'd like to sleep, but I'm not sure it will happen until some of the pain lets up." Frank rubbed his forehead and the bridge of his nose, grimacing through another flash of pain.

"I'm going to remove the board and put a pillow behind your knee for support. That should help it relax into a more natural position. This will hurt, but I promise it will be worth it."

"Do your worst, Doc." Frank braced himself for more pain. "I'm all for the better on the other side."

Megan just kept impressing him. How anyone could talk someone into more pain in the hopes of less pain was beyond comprehension. No easy task for sure.

"Sounds like wonderful news. Do you need me to do anything else?" Sam asked.

"No, thanks." She flashed him a warm smile. "You did great. There is one thing you could do. Can you check on Becca and see how she's handling all this? I know she was worried." Megan hated to ask, but she'd be tied up with Frank for a while.

"I'm on it. I'll get her mind on something else and take her outside to check out those tracks."

"What kind of tracks?" Frank asked, grimacing as another flash of pain shot through his leg.

"Not sure. Becca thought she saw something last night. I'll check it out and put her mind to rest. She's worried a bear is going to appear out of nowhere and eat someone for dinner." Sam chuckled.

"Haven't been any sightings around here this year, not yet anyway." Frank shook his head.

"Thanks, Sam." Megan's look of relief made him wonder if secretly, she'd been worried as well.

"And after that, since you don't need me, I was thinking of going to check on the other neighbors to make sure everyone else is okay. And while I'm at it, I'll stop and lock up your house, Agnes."

"Bless your heart. Thank you. Could you grab my purse while you're there? It's lying on the kitchen table."

"No problem."

"It's an excellent idea to check in on the neighbors." Megan crossed the room to stand beside him. She stepped in close, pressing her hand to his arm. "You're a generous man with a big heart."

The air between them vibrated with energy as their gazes locked.

"You need to let go of the past. It's holding you back from life, and you have so much to give the world. It's a shame to hide it away in solitude."

Megan spoke the words in a hushed whisper, increasing the sense of privacy as if they were the only two people in the room.

"I wish it was that easy, but thanks. You're pretty special yourself." Sam stepped away. "I've got to go." For the briefest second, he imagined kissing her. Thank goodness, he'd stopped before making a huge mistake. But stopping before it happened didn't keep him from thinking about her pretty pink mouth so close to his. In fact, it made him want to kiss her more.

CHAPTER SIX

Sam found Becca curled up under a blanket in front of the television watching cartoons. He kneeled beside the couch, getting level with the girl. He wanted to reach out and comfort her but held back, reminding himself she wasn't Lydia, and it would be far too easy to get attached for all the wrong reasons.

"You okay, kiddo?"

"Yeah. I'm just glad we're back and Mom's taking care of Mr. Frank. But now we won't be able to search for our tree or build an igloo today, and there's nothing to do except watch TV." She pouted.

"I'm sorry. There should be some Christmas specials on. That might make it more fun. I've got to head out and check on the other neighbors and make sure everyone is okay, but I thought first, maybe you and I could check out those tracks."

Becca's face brightened. "That sounds like a great idea. And can I go with you to visit people? Please, Mr. Sam." She reached out and grabbed his hand when he started to stand.

"I don't know." The thought of spending an extended period with Becca scared him. For two years, he'd avoided most children because they were a painful reminder of all he'd lost. To voluntarily allow a child who looked far too much like Lydia to hang out with him for the fun of it, would be insanity. Sam tried to think of a gracious way to say no, but his brain and his mouth weren't in sync.

"Please." Her soft voice wrapped around his heart and squeezed, almost as tightly as her hand on his arm. Any effort to say no vanished.

"Okay. Get dressed, and I'll let your mother know." Insanity won over, and it was an offer he couldn't take back. Becca had been brave throughout today's ordeal, and now it was *his* turn to be brave.

"Yes!" She threw off the blanket and jumped off the couch. "I'll be right back. Make sure you don't leave without me." She ran down the hall in the direction of her bedroom, not giving him a chance to change his mind. Not that he would. Once committed, he wouldn't go back on his word, not to mention he was curious about the tracks.

He knocked on the door of the spare bedroom.

"Come in," Megan called.

Sam poked his head in the room. "Becca wants to go with me when I make the rounds to the neighbors. Is that okay with you?"

"More importantly, is that okay with *you*?" She crossed the room to his side, her brow drawn tight in confusion.

"Yes. She'll be fine."

"It's not her I'm worried about." She reached out and touched his arm lightly.

"I'll be fine. Maybe it's exactly what I need to shake things up in my world and see where they land." He shrugged, but he was feeling anything but indifference with Megan's hand still holding him in check. The touch made him yearn for more, a human connection, something he'd promised himself would never happen again.

"Okay. Let me know when you get back." Megan dropped her hand, breaking the contact between them.

Sam stepped back into the hallway and closed the door, taking a deep breath to recover. He needed to stay focused on one thing at a time, and right now, that one thing was the neighboring people who might need his help.

Becca came out of her room and almost collided with him.

"Let's go, kiddo. You may regret wanting to ride along with me if I put you to work." He patted the top of her head and turned to leave, knowing there wasn't a chance she'd change her mind and stay put.

"I don't mind. I'm big and strong, and I want to help. Do you think there will be any kids I can play with?"

"Already looking to get out of work, I see." Sam shook his head and laughed. "I'm sure you'll find a kid or two."

"Awesome. I wonder if they have sleds."

"Whoa. Slow down. One step at a time." Becca was full-steam-ahead and as talkative as they came. "I did notice a couple of sleds in the shed I can get out for you."

"Yay!"

"Where did you think you saw an animal, and how big was it based on your best guess? He held open the front door, and the two of them moved to stand on the front porch.

"It was about this big—" she held her hand up to her waist, "—and he had big eyes that glowed. He was right over there." She pointed to the corner of the garage.

Sam glanced around but didn't see anything. He focused on the ground, and sure enough, there were tracks in the snow. Becca was right. But judging by the size of the paw print, he wasn't quite as big as Becca thought. They were also fresh tracks, but he wouldn't bother pointing that out to Becca. Any tracks from last night would have been lost in the snow. "Here they are. Look, see this?" He pointed to the pad indentions of the print. "This looks like a canine print of some sort. Their pads are farther apart, and they're missing the extra lobe at the bottom. A feline print would have another arch here."

"What's a canine?" Becca looked up at him, her eyes drawn tight as she tried to figure out what he meant.

"Dog-like. Sorry. You're so smart, I sometimes forget you might not know a big word. But it means like a wolf, a coyote, a fox, or of course, an actual dog. I'm putting my guess on a dog this close to the cabin, but we'll keep watch to be sure."

"Why would a dog be out last night? Wouldn't he be cold?" Her sweetness and caring had no boundaries.

"He could have been out for a walk and on his way home. He'll be fine. Ready to check on the neighbors and help me work?" Sam teased.

"Work is for grown-ups. I'm ready to meet some kids and play." Becca shook her head, grinning up at him in all innocence. They headed for the SUV, and

ELSIE DAVIS

in a few minutes, he had it warmed up, and they were on their way.

He drove down the road slowly, paying extreme attention to the road conditions and trying to stay within the previous tracks to make it easier. Without snowplows to clear the roads, they wouldn't be the best for travel for days to come. Not until the sun came out and started to heat the roads and melt the snow.

It wasn't long before they pulled up to the first house. "Wait here, and I'll find out if they need our help."

"Okay, Mr. Sam."

He slid out of the vehicle and walked up the snow-covered driveway. Knocking on the door, he stood back and waited. The door opened to reveal a young woman with an orange-faced toddler on her hip. By the looks of things, more carrots had ended up on the outside than on the inside of the baby.

"I'm sorry if I interrupted your lunch. My name is Sam Wyatt, and I'm staying at the cabin at the end of the road. Frank and his wife, Agnes, needed some help earlier, and now that we've got them all squared away, I thought I'd check on everyone else."

"Why, thank you. How sweet. I'm Tonia Taylor. And this is Sarah." She wiped her hand on her apron before extending it. "My husband, Jack, is feeding

Susan. They're twins and can be quite the handful. He hasn't had a chance to shovel the driveway."

"It's nice to meet you. Everything else okay here?"

"Yes."

"Then, I'll finish checking on the others, and I'll be back later to lend a hand if Jack hasn't gotten to the driveway yet."

"That would be awesome. Thank you so much." The woman looked as if she'd grown a couple of extra arms trying to keep up with the toddler's antics and keep the slimy muck off her. Mostly off her anyway.

"I won't keep you then. Talk to you later." Sam headed back to the SUV and slid inside, the heat a little overwhelming after standing in the cold. "They had kids, but I think two is probably younger than you had in mind as a playmate." He laughed.

"Well, darn. Maybe at the next stop." He liked her positive attitude.

They pulled into the next driveway about a quarter mile down the road after turning onto Blue Spruce Road. Again, the driveway wasn't cleared, and no one was in sight.

"Wait here, Becca."

"Okay." An exaggerated sigh slipped out.

Sam knocked on the front door and was greeted by an older woman in her sixties.

"Hi, I'm Sam Wyatt." He repeated his introduction to the woman, letting her know what he was doing.

"How kind of you. Come in. Come in. I'm Iris Parker." The woman pulled at his arm toward the warmth inside.

"I've got someone with me, so I really can't."

Mrs. Parker peered around him at the SUV. "Bring her in. Let me fix you and your daughter something to drink. You can meet my husband and my grandson."

"She's not—"

"I won't take no for an answer. We all stick together around here, and it would seem you've made yourself one of us by helping the O'Malleys. Least I can do." The woman waved toward Becca, flagging her to come in.

Becca didn't have to be told twice. She was standing next to him in a split second, her smile hopeful. Strangely enough, she might get her wish, seeing as the woman had mentioned a grandson.

"This is Becca. Becca, this is Mrs. Parker. She's invited us in for a hot drink if that's okay with you?"

"Hi. I would love to come in. Do you have hot chocolate? Do you have kids? Do you have any games I can play? Do you..." Becca pulled off her hat, her eyes shining with excitement. She was the picture of sweet innocence with her rosy cheeks to match.

"Slow down, Becca. One question at a time, or you'll never get any answers." The adults laughed, although he could tell Becca wasn't sure why. But she did stop talking.

"I do have hot chocolate. And you can call me Iris, honey."

"Miss Iris." Sam corrected.

"Miss Iris, do you have kids?"

"I do, but probably not the age you're looking for. My kids are all grown."

Becca's face was an open book of disappointment.

"But I do have a grandson visiting. And he likes video games. Maybe you two can play while I visit with your dad."

Becca's eyes widened as she looked at him and then Iris. Whether at the prospect of meeting Iris's grandson or the reference to him being her dad, he wasn't sure, but Becca didn't say anything to the contrary.

"I'm not her dad. She's with her mother, and they are staying at the cabin for Christmas." There was no way to misinterpret the disappointed look on Becca's face, which answered his previous question.

Sam wasn't looking to be anyone's father. His

first time around had been a complete failure. It was mind-boggling that Becca might have been okay with letting the misconception stand. It was better to set her straight now than to have to nip any ideas she may have later.

"Oh, okay. She looks so much like you. Strange."

An older man Sam assumed was Mr. Parker, walked into the room.

"*Ahhh*, here's my husband now. He likes to nap in the mornings, the afternoons, and just about any time." Iris winked at Sam and then made the introductions. "Why don't we find Devon. Charles, if you could put on the teapot, that would be a big help."

"It's wonderful to meet you both. See you back in the kitchen shortly. It will be a nice change of pace to have someone other than Iris to talk to." It was the older man's turn to grin. Sam saw right through the pair of them. Old and in love. Not something he was familiar with, and yet from the outside, it seemed pleasurable.

They followed her down the hall and soon found the young man. With a game controller in hand, he moved around as if he had ants in his pants as he dodged the bad guy on the screen.

"Devon, can you pause your game, please. I've got someone here to meet you."

The boy glanced up at Becca and, just as quickly,

turned back to his game. Boys and girls had different interests at that age, and it didn't seem young Devon was overly thrilled at the idea of playing with a girl.

"*Hmmm.* I love that game. Level eight? That's all you're at?" Becca stood, arms crossed, and shook her head.

Devon looked up at her with curiosity. "It's a new game. What level are you at?"

"Thirty-three."

"Whatever." Devon shrugged; disbelief etched on his face.

"It's true. Ask me anything." Becca's chin rose a notch.

"Well, how did you get past this fortress?" Devon pointed at the screen.

Becca moved to sit down next to him. "You need to grab the magic sword hidden in the secret chamber. Click on the painting to the right of the fireplace to take it down and reveal the hidden switch to open the chamber." And just like that, the two became friends. It was as though video games had their own set of rules for engagement with other gamers.

Sam and Iris moved back into the kitchen, where they met up with Charles and shared a pot of coffee.

Sam didn't want to spend too much time chatting, but he also didn't want the older couple to feel awkward about getting a helping hand. He headed outside and started to shovel the sidewalk. It wasn't long before sweat soaked the T-shirt under his flannel shirt. He stripped off his outer jacket and started to tackle the driveway. It had been a long while since he'd done this kind of physical labor, and every muscle in his body made sure he knew it.

The driveway was short and took Sam about forty-five minutes to finish. He hoped it wouldn't be too hard to pull Becca away from her new friend. He wasn't her parent, and he wasn't even sure he would remember how to handle a child who didn't want to do something.

Sam went back inside and was surprised to see everyone at the kitchen table talking and laughing. There had to be something special going on to drag the kids away from their video game. By the time he shrugged off his boots, Iris had a fresh cup of coffee waiting.

"Thanks." Sam wrapped his hands around the mug, letting the warmth seeped into his skin.

"No. Thank *you*. I really appreciate you shoveling for me. This old body finds it harder and harder to do every year." Charles shook his head and got up to refill his cup.

"No problem." Eager, smiling faces greeted him as he sat down at the table.

Five minutes later, he knew why.

A Christmas Eve party.

Not exactly high on his priority list, but he didn't have the heart to say no. And since he fully expected to be long gone before Christmas Eve, it didn't really matter.

For the rest of the afternoon, Becca and Sam went from neighbor's house to neighbor's house, Sam checking up on everyone, and Becca telling everyone about the party and playing with any kids available. Many of the neighbors had everything under control and were already starting to take care of business on their own, but everyone was excited about the party.

There wasn't much he could do to stop the freight train, so he hoped Megan wasn't upset about the idea. Especially since with Frank laid up, the Parkers had decided the perfect place for the party was at the cabin—an idea Becca was over the moon about.

Sam pulled into the driveway of the cabin and shut off the engine. He had to admit, the front yard with its decorated flagpole was the perfect place for a party. It would be easy enough to build them a fire pit for a bonfire before he left. As busy as they'd been, he hadn't thought once about checking in for updates on the status of the pass and only just realized he hadn't heard back from the police captain.

"Everyone was sweet. We won't be hungry, that's for sure." He grinned as he grabbed the two boxes filled with food, stacked them one on top of each other, and carried them to the front porch, Becca close on his heels with the third box.

"It was fun meeting all those people. Especially Mr. and Mrs. Parker. I loved her idea for a Christmas party and bonfire. I can't wait to tell Mom. I hope we can play in the snow during the party."

Pressing the boxes against the doorframe for balance and holding on tightly with one hand, he turned the door handle, relieved to find it unlocked. He pushed open the door. "I'll get you the sled from the shed and later, we can let the other kids know to bring theirs to the party."

"And will you sled with me? Like we're family. Please?"

She didn't give an inch when she wanted something. "Maybe. I might not fit, but we'll check it out." It wasn't exactly a promise, but it was the best he could offer.

"Yay!" In her excitement, she'd missed the fact he hadn't agree to sled with her. Hopefully, when the time came, she'd be having so much fun it wouldn't matter he'd already left.

"Mom," Becca hollered. "Where are you? I've got some great news." Within seconds, she'd set the box down and headed for the hall just as Megan and Agnes appeared. Sam chuckled at her enthusiasm.

"*Shhh*, honey. Mr. O'Malley is finally sleeping. He needs his rest. What's going on?" Megan reached out to brush her hand down her daughter's hair and across her cheek. The obvious love and affection in the simple gesture squeezed at his heart.

"We're going to have a Christmas party. Right here in the front yard. And everyone's coming. Mr. and Mrs. Parker. Mr. and Mrs. Taylor, and Sarah and Susan, their twins. They are a lot younger than me, but it'll be fun. Then there's—"

"Whoa. Back up. You lost me at the part about the party." Megan looked up at him for help. "Here, let me help you with that." Her smile warmed him more than any cup of coffee had managed to do all day. Not that he hadn't enjoyed meeting and helping people, because surprisingly, he had.

Even snowed in, people pulled together, Christmas spirit filling their hearts and overflowing. If it was his guess, it would be the same year-round with these folks. It was one of the things he used to love about the country. "Thanks. How's Frank doing?"

"He's been in a lot of pain, but he's doing okay, all things considered. We have him stabilized, and he's sleeping. We just need to keep icing it and hope I'm right and that it's a sprained knee joint and not an ACL tear. Until we can get him to the hospital for testing, we won't know for sure. It's hard to tell with the swelling just by looking at it. So, what's this about a party?"

Becca pulled on her mother's arm to get her attention. "That's what I'm trying to tell you. Mrs. Parker came up with the grand idea of a Christmas party, and Mr. Sam agreed. It's going to be here, Christmas eve."

"Sam agreed, did he? I'm sure there was no shortage of coercion from a seven-year-old." Megan looked at him for answers.

"I'm not sure what co...*coershin* is, but he agreed. And I didn't make him say yes. I think Mrs. Parker made him hungry when she started talking about baking and what she'd bring." Becca giggled.

"She might be right about the food." Sam shrugged. "It sounded pretty good compared to what I brought and what we've been eating. Honey ham, au gratin potatoes, cornbread, peach pie, cookies. Who could resist?"

Megan gazed at him long and hard, contemplating, and then apparently satisfied, her mouth curled into a sweet smile.

"Sounds like fun. So, tell me what you all cooked up, so I know what I need to do."

Agnes had joined the group. "It's a splendid idea. Iris Parker loves having neighborhood parties and normally does something at her place. But this year, her son couldn't make it because he's deployed, and so she decided against it. This will help keep her mind off how far away he is for the holidays."

"Are you sure you're okay with this? I know you've got a lot on your plate with Frank and Becca, and you came up here for a special Christmas." Sam didn't want to make things more stressful for Megan. Her sister's absence had already upset her enough.

"Stop. It's okay. If it will make Becca happy, I'm happy. My mother would have loved the idea, and I'm certain Rachael will, too. It will certainly liven things up around here. It was quiet today after you and Becca left, other than taking care of Frank, that is."

"Okay, then. I guess it's confirmed."

"Yay!" Becca jumped in excitement, clapping her hands. "I've got to use the bathroom. Don't make any plans without me. I'll be right back."

They all laughed as she skipped out of the room.

"They want a bonfire out front by the flagpole, so I'll have to haul some wood out there before I leave. If there's anything else I can do to help, let me know." The party did sound fun, but fun wasn't anything Sam deserved. Solitude was his penance for putting business before his family.

"Leave? You're still planning to if the pass opens?" Megan's brow tightened in consternation.

"This is your family thing. I won't intrude. Besides, I've got work to do."

"Becca seems to think you're staying."

"She has a grand plan, and I didn't have the heart to correct her. She'll be fine when everyone shows up and she's having fun."

"I hope so. She's getting attached to you, and I know it's not your problem, but I worry. Anyway, what's with all the boxes? Are there more in the car that need to be brought in?"

Sam shook his head. "This is it." He'd noticed the attachment as well but wasn't eager to discuss it, so he was relieved with the change in conversation. "You won't believe all the food everyone sent. Once they heard about Frank, everyone raided their refrigerators and pantries and loaded us up. Mrs. Thomas fixed us a hot soup and sandwich lunch and sent the rest of the pot of soup home with me."

Home. He meant to the cabin. It was a slip of the brain and tongue, but luckily, no one seemed to notice.

"That's wonderful!"

Sam headed for the kitchen with Megan close on his heels. Side by side, they loaded the food into the pantry and refrigerator.

"This is great, and I know exactly what I'll serve for supper tonight." Megan's enthusiasm was surprising considering everything she'd been through today helping with Frank.

Like mother, like daughter, they both had an endless stream of energy. "What's that?"

"Hamburger pie. It's an old favorite of mine. It's basic ingredients, but with what everybody's given us, I can make a big batch. Maybe even enough for lunch tomorrow."

"Hamburger pie? Sounds strange. When I think a pie, I think of dessert, not a hamburger." Sam cracked a smile, and for the space of a second, he felt almost normal. He was having a regular conversation with a beautiful woman, snowed in, and in a cabin in the woods. Quite perfect.

Except it was the wrong woman. And just like that, the joy he felt disappeared, and in its place, guilt put a chokehold on him.

"You've led a sheltered life." She laughed. "It's just

hamburger, potatoes, tomato soup, and either corn or beans, all mixed together and baked. And based on what was given to us, it looks as though we'll be using corn tonight."

"Sounds interesting." *Not*. It sounded like a pile of mush, but he wouldn't complain. *Try one bite, and if you don't like it, you don't have to eat it.* Words he'd spoken to Lydia repeatedly, and advice he would take for himself. He made his way to the kitchen doorway, intent on disappearing.

"I haven't called anyone about the pass lately. Did you get any updates on Rachael?"

"They were sure it wouldn't be today, and probably not tomorrow. They're doing the best they can, but they are also watching another storm system threatening to come in. Rachael seems to be doing fine with her new friend, which is weird. I wish she were here, but I'm glad she's not spending the time alone. Who knows, this could be a big step forward for her. So, I'm trying to keep positive about everything."

"Great attitude." Not exactly what he wanted to hear, but it was nice to know she didn't mind him hanging around.

"Was it difficult getting to the neighbors? I take it they are all doing okay?"

"I did a lot of shoveling. It'll be slick come nightfall when it freezes, but I warned everyone to be careful. There are eight houses total, and so far, the O'Malley's were the only ones to lose power, and the only ones having a rough time of it after the storm. I've gone back and shut off the breakers at the house to make sure that if the power comes back on for any reason, there'll be no issues."

"That was sweet of you. I knew you were a nice guy." Megan's smile was soft and tempting, but he knew better.

"You wouldn't think that if you knew me."

"That's just it, you do get to know someone being stuck in a cabin with them. The real person. And I'm thinking there's a whole lot more to you than you let on. I know the man I first met yesterday is not the real you, but we're getting warmer." Her smile widened, inviting him into confidence and friendship.

He didn't want to go down this road with her. "I'm not sure I know who the real me is anymore."

Megan crossed the room and laid her arm on his. It was the second time she'd done this today, and the warmth cracked the ice barrier that held his emotions in check. He could get lost in the blue eyes gazing up at him.

"In the Air Force, I had to learn to read people pretty quick. Especially some of the younger service guys coming into the medical center with a wide array of problems. Most of the time, they were just overwhelmed with what they'd signed on for. They needed reassurance that things would be okay. Sometimes, I sense you're a lot like them. Maybe if you talked about what's bothering you, it would help. I'm an excellent listener."

"I'm not eighteen, and you can't fix me. No one can fix me. But what about you? For all your talk of helping others, what about yourself? I see a beautiful, confident woman determined to take on the world one step at a time. Facing whatever challenges come her way and protecting her daughter along the way. You mentioned your husband died three years ago, but have you moved on and started living life again, or are you still hiding your heart behind the pain of the past?" If she insisted on psychoanalyzing him, it didn't hurt to make her look in the mirror. Megan was made for love and far too special to live out her life alone.

Unlike him.

Megan's smile wavered. "I've had to do everything myself. I've already had one good marriage. I thought we would have forever together—turned out life had other plans. It's by choice that I don't rely on others. I need to stay strong. For Becca's sake, I'm not willing to take another chance and be wrong. Maybe my time will come when she's grown up, but it's just not now." Megan had stepped back, breaking the contact between them.

"And from the outside looking in, I figure you deserve better. I've never known a woman like you, and I figure you're strong enough to handle just about anything."

"That's a lot of advice from a guy who won't even talk."

Point taken. Mind my own business. "Yeah, probably. But maybe I don't deserve fixing, and you do." He shrugged.

"I doubt that's the case. You forget I'm starting to see the real you. Hopefully, when this is over, you will find someone you trust enough to talk to about it. Maybe then you'll have the opportunity to let some light shine back into your life."

"If you say so. I'm going to shower before dinner. I worked up a sweat shoveling snow most of the afternoon." Sam had the urge to reach up and brush back the lock of hair that had fallen across her cheek, but instead, he shoved his hand in his pocket.

He turned and left, afraid that if she psychoanalyzed him any further, she might discover the truth. He liked her. Whether he wanted to be or not, he was attracted to her.

Twenty minutes of hot, scalding water helped his

muscles but did nothing for the torment in his mind. Memories of Laura and Lydia flashed in his head, but so did images of Megan and Becca.

With no bedroom to escape to as a retreat, Sam made his way to the living room and sat down on the couch after stopping to stoke the fire. His heart heavy, he pulled out the well-worn photo of his daughter, trying to remember her smiling face.

"Why do you look at the picture if it makes you so sad?" Becca spoke from the hallway as she entered the living room. The expression on her face softened his heart. She was such a sweet child, and her caring heart continued to amaze him. She never seemed to give up on him, but then again, neither did Megan.

"Because it's all I have left." The words were ripped from his throat. Becca. Lydia. The similarities were amazing. Perhaps that's why Sam couldn't say no to her. Couldn't push her away. His heart softened like melting ice cream on a sunny day with the love reflected in her gaze as she watched him.

"Can I see?" she asked, her request tentative, as if she was afraid to upset him. Becca waited patiently but didn't move.

Sam relented and turned his wallet around, holding up the photo for her to see.

Becca took one quick look before gazing back up at him in confusion. "She looks a lot like me."

"Yes, she does."

"Who is she?" Becca pressed on, a mixture of curiosity and care in her voice.

"My daughter." Sam sat back in the chair; his shoulders slumped forward as he fought the wave of grief threatening to consume him.

"If you're sad, you must be missing her. Is she very far away?"

Sam closed his eyes. "Yes." He forced the word from his lips.

"Heaven far away?" Her intuitive perception of the situation was amazing.

"Yes." Sam rubbed at his temple, flipping his wallet closed and shoving it back in his pocket. He opened his eyes to find Becca still standing there, tears in her eyes.

It was the second time in two days he found himself wanting to talk about his daughter.

"Her name was Lydia. She and her mother died in a car accident a couple of years ago. Every day, I wake up and think about how much I miss them both." Speaking the words, Sam could almost feel their presence. It was as though they were listening.

"I'm sorry. It must hurt your heart an awful lot."

"It does. And because you two are similar, it was a shock I didn't handle well the first day I met you. I didn't mean to be rude, but it was like seeing her again, and I knew it wasn't possible. She would have been right about the same age as you now. I miss watching her play in the snow, running around the yard, or telling me about her day at school when I got home from work. And I miss reading her bedtime stories." Too many times, he'd not been home before she was in bed, and he'd give anything to get back the time lost. They say everyone has a twin somewhere in the world, and Sam believed Becca was Lydia's.

Sam felt a little hand slide into his and squeeze. He opened his eyes and stared at Becca, drawing from the strength she offered him, once again being reminded of Megan.

"Mr. Sam, I have the perfect idea. You should marry my mom, and then you can be my dad. We can be a family. My dad died when I was four, and I don't remember much of him, but I have pictures. I would love to have a new dad, and I think it would make my mom happy. She's been sad since my grandma died. Maybe it would make us all feel better."

Sam didn't know what to say. Sam squeezed Becca's hand, his heart melting bit by bit. He didn't want to hurt her, and it was an incredibly sweet offer, but there was no way he would ever consider marriage or having a family again. He'd had his chance at happiness, and he'd failed.

"Thanks for listening, Becca. I'm honored you would consider me for such a special place in your life, but marriage doesn't work that way. How about you and me, agree to be friends?" It was the most he could offer, and certainly more than he would have been capable of offering a day ago.

"I like it, Mr. Sam." She was a remarkable young lady, and if he wasn't careful, there would be a puddle of water at his feet as the ice around his heart thawed, and a living heart would feel emotions he wasn't prepared to handle.

"I should get us firewood." Sam moved to grab his jacket from the coat rack and headed outside before she could stop him.

CHAPTER SEVEN

Megan focused on putting dinner together, driving thoughts of Sam out of her head whenever they popped in, which was far more often than she liked. She didn't want to think about the warm, kind, and caring man who'd gone out of his way to help others today. She didn't want to think about the growing attraction she felt, an attraction she was quite positive went in one direction. Each time they shared a moment, she was never sure if he was thinking of her or his deceased wife, but odds were on Laura.

She thought about what Sam said. Was he right about her? Was she missing out on life? And what of him? It seemed they were more alike than they wanted to be, and not in a good way. At this point, it was the only way she knew how to operate. But what about the future? The truth was, one day, Becca would be all grown and move on with her own life, whereas Megan had put life on hold. What then?

Sam had his own set of problems. The two of them made quite the pair. Not a pair in the sense of a couple, but a pair in the sense of two totally messed-up people. He had no idea the price Megan had paid to put her life back together, especially that first year after Andy died. The only time she could let herself grieve had been in the wee-dark hours of the night, only to have to wake up strong and ready to take charge the next morning. Her day had no room for weakness.

But what of the price he'd paid? And was still paying? Sam didn't have a daughter to keep him grounded and moving forward. *Poor Sam.* He wouldn't want her pity, but the man needed a friend. Something she could give him, and maybe in the long run, it would help them both move forward.

Megan topped the casserole with the whipped potatoes and added a dab of butter as a finishing touch. She placed it in the oven and set the timer for thirty minutes. The back door closed, the sound drawing her attention. Glancing out the window, she checked to see who'd gone outside.

She spotted Sam and watched him as he headed toward the woodpile. He picked up an axe and swung it up over his head and then back down, landing with precision and power, busting the log in two. One by one, he split the logs and stacked them. The pile looked high already, leaving her to wonder if there was more to his sudden desire to split logs.

"Becca?" Megan went in search of her daughter.

The bedroom door opened, and her daughter stepped out into the hallway. "Did you call me, Mom?"

"Yes, honey. It's almost time for dinner. Can you get washed up and come set the table, please. I'm going to fix a tray to take to Mr. Frank, but you should set a place for Miss Agnes."

"Okay." Becca walked toward her, a solemn expression on her face.

"What's the matter?" Talk about a lack of energy, something completely unlike Becca's normal cheery self.

"It's Mr. Sam. He's so sad, and now I know why."

"I thought we discussed that you weren't going to bother him with questions."

"I know. And I'm sorry, but he was just sitting there with a sad look on his face. I wanted to help him. I don't think I made things any better. Did you know he had a daughter? She died."

"He told me, honey. He lost his wife and daughter two years ago. I think he's still really hurting inside."

"Like us? With Daddy?" Becca asked, her voice barely above a whisper.

"Yes. Like us. Time helps, but we had each other. He doesn't have anyone to share his hurt with, and so it might be taking him a little longer. He'll be all right in time."

"I hope so. He's a nice man."

"Yes. I agree." *Not to mention attractive.*

"Just be his friend. I'm sure he could use a few." Megan glanced out the window to see Sam still swinging the axe.

"He told me I was his friend." Becca had made more progress than she had, but there was no way her daughter would understand the healing process or just how much she'd helped Sam in the short amount of time they'd known him.

"Why do you think you made it worse? It seems to me, if he told you he wanted to be friends, things between you can't be as bad as you say. You have a way of wiggling into somebody's heart, and maybe you've managed to creep into his. I'm proud of you for trying, honey. I know it couldn't have been easy."

"I told him he should marry you, and then we could be a family. And..." Becca picked at one of the buttons on her shirt. The offer totally explained Sam's current interest in the woodpile. Her daughter's innocent comment had been made with the best of intentions but wouldn't change the net effect.

"And what? It's okay, you can tell me anything."

Becca looked up at her nervously. "And that he could be my new dad." She looked away as she said the words.

Be her dad? Megan closed her eyes for a second, needing to regroup and not wanting Becca to see her confusion. She tried to find the right words, but she had no clue how to respond.

"That's not how things are done. People date based on common grounds and interests, and Sam and I barely know each other. We only met yesterday. I think it was a sweet offer made with the best of intentions, and he must feel the same way since he offered you friendship instead." That was the easy part of the talk they needed to have.

"People fall in love at first sight in my fairy tales, why can't you and Mr. Sam?" Becca persisted.

"Sam's family is very much alive in his heart and mind, and neither one us is looking to get married." *Now for the hard part.* "But we need to talk about you wanting a new dad. I had no idea you felt that way." Megan pulled her daughter into a hug and kissed the top of her head. This was something Megan hadn't considered in the years since Andy's death. Her focus had been on raising her daughter as both mother and father, never considering Becca might want both again. Or feel as though she were missing out.

"I think it would be nice to have another dad since mine's in heaven. Do you think he'd mind?" Becca bit her lip as she waited for an answer.

Megan's eyes filled with tears that threatened to spill over. "No, honey, of course not." Her daughter's words drove straight to the heart, opening Megan's eyes for the first time. It seemed that no matter how hard Megan tried, she wasn't getting it right. The question was, did Megan have enough heart left to love again? Because one thing was for certain, it couldn't be *for* her daughter, or *because* of her daughter, for that matter. It would have to be for herself. And when was the last time she thought of herself?

And then there was Sam.

He would be gone the minute the pass opened, even sooner if he could find a way out. The ounce of attraction she felt was not enough reason to even remotely put herself and her heart on the line, not when she'd be resigned to playing second fiddle in his life. Sam wore emotional unavailability like a second skin.

"I've just been busy having fun with it being just the two of us, honey." The timer dinged. *Saved by the bell.* "We can talk more about this later. Run along and set the table. I need to take a plate to Frank."

Megan glanced outside and noted Sam was still chopping wood. She fixed Frank's plate and headed down the hall to the O'Malley's bedroom door, juggling the tray in one hand as she knocked with the other.

"Come in," Agnes called out. "Everyone's decent." The older woman had a wonderful sense of humor now that her husband was in good hands and doing better. The pair of them made a game of word banter, and Megan couldn't help but find it highly entertaining. The humor was just what she needed right now.

She pushed the door open and entered the room. "I've got Frank's dinner."

"I might not be so decent after I eat. After she strips off my dinner-covered shirt to rinse it out like a mother hen, I'll be naked for hours. My shirt is barely dry from lunch." He winked.

"Maybe I should let you eat alone and join the others. Then you'll miss my attention. And it's wifely, not motherly. There's a difference." Agnes frowned.

"I don't think I married you forty-two years ago to wash my shirt."

"Frank!" Agnes blushed and huffed out of the room, but not before Megan saw her smile.

"Your incorrigible, Mr. O'Malley, but I think she likes it." Megan laughed. "We're having hamburger pie, and if you end up wearing some of it, I won't tell anyone. Tomorrow, we need to get you some fresh clothes."

"It's a good thing you hadn't already given me the tray, or the missus may have dumped it on me." He chuckled.

"You're probably right. I'll be back to check on you in a bit. I need to get the food on the table for the others." Megan headed for the door.

"Thanks. You're a keeper, and Sam's a lucky man."

She turned back to Frank and shook her head. "Oh, we aren't together. And don't be getting any ideas. We just met, and not under the best of circumstances."

He grinned, more than enough proof he didn't believe a word of what she said.

"Don't matter how or why, it only matters that you did. The rest, well, it just happens. I knew I was in love with Agnes the day after I met her. It just took me a few days to convince her I wasn't insane."

"Well, you were certainly right in your case, but it doesn't normally happen that way. Besides, I've been married already. Chances of me finding the right guy twice is next to zero."

"Time will tell. Heed the words of an old man who knows what he sees. Now skedaddle so I can eat." There was no sense in arguing the point because he was right—time would tell.

She entered the dining room and discovered Sam had already come inside, and everyone was seated at the table waiting for her. "Sorry to keep you waiting. Frank likes to talk." Megan grinned.

"Don't I know it. That's why I escaped when I could. I talked to my boys, and everything's business as usual in town. We own O'Malley's Charm in town, but the kids manage the restaurant and they say everything is going fine without us. Don't tell Mr. O'Malley, though. He likes to feel useful helping in the kitchen and talking to customers. Keeps him young at heart, I reckon." Agnes chuckled before taking a bite of her bread.

"I think you do that for him." Megan winked at the older woman.

"Can I ask a blessing?" Becca asked as Megan ladled a small portion of the casserole on her daughter's plate.

"That would be sweet. You go right ahead." Agnes smiled and held out her hand to take Becca's.

Megan sat across from Becca in the empty seat.

Her daughter reached for Sam's hand, and much to her surprise, Sam took it, almost as if it was a natural thing to do.

"We need to close our eyes." Becca looked around to see if everyone was doing what she asked. When Becca's gaze landed on Megan, she joined the others and closed her eyes.

"God, please help Mr. Frank's leg so it won't hurt anymore. I pray Aunt Rachael will be here tomorrow so we can build an igloo and have an igloo lunch. And I pray...I pray Mr. Sam's hurt goes away and that you take good care of Lydia for him. Oh, and bless the food we are about to eat. Amen."

"Amen." The others all echoed the sentiment.

Megan opened her eyes and zeroed in on Sam, afraid of his reaction. She needn't have worried. Tense, yes. Angry, not at all. Becca really was working a miracle on him.

Agnes's curious gaze landed on Sam. "What lovely prayers. It was sweet of you to remember Frank. Thank you." To her credit, Agnes didn't say a word about Sam's part in the prayer. Her sweet sensitivity was much appreciated.

"Thank you, Becca. I don't know about everyone else, but I'm ready to eat. Chopping firewood made me hungry. Oh, and guess what? I'm pretty sure I caught a glimpse of your wild animal while I was outside." And just like that, Sam had moved on, letting the awkwardness of the moment fall away.

"And? Was it a dog like you thought?" Becca asked, her eyes lit up with excitement.

"Yes. Scrawny looking little white dog with brown ears. But he ran off when I started toward him. He's skittish for sure."

"What's skittish?" Becca looked up at Sam as if he hung the moon.

Sam smiled. "Means he's afraid of people, or maybe just me. We need to keep an eye out for him, though. I swear he looked hungry."

"Maybe we could put some food out for him?" Becca asked hopefully.

"We could, but I'm afraid it would confuse him, and he won't return to his own home." Trying to rationalize with a seven-year-old wasn't the easiest thing to do, but Sam was holding his own.

"But what if he's lost. It's cold outside, and he'll starve. Or freeze. We have to help him. Please." The persistence thing was a trait Becca had gotten honestly—from her.

"Fine. We'll find something to put out by the garage. And some water. Maybe when I make the rounds tomorrow, we can ask the others." Sam caved just as she'd known he would.

"At least now we know it's not a bear." Megan grinned. "What a relief."

Becca was the center of attention the rest of the evening as she regaled the others with tales about her school, her teachers, and her friends. Most surprising was Sam's occasional smile, and even an occasional comment slipped into the conversation, all of which kept Becca on a roll.

"You all know you can't lick a flagpole, right?" Becca looked around the table at everyone for confirmation of her newfound fact. "There was a boy at my school that tried to get me to do it, and another boy in my class told me my tongue would get stuck. I was afraid, so I didn't do it. Mom tells me I made the right choice. A better choice than she made—" Becca giggled "—because she did it, so she knows." *The little rat.*

That had been information shared between the two of them, and now Megan felt foolish, just as she had when she was a child, and everyone had made fun of her. Only now, it was Sam who laughed, something she hadn't seen him do before. For that, she'd let her daughter embarrass her a hundred times over.

"It sounds to me as if the boy who told you not to do it, likes you." Agnes grinned, winking at Becca.

"I don't think so." Becca grew quite serious.

"Besides, I'm not interested even if he is. Mom says I am too young to worry about boys, and I agree." Another round of laughter filled the room. Megan hadn't foreseen having this much fun being snowed in with strangers. Or almost strangers.

"I agree with your mother. You're too young. Wait until you're older, and then you can be like your mom and find a wonderful man like Mr. Sam. I can spot a good man a mile away, and he's one of the keepers. They don't make them like they used to." Agnes shot Becca a conspiratorial grin.

"Oh, no. We're not together." The conversation turned into an echo of Frank's comment to her earlier, leaving her to wonder exactly what the O'Malleys talked about behind closed doors. They were wrong about her and Sam, and Megan didn't want Becca getting any ideas. "My sister, Rachael, is in Hallbrook, stuck on the other side of the pass. We're supposed to be spending Christmas up here with her. Sam and I had a mix-up with our reservations, but then he got stuck here because of the avalanche."

Agnes looked back and forth from one to the other. "Really? You could have fooled me. You two appear as though you belong together."

"I assure you; she's telling the truth," Sam spoke up, the gleam in his eyes an indication he wasn't upset with the turn the conversation had taken. It was probably the closest he would get to admitting he was having fun.

"Mr. Sam is my friend, but I'm good at sharing. He needs more friends."

"Thanks, Becca." Sam winked at her daughter.

Winked. Megan would never have believed it if she hadn't seen it.

CHAPTER EIGHT

Megan yawned and looked around the room but didn't see Becca. It came as no surprise because her daughter was an early riser and an early eater. She ran a brush through her hair, rubbed the sleep from her eyes, and tightened the belt of her robe just in case she ran into Sam.

Just as expected, Becca was sitting at the table with a bowl of cereal. "Good morning, honey." Somethings didn't change. Megan smiled at her daughter, excited for the fun they would have today making an igloo and picking out a Christmas tree.

"Morning, Mom. Mr. Sam made coffee, and I was going to bring you some, but he told me I needed to let you sleep in this morning. So, I tried to be quiet."

"You did a great job, and I appreciate the extra

sleep. Thank you." She kissed the top of her daughter's head on the way into the kitchen. Sam's coffee yesterday had been strong enough to wake the dead. Megan liked hers more on the Hazelnut light side of life; however, the aroma of black drudge filled the kitchen, promising her more of what she'd choked down yesterday.

Megan looked around but didn't see Sam anywhere. She didn't want to hurt his feelings or appear ungracious, but two days in a row was more than she could bear. Taking a leap of bravery, she chucked the liquid down the sink and proceeded to make a fresh pot. She measured out six scoops into the filter, aiming for a balance between the way she would want it and the way he would. Compromise was important when you were snowbound with a stranger.

"Mr. Sam told me we could check the food bowl we left out for the dog. He won't let me go out alone. You should tell him I am seven and can handle going outside." Seven going on thirteen.

"He's being cautious, which is a good thing. Remember, whoever's in charge makes the rules."

Becca frowned. "Fine. But I'm not a baby."

Megan laughed, shaking her head.

The coffee gurgled as it finished brewing. She

poured a cup, adding some of the cream one of the neighbors had graciously supplied. Then she added a little more cream and stirred, trying to get it to the caramel color she liked. She took a sip. *This I can do.*

Thinking of the neighbors reminded her she needed to plan a menu for the Christmas Eve festivities. Everyone was bringing a dish or two, but she had to do her share as well. Luckily, she'd found plastic forks, spoons, and knives, as well as paper plates, all in the laundry storage cabinet. That at least would save on the cleanup and make the whole affair less stressful.

It was a wonderful idea, and she was glad Iris Parker had suggested it. Having kids to play with almost guaranteed Becca's level of fun would multiply exponentially.

"Good morning." Agnes joined her in the kitchen.

"Good morning. Help yourself to some coffee."

"Um, we may pass this morning." Agnes shifted uncomfortably and looked away.

"Don't worry. Yesterday's brew was Sam's attempt at making coffee. I made it this morning, and I think everyone will be able to tolerate it." Megan grinned.

"In that case, don't mind if I do." The older woman laughed as she grabbed two cups. "I didn't want to offend anyone, so I'm glad I'm not the only one who found it intolerable."

Megan held out the creamer, her cheeks hurting as her grin widened. "How's Frank this morning? Should I check on him?"

"No, no. He's doing fine. Slept better. I'll take him more pain relievers. Just wish you had good-temper pills. He's bored stuck in bed and a little irritable." Agnes rolled her eyes and picked up the bottle of pain relievers from the counter.

"We could carry him out to the living room so he can watch TV. Change of view. I don't want to hurt him or aggravate anything in his leg, but sometimes the mental condition of a patient is even more important in the healing process."

"He'd appreciate that. I'm going to see if Sam can run me to the house today to get more clean clothes and pick up a few books for Frank."

"Sounds like a plan." Megan nodded her head in agreement.

"Speaking of Sam, if you two really aren't a couple, you should think twice about letting him leave without trying to start something. He's got a big heart and cares for your daughter. I'm thinking he could care for you also if you let him know you're interested."

Put two single people together, and suddenly everyone wants to play matchmaker. "It's not like that. He's lost without his wife and daughter, and I'm not sure I'm the best person to help him. I tried once. He was quick to point out that I was big on words and light on action." She and Sam were at different places in life and the timing was all wrong.

"Well, then maybe it's time you stepped back into action. He's the perfect person to test your dating skills on. Flirt a little, for goodness sake! At least let him know you're interested. I've seen the way you watch him."

"You're imagining things. Even if I was, it's not that easy. I have a daughter to consider."

"You can't hide behind Becca for the next ten years. Don't let life pass you by." Agnes tapped out two pills into her hand, grabbed up the mugs, and walked out of the kitchen, leaving Megan staring after her.

Easy for you to say. You're still married and don't have to open your heart again, wondering if you'll get hurt or if you'll even survive it the next time around. Besides, she wouldn't have a clue what to do. Her knowledge of modern day flirting and dating rules amounted to zero.

Becca came into the kitchen and headed for the sink with her bowl. "Mom, I'm going to watch cartoons."

"Okay, I'm going to make pancakes for breakfast. I'm assuming you want some of those and that cereal was just your first course?"

"Yes, please. Oh, and remember, we need to build the igloo today and go on a tree hunt and go sledding. And we should build a snowman." Becca smiled, her blue eyes twinkling with excitement.

"I remember, but I'm not sure we can do all that in one day." Megan laughed. "We can start by picking out the tree. We'll tie a ribbon around it, and when Aunt Rachael gets here, we can take her there to get her approval. With any luck, she'll show up today. The property manager said we were free to cut down a Christmas tree and bring it back to the cabin to decorate with all Grandma's decorations."

"Awww, shucks. I was hoping to get it now and bring it back. Please?"

"You know the rule—everyone has to approve."

"Okay. Maybe she'll get here soon." Her daughter's smile brightened before she headed for the living room.

There was no reason to tell Becca that wasn't going to happen, at least not based on the last conversation she had with her sister. Megan took out the box of pancake mix and the other ingredients and mixed everything together. She sensed someone behind her and turned around.

Sam. Freshly showered, his hair still wet. The man looked...scrumptious. The bulky, corded sweater he wore molded his chest and hung low on his hips. Dark-blue jeans completed the rugged outdoorsman picture.

"Good morning," he said, his voice husky. And judging by the shiver of pleasure racing down her spine, she liked husky. *A lot.*

"Good morning. Coffee's, um, ready." She turned away. The last thing she needed was him to see her blushing like a schoolgirl. Drat Agnes and all her talk of flirting.

"I know, I made it this morning, but thanks." *Uh oh.* She'd almost forgotten her coffee redo while she took mental stock of the handsome man, and he might not be so happy when he discovered what she did.

"Umm... I sort of remade it...in the best interests of the rest of the household adults."

His brow wrinkled as he looked first at the coffeepot and then back at her. "It looks a light."

"It's called compromise. Not everyone enjoys coffee made like syrup." She shrugged, standing by her decision. He was outnumbered.

"It might have been a little strong, but it couldn't have been so bad it warranted being thrown out."

"Wanna bet?" She looked up and laughed. His expression was priceless. Apparently, Sam wasn't in the habit of hearing brutal honesty. "I made it stronger than I normally enjoy, hoping to meet you halfway."

Sam took a sip and grimaced. "It'll be fine."

"I'm sorry. Maybe I should have kept yours and put it in a cup."

"I said it's fine. Less caffeine won't hurt me, that's for sure." He shrugged.

"If you say so." Megan felt better and turned back to finish mixing the batter.

"I do. What's for breakfast, and can I help, or have I been banished from the kitchen for a lack of culinary skills?"

"Pancakes. And, no, you're not banished, as long as you promise your cooking skills are more refined than your coffee-making skills." She flashed him a smile, hoping he wouldn't take offense.

"Just tell me what to do. If I'm following orders, I can't go wrong. Right?" He chuckled, and the sound was one she liked *and* one she could get used to.

"First, you should probably take Becca outside to check on the dog's food. She's worried."

"Okay. She was disappointed I wouldn't let her

go out there alone—in the dark." Sam started toward the living room.

"I knew there had to more information I wasn't getting. Good call." Megan nodded.

"Be right back." True to his word, he was back in less than five minutes.

"The dog came and ate and drank everything we put out last night and we've refilled both bowls. I didn't say anything to Becca, but I'm worried he's a stray by the looks of him."

"Well, if he is, I hope we can catch him and run him into town when the pass opens."

"I'll check with the neighbors to see if they know of anyone missing a dog. Becca seems to love the idea of a dog. Maybe if he's a stray, you could always adopt him."

"No. And don't be putting any ideas in her head. She's been wanting one for a long time, but with my job and our schedules, it wouldn't be fair to the dog."

Sam stared at her as if he wanted to say something but then didn't, instead refilling his cup of coffee.

"Tell me what I can do to help in here now." The change in subject left her wondering what he wasn't saying. Megan knew far better than anyone else, a dog was not the answer. Sam didn't understand, and she didn't see him lining up and raising his hand.

"There's fresh maple syrup from one of the neighbors that should make the box mix almost palatable. And there are some peaches I was going to cut up and put on the table if you're serious about helping."

"I am. I think I can handle maple syrup and peaches and keep everyone safe from me." Sam's easygoing smile reached his eyes, the corners crinkling upward.

"It would seem so." Megan scooped out quarter-cup servings of batter onto the skillet and turned the heat up a notch. Now was the perfect time to talk to Sam, especially knowing Becca was glued to the TV. "I've been meaning to talk to you about Becca. I'm sorry if she's been intrusive. She's just a child and doesn't understand boundaries as well as grown-ups do." She flipped the pancakes one by one, finding it easier to keep her focus on the task and not on the man.

"Don't worry about it." His voice changed from one of humor to one of a more somber nature. The mood in the kitchen had been ruined by the discussion. She shouldn't have mentioned it, but felt she owed him an apology.

"I do worry. She told me what she said, but she didn't really understand what she was asking or how it would make you feel. She means well." Megan dared a glance in Sam's direction and then wished she hadn't.

Clearly, talking with a seven-year-old about the issue was entirely different than talking with another grownup. Every second of his silence made the gnawing in her stomach grow. She flipped the pancakes over. *Again.* Anything to keep her hands busy and her mouth shut.

"Thank you." Sam's voice wavered when he finally spoke.

Megan reached out to touch his arm, hoping to comfort him. Human touch was reported to be an amazing healer, and it was a risk she was willing to take for Sam.

He stared down at her hand, and then back at her, his eyes full of confusion. Everything around her disappeared except for the two of them. Was he about to kiss her? Did she want him to? Who was it he wanted to kiss? Her or Laura? It was an answer she desperately needed but didn't have a clue how figure it out.

Sam's eyes darkened. He stepped back, breaking the contact between them. The shuttered look in his eyes was a clear signal the moment was over. "It looks as if those pancakes are done, unless you're aiming for blackened." He smirked. "I'll let the others know breakfast is ready. When it warms up a bit, I'm going to head out to the neighbors again and work on a few more driveways and sidewalks."

Clearly, the answer had been Laura. Agnes and Frank had it all wrong. You couldn't have a relationship with only one person interested. One thing for sure, the urge to kiss him meant she was the interested party. The idea was both scary and exciting at the same time. She wondered what he would have done if she had raised up on tiptoe and kissed him first.

She hadn't planned on her life including anyone after Andy. This new twist in her road wasn't something she prepared for, but she was clearly more prepared than Sam.

"Why don't you go ahead and sit down for the first batch. Becca's already had cereal and won't eat but one or two. Before I forget, while you're out today, will you see if you can get a headcount for the party?"

"Will do." Sam started to leave the kitchen, pausing at the door. "How's Frank?"

She could do small talk as well as the next person, letting him set the pace for the moment. "He's making progress. I'm thinking now it's a bad ACL sprain, which is far better than a tear, especially at his age. The swelling has come down. Enough for me to examine it better. Agnes says he's getting stir-crazy. Is there any chance you could help us carry him to the living room before you leave?"

"Sure thing." Sam smiled and headed for the dining room, taking the plate of pancakes with him. The renewed peace between them filled her with satisfaction.

It wasn't long before Becca showed up. "Is breakfast ready, Mom?" It was as if she had an extra nasal sensor to sniff out food when it was ready.

"Yes, honey."

Sam came into the kitchen. "I'm about finished here, and I can spare a few more minutes. Why don't you check in on Frank and take him his breakfast, and I'll finish cooking up the rest of the pancakes for you and Becca." An image of blackened pancakes stacked high and drizzled with maple syrup came to mind.

"Um, we're okay. You can help the neighbors."

"I know what you're thinking, your face gives you away. Contrary to popular belief, I can cook. Besides, Becca's here to help. Between the two of us, I'm sure we can get it right." Becca had a way of bringing out the best in Sam. His sour mood disappeared in a flash.

Megan wasn't used to giving up control or sharing her responsibilities, but she'd be a fool to say no. The proverbial gift horse was knocking at her door. "Deal. Becca don't let them burn." She shot another quick glance at Sam, satisfied to see him smiling. She picked up Frank's tray and headed down the hall.

Knock. Knock.

"Come in," Agnes called from the other side.

"Hope you fancy pancakes, Frank." She set the tray in place on the bed. "How are you feeling?" Megan reached out to touch the palm of her hand to his forehead.

"I'm okay. Knee hurts like a son of a gun when I move it, but not like it was earlier."

"You don't have a fever, which is excellent news."

"I'm tired of lying here. Driving me crazy with the wife dancing in attendance." He winked at Agnes, the corners of his mouth twitching as he tried not to laugh.

"I have some news on that front. Sam is going to carry you to the living room. We can wrap your knee up tight to protect it. There's a TV with your name on it. Then when you're tired, I'll have him bring you back in here. Like a wheelchair on two legs." She grinned.

"Hallelujah! No offense, darling."

"None taken. I'm going to get breakfast. You complain too much." Agnes laughed as she headed out the door.

"Do you need any help getting to the bathroom?"

Frank's face turned beat red. "No. Between using the wall for support and Agnes, I managed to take care of business this morning. Thanks."

"Great." She wasn't trying to embarrass him, but she did want to make sure the situation was handled before Sam left, just in case they needed his help.

An hour later, breakfast and cleanup completed, Becca was more than ready to head outside, eager for the annual tree hunt. Only this year, the tree lot was just down the street and not an hour outside of town.

Agnes chose to stay inside by the fire and read, preferring to stay close in case Frank needed her. Megan called Rachael, hoping for good news. "Hey there, what's going on? Any updates?"

"Good morning to you, too. Don't you know what time it is? This is my vacation. I cherish the mornings I can sleep in." Megan could barely make out the words through Rachael's barely concealed yawn.

"Sorry, sis. There is no such thing as sleeping in when you have kids. You'll find that out soon enough when you have your own family." Megan chuckled.

"Knock it off. You know I'm not looking for Mr. Right. Just Mr. Right for right now."

"You need to get out and meet people. You might change your mind. You can't work all the time." They'd gone back and forth on this subject for years, and lately, her sister had gotten worse about it instead of better.

"You're one to talk. I don't see you getting out to meet people."

"We've had this discussion before, and the answer is no. The difference between us is that I've had that once before, and I'm not looking for a repeat. I've got enough on my plate as it is."

"*Hmpphh*. Whatever. So, how's Mr. Handsome? Sam, I think you called him."

"I wouldn't know." Megan had walked into the laundry room where Becca couldn't hear this part of the conversation. "The guy lost his family a few years ago and has some serious issues in dealing with it. He doesn't talk much, at least not to me."

"Maybe because he likes you, and you scare him?"

"Stop. Between you and Agnes, you'll have us married off in no time at all."

"Interesting. I can't wait to meet her." The two of them together would be a nightmare as far as Megan was concerned. It was a good thing that when the pass opened, and her sister got here, Agnes and Frank would be able to get to the hospital.

"Have you heard any news about when the pass

will open? We are going to pick out a tree, but I told Becca we had to wait for your approval before cutting it down."

"I haven't heard anything because I'm still in bed. Give me five minutes to get some coffee and make a phone call, and then I'll call you right back."

Five minutes later, her phone lit up, Rachael's ringtone filling the kitchen.

"Hi, Aunt Rachael!" Becca hollered into the phone. "Hurry up, Mom. I'm going to put my coat and boots on. I'll be ready." Becca skipped out of the room.

"Give me a few more minutes, and I'll be right there," Megan called out after her. She held the phone to her ear. "What did they have to say? When will you be here?"

"I'm not. At least not today, and probably not tomorrow. I'm sorry. Brandon mentioned they have no way of knowing when the pass will reopen. It could take days, depending on the stability of the snow as they dig through it. With all the new snow-fall, they are concerned with setting off a secondary avalanche. Plus, most of the road crews are busy clearing out the roads here in town. Apparently, you're in an area referred to as Christmas Cove and the only two streets there are dead ends, making them low on the totem pole for digging out."

"You've got to be kidding. You can't possibly be stuck in Hallbrook just a few miles away from us. This is ludicrous." Megan paced the kitchen floor.

"I'm going to have to wait it out. I'm so sorry. I wish I hadn't stopped for food last night. Oh, no. Do you have food? What will you eat?" Rachael's voice rose a notch.

"Stop. We're okay on food. Sam stocked the place when he got here, and the neighbors have been amazing. You do realize Christmas is three days away?" Megan shook her head and sat down at the dining room table. This was unbelievable. It was supposed to have been a happy family get-together with her sister and daughter to honor her mother's traditions for Christmas. How could she do any of that now without Rachael? This was a disaster. Megan closed her eyes and drew in a deep breath. They should have never come here.

"I'm sorry, Megan. I'm sure the authorities are doing everything they can. At least the people in Hallbrook are warm and welcoming and all too ready to help. It's been nice considering the situation. I was at Sally's Diner this afternoon, and they were rounding up volunteers to help the rescue squad dig out the pass. Quite a few signed up, and it sounded as if more people would be helping after they got off work. There's nothing else we can do but wait it out. We can talk all the time, and I'm sure the pass will be cleared before Christmas morning. Everything will be okay."

"It doesn't sound as though I have much choice. I guess when we pick the tree, Becca and I will have to cut it down and haul it back here. She will be so disappointed you're not coming today."

"What about Sam? Ask him to help." An image of them out tree hunting flashed before her eyes and made her smile. It was an idea, but one that wouldn't work.

"Becca and I can handle it. Sam's leaving to help the neighbors with some more of the shoveling, and I don't want to make Becca wait any longer. I promised her we'd go now. But what about you?"

"I'll be fine. Trust me." Her sister sounded different. Off, but in a good way.

"What's going on, Rachael? That sounded… Well, interesting."

"It's nothing, really. He took me to a restaurant and tavern place here in Hallbrook. O'Malley's Charm. I think Brandon Stewart has a bit of his own charm going on. I'm meeting him after his shift tonight to go out again."

"The O'Malleys are the folks staying here with us. Their two sons run the place."

"Nice. Let Mrs. O'Malley do the cooking, 'cause her food is scrumptious. Just saying."

"I'll pass that along, but I want to hear more about your charmer."

"There's not much to tell. We talk. We laugh. There's a bit of attraction, I'm not going to lie. Considering I'm staying at his place, it makes things a bit awkward." *Interesting and unexpected.*

"Oh, so that's it. You want me to do all the work here at the cabin while you play with Romeo in town. Lucky for you, you have an excuse this time." Megan laughed.

"It's not like that. I'm not into dating, and you know it. Nothing's changed."

"If you say so." Megan wasn't quite so sure. She hadn't heard this kind of giddy excitement in her sister's voice in quite some time.

They hung up after promising to keep each other posted. Megan headed for the bedroom to make sure Becca was dressing warm enough to be outside for a while.

"Aunt Rachael's not coming today. I'm sorry. The pass won't be open for a couple of days, so she's tasked us with getting the place ready for Christmas. So, it's up to you and me, kiddo."

"Poor Aunt Rachael. We'll make it super special for her. Right? Starting with the tree."

"Yes. We need to stop at the shed and find a saw and some rope." Hopefully, there was a handsaw, because operating a chain saw was way out her repertoire. Not that she would admit it to her daughter, and not that she wouldn't try.

"Put on some warmer clothes. I'll find Sam and let him know about the pass, and then we can head out."

"Yay! And maybe we will spot the dog." Becca ran out of the room, ready for action.

Becca hadn't even seen the dog yet, and she was hooked. Megan hoped he'd gone back to wherever he belonged. The last thing she needed was for Becca to get attached to a dog.

Megan went in search of Sam and found him in the garage. "I just wanted to let you know I heard from my sister. The pass is going to be closed for a couple more days. Sounds like it's dangerous to work on because of the extra snow and they are having to go slow."

Sam's face tightened, the lines between his brow deepened. Still, he said nothing.

"And they are trying to round up volunteers to help because the main road crew is focused on clearing the streets in town."

The corded muscles of his neck popped out like buoy lines in a storm, his fists tightly clenched.

"Days? I can't stay here that long. I need to get back to New York."

"I'm not sure how to take that." She frowned. "You're welcome to stay here, and I'm sorry you're stuck with us. Maybe someone else on this side of the pass will be happy to put you up." She was tired of the on and off switch that tripped every so often in him.

Sam ran a hand through his hair as he let out a deep breath. "It's not that. Honestly. It's not you. It's me and the situation." The words came out stilted. "It's just doesn't work for me."

"But it could if you relax and try to open up. You need to let go of the past. Trust me."

"You have no idea what you're asking. It's not that easy."

"Whatever." She shrugged. "Becca and I are going on a hike to find the perfect Christmas tree and cut it down. When we get back, we're going to decorate it and decorate the house to bring some Christmas magic and cheer into the cabin. Maybe some of the magic will rub off on you. Until then, we'll be out of the house and out of your hair."

Sam looked at her as if she'd grown horns. "We've just come through a snowstorm. You can't possibly trudge around out there by yourselves in a strange place looking for some magical tree, expecting to cut it down and haul it back by yourselves."

"But that's where you're wrong. I do expect to do just that. And when I have expectations of myself, I deliver."

"I can't let you out there alone. I wouldn't forgive myself if anything happened to you or your daughter. If you insist on this lunacy, I'm coming with you."

"You don't need to feel obligated. I don't consider it lunacy, and I'm pretty levelheaded."

"Humor me." He shook his head, grabbed up his jacket, and started to pull it on.

"We would love for you join us, and maybe, just maybe, this will put some Christmas cheer in your life. You look as if you could use a healthy dose." She hadn't meant to say the last part, but his attitude rankled her.

"You have no idea what I need." He followed her through the kitchen to the back door.

"You're right. But I do know grumpy and withdrawn won't fix it, whatever it is that ails you."

"I said I'd go with you, no one said I had to be happy about it."

"And no one said you had to come. If you want to be Mr. Grumpy, it's your choice. But Becca and I are going to have fun, with or without you." The nickname she'd given him slipped out, but it gave her a sense of satisfaction when he stopped to peer back at her, his eyes wide in shock.

Apparently, Sam wasn't used to people calling him out for his shortcomings.

CHAPTER NINE

"He's coming with us?" Becca asked, her face lighting up with excitement.

"Yes. He wants to keep an eye on the womenfolk. He's a bit old-fashioned, but let's humor him." Megan rolled her eyes, but only for Sam to see.

"I'm just here to make sure you don't get in any trouble. That's a lot of acreage out there, and I wouldn't want it on my conscience if you get lost and freeze to death."

"Yes, Mr. Grumpy," Megan teased, her voice patronizing. "I told the O'Malleys we're headed for the tree lot. We need to stop at the shed first. The property manager told me everything we needed would be in there. I was hoping to find a handsaw and some rope."

"Unless you're planning on a skimpy tree, you'll

be cutting it down all day. Hopefully, there's a chainsaw available. It'll make your job easier."

So, Mr. Grumpy *was* here to watch, and Megan hoped she didn't make a fool of herself. Her bold boasts would need to be followed by some bold action.

"Mr. Sam, you can help us pick out the best tree. And then you can help us decorate it. This will be lots of fun." Becca reached out and put her hand in Sam's.

Megan saw him flinch in surprise, but then to his credit, he didn't pull away. Megan's respect for him rose another notch.

"You can have my share of the fun, and I'll watch. Christmas isn't my thing, and I've got to shovel some snow when we get back." Sam's words were a solemn declaration.

"But Christmas is everybody's thing." Becca giggled, dropping his hand to run ahead toward the shed, dancing in the snow along the way.

Sam grabbed the shovel standing against the side of the shed and dug a wider area for the door to swing open. His breath looked like smoke as he exhaled from the exertion.

Megan chased after Becca, laughing as they tossed handfuls of snow at each other. She couldn't help but notice each time Sam stopped to watch, his expression was hard and unreadable.

He pushed open the door and stepped inside, Megan close on his heels. She searched for a hand-saw, but Sam had other ideas. He looped some rope into a coil, hung it over his shoulder, and leaned down and picked up the chainsaw. "After you." He gestured for her to lead the way.

She walked around to the front of the house and down the driveway, turning right at the end of the pavement. "Mr. Harper told me the best trees are over there." She pointed to the left and down the road a little way. The snow made trekking through the yard difficult, and the road wasn't much better, but it was all part of the fun.

The chill of the air perfectly complemented the dark evergreens that were frosted white with snow. Birds danced and sang as they searched for food. Fresh animal tracks made it clear they weren't the only ones out on a mission.

Becca kept the conversation flowing, painting the picture of her perfect Christmas tree for Sam. Some-where between North Pole perfect and the Charlie Brown special, her daughter had high hopes of finding the tree of her dreams.

"Yellow light," Megan called out.

"Yes, Mom. I know the rule. I can still see you.

And I'm too old for the red-light, green-light game. I'm not a baby anymore."

"I'm sure you're right. Sorry." Megan shook her head. Her baby was growing up.

"Good kid." Sam spoke from behind her, his kind words giving her a rush of satisfaction.

"Thank you." Except she'd just called him Mr. Grumpy to his face, and now he was making her eat those words.

"How would she play red-light, green-light alone? I thought that was a group game for children."

"Normally, it is. But when she was growing up, I made listening to me into a game. Red light is stop immediately. Yellow light is walk slower. And green light means go. She can run ahead as long as she can still see and hear me."

"And it worked?" he asked, his tone incredulous.

"Like a charm. It gave her the freedom she craved, but within my boundaries."

"Nice. So how far do you intend to go looking for a tree?"

"As far as it takes. Finding the perfect Christmas tree is like finding the Christmas star in the sky. You search long and hard, and then lo and behold, it'll just be there. Bright. Shiny. Perfect. Or in this case, tall, green, and bushy. Preferably a blue spruce."

Megan laughed, the expression on Sam's was face priceless.

"This could be a long morning." *He had no idea.*

"Since it looks as if we're going to be stuck together for a couple of days, can I ask you a few questions?"

"You can ask, but I'll only answer if I want to." His lips curled into the hint of a smile; one she'd come to recognize meant he was teasing.

"Fair enough. We didn't get to finish our conversation the other night, and I'm curious about something you said. You mentioned you were an investment negotiator and that you owned the company, but you didn't sound happy about it. Why do it, if you don't enjoy it?"

Sam snorted—half laugh, half something else she couldn't put her finger on.

"Doesn't matter, and it doesn't pay to dwell on it. I do what I have to do." In other words, he wasn't going to elaborate.

"Becca! Yellow light," Megan hollered, forgetting her daughter's earlier admonishment about hating the childish command to slow down. It's not that Megan considered herself overprotective, but she was careful. Becca meant the world to her, and she would do everything in her power to keep her safe.

"Sounds awful." A silence fell between them,

Megan searching her brain for another question to bridge the gap between them. "Why do you come up here if it makes you sad?"

Sam stiffened his shoulders and back as he continued to trudge through the snow without answering her question. It was a weak attempt to get him to tell her more about himself. Judging by his reaction, she'd stepped on a minefield. Another link to the man inside.

"I'm sorry if that was off-limits. I'm just trying to understand you better." Silence. This was going to be a long morning. "Well, in the interest of keeping the conversation going, and since you didn't ask about me, I'll tell you our story. We live in Boston. I'm a nurse at the hospital, and in my free time, I love photography. Not that I have much time to pursue a hobby with Becca around. She keeps me hopping."

Sam looked at her as if he wanted to ask a question.

"I found it! I found it! Come on!" Becca shouted with excitement and came running up to them.

"Show us, but don't forget we both have to agree." Megan reminded Becca of the tree-picking rule established years ago.

"Yup. We all must agree. That's the rules. And that means Mr. Sam has to agree because he's here too." Becca ran ahead, waving her arms for them to follow. Her excitement was contagious, and Megan ran after her daughter.

It was a lovely tree, the branches well balanced and full of dark-green needles, but by the time Sam caught up, Becca was off and running to the next perfect tree. Three trees later, Becca stopped. "Mom, it's beautiful. This is just like the tree I pictured. It's perfect." This time, her daughter's voice was a mixture of determination and awe.

Megan couldn't help but agree with her daughter's choice. This one *was* special. There wasn't any one thing that made it special. The entire tree was wonderful. The needles shimmered in the sunlight with a touch of snow here and there on the branches. It was as though an angel had marked this tree and had been guiding them to it. And it was a blue spruce on top of everything else.

Becca dropped to the ground and put her arms above her head. She started making sweeping motions with her arms and legs to make a snow angel. It was one of her favorite snow activities and something she did several times every winter. Megan had asked her once why she made so many angels, and she'd never forgotten her daughter's sweet but simple reply. *The world needs more angels.*

Megan turned to wait for Sam, anxious to see what he thought. Becca valued his opinion, and it would be awful if he didn't admire the tree she selected.

He'd stopped dead in his tracks twenty feet away. His eyes darkened as he watched Becca. He opened his mouth to speak nothing came out, a blank look crossing his face. It was as if he'd seen a ghost. Megan looked around, but she knew his gaze was still locked on Becca. What she didn't understand was why.

"Sam?" She bit her lip until it hurt, waiting for his response. Luckily, Becca was having too much fun to notice.

"Sam?" she tried again.

He blinked and looked over at her as if lost. Sam shook his head and rubbed his hand over his eyes. "I can't do this." His voice was tight, almost distant.

She'd walked back to his side. "Yes. You. Can. Do you have some sort of medical issue I should know about? Should I be calling 9-1-1, not that it would do much good right now, but still, what can I do to help?"

Sam focused on her. It was as if he was drawing life directly from her, blocking out the rest of the world.

"It's okay, Sam. Please. You don't have to pick out the tree with us. Just take a short walk and take deep breaths. Or sit down. Give me the saw, and I'll take care of getting the tree cut."

He looked down at the saw and back at her. "My health is fine. I'm sure you think I'm crazy, and maybe I am, but it's just some things remind me more than others of all I've lost. It hurts." She was sure the admission had cost him a great deal. The worn-out expression on his face was an easy read.

"Talk to me. I'm an excellent listener."

"Talking won't help. Nothing will. But thanks for the offer." Sam seemed to be moving past whatever had gripped him in cold terror, and Megan was relieved for Becca's sake. This was supposed to be a fun Christmas tree hunt.

Becca came to stand beside them and pointed at her freshly made angel. "Look. I made a new angel for Earth."

"Sweetheart, it's beautiful." Megan was quick to reassure her daughter, knowing Sam wasn't likely to say anything.

He edged his way around the angel, keeping his eyes on the tree. He looked back at Megan and then at Becca, his face drawn tight. "Is this the one you all want?"

"Becca loves it, and so do I, so yes."

"Wait. Mr. Sam has to love it," Becca chimed in. "It's the rule."

"What do you think, Sam? Is it the perfect tree?" Megan hoped he would play along with the game.

"If it means I can cut it down and haul it back to the cabin, it's the perfect tree."

"Bah, humbug. But I guess that means this is our tree." Megan laughed and joined hands with Becca.

"If you two will stand back, it shouldn't take me long to cut this down." Sam flipped a switch on the chainsaw and then pulled the rope cord a few times. Nothing happened.

"Is it broken?" Megan frowned.

"I'm just priming it and I'm waiting for you to step back out of the way."

Nothing like letting him know how little she knew. Oh, well. "Okay. We'll be over here making a snowman in order to keep moving and stay warm. I think we'll call him Mr. Grumpy, the snowman." Megan grinned, shooting Sam an it-will-look-just-like-you look.

Sam fired up the chainsaw and kneeled in the snow to get to the trunk of the tree. The whir of the chain increased as he moved in to make the first cut. Vibrations shook the tree limbs, sending snow flying and landing on top of Sam's head.

"What the heck?" Sam shouted the words as he brushed the snow from his head. Becca and Megan couldn't help but laugh even though it earned them a stern look.

Ten minutes later, Sam had the tree cut down and wrapped up with the rope. He insisted on hauling the tree and the chainsaw back to the cabin. *Mr. He-Man.* Except it was slowing down their return trip quite a bit.

"Let me carry the chainsaw since you are dragging the tree. It will be so much easier," Megan insisted, reaching for the power tool.

"I can do it. The snow is deep, and if you fall, you might get hurt on the chain." His tone brooked no opposition, even if it was a ridiculous line of reasoning.

It's not like she couldn't handle herself, after all, she was ex-military. "Well, based on the snow starting to come down, if we don't get a move on, we may not get back. I'm not a fragile flower, just give me the chainsaw, will you?"

Sam looked up at the darkened sky, grimaced, and shook his head. "Fine. But be careful. It's not light."

"I'm sure it's lighter than the forty-pound rucksack I used to carry in the Air Force. I've got this." She could only describe his expression as one of appreciation, which made her more determined to do it right.

"Just watch your step. Please." The last word rang with sincerity, driving away any irritation she might have felt at the command.

Becca started to sing Christmas carols, and Megan joined in.

"Sing with us, Mr. Sam. You must know 'We Wish You a Merry Christmas'?" Becca stopped walking and turned to look at him. Sam was up against a powerhouse when Becca turned on the charm.

"I don't have much of a voice and I'd much rather hear yours."

"Nope. It doesn't work that way. It's not about your voice, it's about singing with me. And having fun. Come on, please." Becca's smile grew bigger, her dimples irresistible.

Sam glanced at Megan for help, but she didn't feel the inclination to butt in. He was on his own.

"*We wish you a merry Christmas, we wish*'—you're not singing." Becca stood with her hands on her hips, determined to get her way.

"*We wish you a merry Christmas, we wish you a merry Christmas.*" The low baritone of Sam's voice joined with her daughter's was a beautiful sound. She had to give him credit—he'd surprised her in a good way.

Sam had more Christmas spirit and kindness in

his heart than he wanted the world to see. He only sang the one song, but it was enough to make Becca happy before she took off running ahead and singing more holiday favorites. By the time they got back to the house, they were cold and covered in wet snow. The muscles in Megan's right arm ached from carrying the chainsaw. She'd clearly grown soft after leaving the Air Force. Sam, on the other hand, seemed unfazed by any of it. But there was no way she would let on how tired she was. She had an image to protect.

Agnes greeted them at the door. "Good heavens. Look at the lot of you. You were gone longer than I expected. I've got a pot of coffee on and some warm milk on the stove to make hot chocolate for Becca." Agnes helped them with their coats as Sam stood the tree in the corner before shucking his boots and coat.

Becca's cheeks were pink with a chill.

"Thanks, Agnes. Finding the perfect tree takes time. Ask Becca." She winked at the woman. "Run along and get out of those wet clothes, and then we can set up the tree. I'll be right behind you to help."

Becca wrapped her arms around Sam's waist. "Thanks, Mr. Sam. I love our tree."

Megan watched from the doorway. Sam's gaze

softened as he reached up and stroked her hair ever so lightly. "You're welcome."

But then just as quickly, he stepped back and cleared his throat, dropping his hands to his sides. He picked up the tree, and without so much as a backward glance, carried it to the living room.

CHAPTER TEN

Mr. Grumpy had a heart, even if he didn't want to admit it or show it to the world. The tenderness she'd glimpsed for a fleeting second in his expression couldn't be mistaken for anything else.

"Becca, I'm going to run out to the car and bring in our boxes of decorations. Do you want to help me?"

"I think I should watch Mr. Sam and make sure he gets the tree up straight. Um, unless you need me to help you." It was an afterthought, but it counted in Megan's books.

Her mother had been sweet, kind, and helpful, and Becca was a lot like her. "You're fine. Just don't get in his way, and don't ask him a million questions. Remember, respect his privacy."

"Thanks." Becca flashed a smile and was gone in a

split second.

One by one, she hauled the boxes into the house, grateful her SUV was in the garage and not outside covered in snow. With the last box in her hands, she gently pushed the door shut with her foot. Turning back to the kitchen, she ran smack dab into Sam.

His hands came up to steady her as she pulled back, trying to balance the box. "I didn't mean to startle you. I was just coming to see if you needed help. I didn't realize you had so much to bring in. You really should've asked."

Toe to toe, with just the box between them, Sam's musky cologne invaded her senses as his words sunk in. She shook herself free of the awareness crackling between them.

"You were busy putting up the tree, and I can handle carrying in a few boxes. I like to think I can handle things on my own." She sidestepped around him and crossed the room to put the box on the table with the others.

"Clearly." His disapproving tone rankled.

"There's nothing wrong with being self-suffi-cient. I'm a single mother, and it's more a necessity than an extravagance," she huffed. Her response might have been a tad defensive, but she didn't appreciate people thinking she couldn't make do on her own.

ELSIE DAVIS

Sam gazed at her but refrained from comment. He crossed the room to the table and started to open one of the boxes, pulling back the tape. "So, what is all this stuff?" She appreciated his restraint in shoving any macho attitude back at her.

"All this—" she waved her hand over the piles of boxes, "—is my mother's Christmas decorations. My sister and I were going to decorate the cabin as our way to honor her." Every decoration her mother owned told a story about her life.

"I see. Who are you really doing this for? You, your sister, or perhaps Becca." She would have taken offense if his tone had been anything other than concerned.

His words came too close to the truth. "It would be hard to explain in a way you would understand, but in keeping her part of our traditions, we feel closer to her. A connection that can't be labeled as *nothing*."

Sam shook his head and shrugged. "If you say so. But these things won't bring her back." He spoke as though from experience and resignation, but his reminder intensified the emptiness dwelling within her.

"No, but it does keep her alive in our hearts."

She'd told Becca to respect his privacy, and Megan forced herself to do the same. The man had

164

issues, but they were his own and he'd made it clear he didn't like interference. Megan remembered the pent-up anger after Andy's death and how it had held her back from life. It had taken her time to get over the intense pain and loneliness, but in its place, she'd found joy in the everyday happiness of spending time with her daughter.

Megan prayed he'd get the help he needed to push past the pain. He was too kind to be left alone, walking in the shadows of life. Just as she believed honoring her mother this Christmas would help bring closure to her mother's death by rejoicing in her life, he needed to embrace the past to move forward.

Sam grabbed a box and headed for the living room.

Megan took a deep breath, picked up another box, and followed him. There was nothing else to say, and she wanted this to be a fun time. Whether he chose to join in or not would be up to him. "Look, Becca. Grandma's things. Once you unpack the boxes, we can decide where to put everything."

"What's going on here? Looks like fun." Agnes spoke from the hallway as she entered the living room.

"We got a tree, and now we're going to decorate

it. You can help." Becca moved to Agnes's side and pulled her by the hand farther into the room.

"Pretty tree." Agnes looked around at all the boxes. "And it looks like a big project. There's a Christmas shop in town, but by the looks of it, you won't need anything else."

"I always add one special ornament each year for Becca, so hopefully, Tinsel Pass opens, and I can see what they have. I was hoping to check Artisan's Creations. My mother always told me what a wonderful woman the owner was, and that she had some of the most unique crafts for sale in the state of New Hampshire. Not a place to be missed."

"Mrs. Bradley was a gem in this community, God rest her soul. But now her son has moved back to town and taken over the business, so it remains open and flourishing, just like his mother would have wanted."

"Sounds like a thoughtful man."

"He is, at that." Agnes nodded.

"How's Frank?" Megan asked, the nurse in her needing an update.

"He's sleeping. Time for me to make my escape." The older woman laughed, moving to sit down in the chair next to the tree. "I'd rather watch if that's okay with you, young lady?"

"Sure thing. I'll show you everything." Her

daughter's excitement was contagious.

Megan watched as Sam laid a box on the couch and pulled back the tape. It didn't take long for Becca to pull out the first ornament and hold it up for inspection. Megan tried to squash the rush of emotion, seeing one of her mother's treasures.

"Look. It's her special antique snow globe. Every year, she played the music over and over while rocking in her chair." Becca turned the tiny metal switch at the bottom, starting the music. The instrumental sounds of 'Silent Night' played, filling the room with the peace and goodwill of Christmas spirit.

Megan reached out to take it from her, worried she might drop it.

"I've got it, Mom. I'll find a spot." Becca held tightly as she shook the globe to watch the snow falling.

"Make sure it's a safe one so that it can't get knocked over or broken." The first time Megan had seen the snow globe, she'd been about Becca's age. She could hear her mother as if she were standing in the room.

"This isn't a toy, but you should play the music and listen. If you listen hard enough, you can hear the angels singing."

Megan had told Becca the same story years ago.

It was around the same time Becca had become obsessed with making angels. Paper. Snow. Pretend. It didn't matter. To Becca, there could never be enough angels.

And just as her mother trusted her to cherish it, Megan had to trust her daughter. It wasn't easy to give up her need to control everything, but she continued to try—especially when it involved Becca. She wanted her daughter to grow up strong and independent, and for that to happen, Megan had to give her some freedom. Mistakes would happen, but Megan would be there to help her learn from them.

Megan had Rachael to teach her things when they were growing up, but Becca didn't have that option. Andy's death eliminated any chance for Becca to have a sister or brother. One more regret Megan could add to her list. She'd always imagined having two or three kids.

"Look, Mom. This is one I made for Grandma." Her daughter glowed with pride.

"Yes, I remember. I'm almost finished adding the lights, and then you can hang the tree decorations up to where you can safely reach while I get the other boxes. I'll hang the higher ones in a bit."

"Look, Miss Agnes. I made this." She held the paper angel out for inspection.

"What a beautiful angel. No wonder your grandmother treasured it." Agnes handed the doll back to Becca. Her daughter had also made similar paper angels for her and Rachael that should be somewhere in one of the other boxes.

Thinking of her sister reminded her it had been several hours since they'd spoken. Rachael must not be lacking for company or fun with her new-found friend. Hopefully, the guy wouldn't get too attached, because her sister's anti-commitment philosophy didn't bode well for any type of real relationship.

Megan stopped to queue up her Christmas playlist on her phone before returning to the kitchen for another box and discovered Sam had beaten her there. "You don't have to do this."

"Yes, I do. I'm not going to stand by and just watch you do all the work. I'll leave you two to the decorating, however, if you don't mind." Box in hand, he started walking without waiting to hear a response.

She grabbed the last box and hustled after him. "Any chance you would want to be on coffee and hot-chocolate duty? You can use milk to make it since the neighbors gave us plenty, and there are miniature marshmallows in the kitchen. Just don't make it too hot."

Sam pondered her suggestion, one eyebrow raised slightly. "I guess I could do that, but just so you know, I can make hot chocolate without directions. Are you always this controlling?" The corners of his eyes lifted as a gentle smile crossed his face, making him seem quite approachable. His tanned complexion complemented the brown of his eyes. And those eyelashes. Completely unfair, when every day she had to use mascara to get hers to appear half as thick and full.

"Maybe. Probably. It's a bad habit I've developed out of necessity." She shrugged.

Sam headed for the kitchen as Becca began to lay out all the decorations, *oohing* and *aahing* as if she hadn't seen them every year. They both glanced around the room and plotted possible sites that would highlight each one.

Sam returned with hot drinks, surprising her when he sat down to watch the fun. True to his word, he didn't join in the decorating, although it wasn't from the lack of Becca trying to get him more involved. After showing each piece to Agnes, Becca would show Sam the ornament, repeatedly asking him where she should put it—all while ignoring Megan's opinion.

Normally, that might have been a bit irritating, but in this situation, she could read into her daughter's actions and applauded the way she tried to include Sam. Becca had a big heart. At first, Sam's reticence was tangible, making it awkward for all four of them. But by the time they'd gotten halfway through the boxes, Becca had managed to get him to relax and join in the fun, even if from the couch.

Agnes didn't fare as well when it came to resistance. She succumbed to Becca's continued pleas and joined in the festivities.

Hours later, the tree was finished, and the room sparkled with hints of Christmas everywhere you looked. Becca and Megan held hands as they stepped back to admire their handiwork, Agnes standing next to them.

It was time for the grand finale. "Becca, why don't you plug in the lights, and let's officially kick off this year's Christmas celebration." Megan dropped a kiss on her daughter's head.

"Really? I get to do it this year?" Her daughter twirled about, clapping her hands as she made her way to the wall to plug in the lights.

Megan exchanged glances with Agnes, the two of them understanding the excitement and joy associated with being assigned big-girl tasks.

Sam came to stand next to her, and Megan couldn't deny the tingling awareness rippling down her spine.

"Three. Two. One. Tada!" Becca giggled.

"It's beautiful. Grandma would have loved this."

Megan wiped away the tears threatening to spill over.

"It's okay, Mom. Grandma's watching from heaven. You always told me she's never really gone because she's in our hearts." Becca touched her hand to her heart.

And here she thought she had to be a tower of strength for her daughter. Instead, it was her daughter who was giving her the strength. It was Megan's turn to listen to her own words. "Thank you, sweetheart. You're right."

"You ladies did a fine job. Much better than if I'd helped." Sam's attempt at humor surprised her.

"Wait. There's one thing missing. Mr. Sam, you have to put up the angel."

"I'm pretty sure that's your mother's job. I wouldn't want to usurp her position. Besides, I might not get it up there properly." He shot her a grin and winked. His dig hit home, although she wasn't that controlling. Or at least she didn't think she was.

"What's usup?" Becca scrunched up her face as she said the word, trying to figure it out.

"Usurp." He laughed. "It means to take over."

"Oh, well, then you have to usup, I mean, usurp. Everyone needs to help," Becca pleaded, her hand on his arm, tugging him toward the tree.

"Yes, Sam, everyone needs to help." Megan issued the challenge, knowing it would be almost impossible for him to say no.

"This isn't elementary school. Everyone doesn't need a participation award." He smirked, the words whispered softly and close to her ear, sending a ticklish shiver down her spine.

Much to his credit, he stepped forward, taking the angel from Becca's hand. He reached up effortlessly, placing the angel on the top of the tree.

"She's beautiful."

"Yes, she is," Megan and Agnes said in unison.

"Yes, she is." Sam's deeper voice chimed in, but he wasn't looking at the angel. In fact, his eyes were closed, leaving her to wonder who he was thinking about.

"Mom, where's that bag of the craft stuff we brought? I want to make a paper chain to hang outside on the porch. And maybe when Aunt Rachael comes, she can bring popcorn, and we can make a popcorn string for the birds." And just like that, the tree decorating was over, and her daughter was ready to move on to something else.

"I put it in the closet in our bedroom. Go fetch the bag, and we can work at the kitchen table if you don't mind me making a decoration or two with you. Maybe Miss Agnes and Mr. Sam would like to join in our fun." Her daughter's excitement brought joy to her heart. This is what Christmas was all about. Love. Family. It was a shame Rachael wasn't here for all this.

"That's a great idea. Wait right here, and I'll get the bag." Becca ran down the hall and disappeared into the bedroom.

"It's time I checked on Frank, so I'll leave you two to your fun." Agnes left the room.

"Sounds like my cue to haul in more firewood. I'm concur with Agnes. You two are on your own. I'm not a crafter kind of guy." Sam didn't wait for an answer and practically ran out of the living room toward the laundry area. Poor guy was afraid he'd get roped into a Christmas arts and crafts session. Or was it that he was trying to get out of the room so as not to be alone with her? The second option stung a bit. *Or a lotta bit.*

Becca ran down the hall and came back minutes later to dump the entire contents out on the table. Megan shifted her Christmas playlist to an upbeat holiday-favorite station and pressed play. Strains of 'Have a Holly, Jolly Christmas' filled the room.

"Look, Mom. Candy canes from last year." Her daughter's excitement mirrored her own.

"Let me have one." She held out her hand. "What a great find." Megan peeled off the plastic wrap and stuck it in her mouth. "*Hmmm*. Just what we needed. What's Christmas without candy canes. Are there any we can put on the tree?"

"No. There's just one more."

"Then we need to savor these and make them count." She laughed and took another lick.

Becca kept the wrapper on hers, peeling back the tip. Since when did she get smarter than her mom? Megan's hands were already getting sticky. Becca went to work on her paper chain, cutting out rectangles to glue into a chain and alternating the red and green, stopping on occasion to get a sweet peppermint lick off her candy cane.

Megan went to work on her own decorations, trying to remember how to cut out snowflakes the way she'd learned in elementary school many moons ago. She folded the sheet of paper in half, cutting off the excess. Then folded it again and again. Using scissors, she cut into the edges here and there, all the way around before unfolding her snowflake.

"Look, my first one's done." The paper was starting to stick to her fingers from the sugary peppermint mess she was making of her candy cane.

Becca stopped to glance at her creation. "Pretty. We should hang them from the ceiling."

"Great idea. I'll have to make a lot more."

Becca's chain became longer and longer, and

Megan's mountain of snowflakes grew over the next couple of hours. In between crafting, singing, and laughing, the pair had almost forgotten Sam had come back in and was hiding out in the living room.

'I Saw Mommy Kissing Santa Claus' started to play, and Becca stopped what she was doing and looked up at Megan, a strange expression on her face. Her daughter grinned and joined in the chorus, laughing as she sang.

"How on earth do you even know that song? Brenda Lee goes way back before your time."

"It plays every year. Maybe Santa Claus will bring you someone to kiss this year."

"I have you, sweetheart. And you're all I need." Megan laughed.

"But I want to be like all the other kids at school. I want a dad, so you need to kiss a man if that's ever going to happen."

This was the second time Becca had brought up the subject in as many days. "You're incorrigible."

"What's that mean?"

"In your case, I can't get you to change your line of thinking and persistence." Megan shook her head. She inhaled the fresh pine scent that filled the air, laced with warm vanilla from the candle she'd lit, while searching for the right words. "I don't want a new man. Your dad was special, and no one could ever take his place." *But there is one person I can't stop thinking about.*

Becca looked up past Megan's shoulder. Megan turned around to discover Sam standing behind her. *Great.* Their gazes locked. He had to have heard her declaration, but hopefully, he had the good sense not to comment.

"I'll get another load of firewood." He shrugged on his jacket and reached for the back door.

"But you just brought some in, Mr. Sam." Exactly what Megan was thinking. *Way to go, Becca.*

"You can never have too much. It's going to be another cold night, and we'll need it to help break the chill in the cabin." The few seconds of silence before he spoke had seemed an eternity, and she was grateful for his recovery.

"Not that I don't love the idea of a fire, but won't the heater do the trick?"

"Yes and no. When it gets this cold, heat pumps don't work as efficiently. They switch to emergency heat, which can be costly and really taxes the system. It's easier just to build a fire to help it out."

"Need any help?" Not that she wanted to go outside, but she wouldn't shirk from any responsibility.

"No. You two seem as though you're having fun." He glanced at her pile of cut-up paper. "Although,

I'm not sure what you are trying to accomplish. Becca's, I get. I've seen paper chains before, but you look as if you're just making a mess cutting up paper."

"They are snowflakes. And each one is original. Look." Megan stopped cutting and picked one up from the pile and held it for up for inspection. Sam moved closer.

"Very nice. If you need help hanging them, let me know." For a moment, he looked as if he wanted to say something more, but then just as quickly, he turned and pulled open the door.

"Wait, Mr. Sam. Look at what I made. It's finished."

Sam turned back, and Becca held up her paper strand for inspection.

"Nice. I'm sure the birds will love your thoughtfulness."

Megan smiled at her daughter's creation. "It's beautiful, Becca. Good job." Without another word, Sam turned and went out the back door. His high praise left Becca beaming long after he'd left the room.

"I need to make something else before we go outside to hang this." Becca grabbed more paper and started cutting.

"What's that?"

Her daughter glanced at the back door and then at her. She leaned in toward Megan, finger pressed across her lips. "*Shhh*. Since Mr. Sam doesn't have any of his own decorations here, I'm going to make him something special of his very own."

"Oh, honey, that is so sweet of you. I'm sure he will treasure it forever." At least she hoped he would for the remainder of the time he was stuck with them here in the cabin. She didn't want to see Becca get hurt. Megan picked up her candy cane her fingers sticking to the sugary mess. "But don't forget, he might be gone any time now and not be here for Christmas."

"He'll be here. I've sent an angel wish to Santa, asking to keep him Mr. Sam here for Christmas. He seems so sad, and I think Christmas with us will cheer him up."

Her daughter's intuitive instincts were spot on. Megan was blessed to have a daughter with such a caring heart. She hoped it wouldn't ruin Christmas if the pass opened and Sam left anyway because Megan was pretty sure when it did open, he'd be gone faster than a shooting star.

"While you're doing that, I'm going to wash my hands and start dinner. I think I saw some spaghetti sauce and pasta. Would that be okay?"

"Of course! I love spaghetti." *What kid didn't?* It

had also been one of the few dishes Andy made well, and the pair of them had eaten it repeatedly while Megan was deployed.

Megan made a move toward the kitchen.

"Oh, I almost forgot something. Did you put my coat in the laundry room?" Becca lifted her head, waiting for the answer. The glow on her face made Megan pause.

"Yes. Why? What do you need? I prefer you not to be out in the cold right now."

"No. It's not that. There's something I need to do. You'll see." The glow almost radiated from her grin. Megan watched with curiosity as Becca went into the laundry room and returned moments later.

Becca pulled a dining room chair up to the doorway between the kitchen and the dining room and stood on the seat.

"What are you doing? Be careful." Megan started to step forward, prepared to catch her daughter if she fell.

"You'll see." Becca pulled something green from her pocket and then reached into her other pocket for something else. She stretched up high, trying to pin the greenery to the top of the doorway. It was then Megan realized what she had. Mistletoe.

First wishing for a new dad, then wishing Sam would stay for Christmas, and now, the mistletoe.

Nothing good would come from her fanciful notions, and Megan needed to put a stop to her matchmaking efforts.

"If you and Mr. Sam walk under this, you have to kiss. I saw it in a movie." Her daughter giggled, jumped down, and pulled the chair back into place, a satisfied smile on her face.

"It doesn't always work that way. Sam isn't here because he wants to be, and I don't think this is his idea of fun."

"But it's a Christmas tradition. You have to."

"Where on earth did you get mistletoe?"

"In the woods, when we were picking our Christmas tree. I saw it and recognized it from my storybook. You two talked a lot, and I noticed him smile at you. He doesn't smile much, so I think he likes you."

"It's not that easy. We're here to celebrate Christmas, and Mr. Sam is a stranger who is stuck here. You can't make people kiss, honey."

Becca's answering grin was outdone only by the sound of her humming 'I Saw Mommy Kissing Santa Claus.' The kid was ignoring everything Megan said on purpose.

She wouldn't make Becca take it down, but the last thing she expected was for Sam to kiss her because of her daughter's far-fetched Christmas tradition ideas. It was cute, and secretly, Megan had to admit she wouldn't mind kissing Sam. He was a terrific guy, and other than his occasional melancholy and distant behavior, she liked him.

Megan had her daughter and her sister to help keep her grounded when she started down the pity-party path, but who did Sam have? To her knowledge, he hadn't called or talked to anyone other than the local authorities. Wasn't anyone the least concerned he was trapped in a cabin in the mountains because of an avalanche? Not to mention at Christmas time.

Sam came in through the back door, his arms laden with firewood. He didn't say a word as he passed through the room and dropped the wood next to the fireplace, the sound echoing through the house. It was a stark reminder of the first night they'd met.

Megan took another bite off her candy cane as she stirred the spaghetti sauce. She noticed movement off to the side and turned to find Sam standing in the doorway watching her.

"Nice appetizer." The barest hint of a smile crossed his face. "I see you found something to make for dinner. How much longer until we eat?"

"I'd say give it fifteen minutes." She stopped stirring, and looked over at him, her gaze going to the mistletoe." "You might not want to—"

"Mr. Sam. Mr. Sam." Becca danced excitedly from behind him, pointing at the mistletoe above his head.

Her warning came too late. Becca wasn't letting this one go. Her face felt warm as the blood rushed to her head. She waited for him to put it all together and realize what Becca was up to.

Sam looked up and froze. Lines of tension etched across his face, and he ran his hand through his hair. His gaze landed on Megan, an apologetic expression in his eyes. "I...I...need to wash up." He turned and bolted down the hall.

Becca's face was crestfallen, but no more so than the wave of disappointment that washed over Megan. She'd known nothing good would come of it, but she hadn't put a stop to it for two reasons. One, she didn't want to spoil Becca's fun, and two, Megan herself was curious about what he would do. Not to mention, the idea of the kiss intrigued her. Not that it should, so it was just as well it didn't happen.

"Sorry, honey. I told you not to get your hopes up. Some people just don't know how to have fun."

CHAPTER ELEVEN

It had been a narrow escape, one that left him confused and angry—with himself. For one split second, he'd wanted to kiss Megan. Wanted to know if her pink lips tasted like peppermint from the candy cane. And it wasn't the first time.

But it felt disloyal to his wife's memory. He stood in front of the window and gazed out, unseeing, lost in a haze of the past. *I'm so sorry, Laura.*

The pass couldn't open soon enough as far as he was concerned, but he was stuck here until it did. It wasn't Megan or Becca's fault he was in this situation, and he didn't want to ruin their time here. They were wonderful people, and it was rotten of him to be an ogre.

Sam returned to the dining room; a firm resolve in place to be more gracious. "Becca, do you want to come with me to put out food and fresh water for the dog?"

"Yeppers. And do you think we could put out a blanket in case he's cold? Maybe fix a box or something."

"Sure thing. That's a terrific idea." Anything to wipe away the look of hurt he'd seen on her face as he bolted.

"Just don't get your hopes up the dog will come every day, honey. Since he's still hanging around, he either belongs somewhere, or he's a stray that's nervous around people."

"That's okay, Mom. I just want to help him if I can. Maybe he's lonely."

"Go on. And take some of this cheese and put it in his bowl as a treat." Megan sliced off a few pieces.

Sam had already talked to the neighbors and discovered none of them were missing a dog or knew of one in the area that fit the description, Sam was pretty sure it was stray. Or worse, someone had dropped the dog off, hoping he'd find himself a new home. It was wrong, but it didn't stop people from doing it.

"Thanks, Mom." Becca zipped up her coat and took the cheese.

"We'll be right back."

Sam and Becca headed out the garage door. The

neighbors had given them the canned tuna and chicken for their own meals, but he had a feeling the dog needed the food more than they did.

"Let's search around and see what we can find. I saw a blanket in the cabinet over there." He pointed to the brown cabinet on the side of the garage.

"Okay." While Becca grabbed the blanket, Sam looked around, his gaze landing on a storage container.

Laying on its side, it would make the perfect shelter from the wind and help fight against the cold if they put it up against the house. "I found a box we can use." Sam set the water container and the food down in the box and picked it up to carry outside, Becca following closely behind.

She looked around, her shoulders drooping when there was no sign of the dog. "Don't worry. He'll be back for his food and find the blankets."

"But why won't he come around more? Is he afraid of us? I won't hurt him." Her voice took on a whine.

"No, it's not you. He's just nervous around people. We don't know how he got here, but we're doing what we can to help. You've got a big heart." His sincerity earned him a smile, one that reminded him of an angel.

They finished adjusting the box and blanket,

turning the opening in the best direction to protect it from the wind. Satisfied, they both stood back and looked around once again for their furry friend.

"Come on. The sooner we head back inside, the sooner he may come to check things out."

"Okay." She slid her hand in his, and they headed back toward the garage.

Megan looked up as they entered. "Any luck?"

Becca shook her head, the expression on her face a reflection of her disappointment. She'd really thought this time they'd get lucky and see him again. "He eats everything we put out, but then he's gone. Like a ghost dog."

"We found a container in the garage that works perfect as a shelter and laid out a blanket. I'm betting he'll be happy for the extra protection and warmth from the elements unless he already has a better place to stay."

"I think when I talk to Rachael tomorrow, I'll ask her to put up some posters around town. Hallbrook's not that big, and if someone is missing a dog that matches your description, it might put them at ease to know where he is." With the pass closed, no one could come looking.

Although, truth be told, the dog was a long way from home if he lived on the other side of the pass. More likely, someone had abandoned him. Sam

ELSIE DAVIS

knew what it was to have a family and then suddenly be alone. His heart went out to the dog. Tomorrow, if the dog didn't turn up and Sam was still here, he'd start looking for him. The scared look in the mutt's eyes was still fresh in his mind.

"Great idea. What can we do to help you get ready for dinner?" Laura might have done all the cooking, but it didn't mean he was a stranger to the kitchen.

"Setting the table would be fantastic. Agnes will be joining us, so set a place for her. I'll take up Frank's plate and run it in to him. Becca, if you can clear the table of your craft supplies, that would be a big help. Dinner's almost ready."

Sam grabbed plates out of the kitchen and carried them to the table, returning for silverware and glasses. Megan glanced at him, acting as though she wanted to say something but then thought better of it. She poured the sauce into a serving bowl.

His curiosity wouldn't allow him to let the look pass. "What's wrong?" Sam took the pan from her and started to rinse it.

Megan's hand froze mid-air as she prepared to taste the sauce. "I just wanted to say I'm sorry, for earlier. You know, when she got more personal than she should have. Becca means well, but she doesn't understand."

"It's okay. My reaction was rude, and for that, I'm sorry. It was nothing personal, I hope you understand. It's just my wife..." The words tumbled out, and he couldn't stop the flow. "It just doesn't feel right for me to kiss someone." He returned his focus to the pan, scrubbing hard, back and forth, trying not to show emotion.

"I completely understand," she said softly.

He made the mistake of looking up again, only to discover her eyes were filled with tears. Maybe her husband's death was still considered *recent* in her mind. It would explain the comment he'd heard earlier between her and Becca. Maybe they were both kindred spirits walking a dark and lonely path, destined to be alone forever.

"Thank you." Sam finished setting the table and carried out the bowl of sauce.

Becca rejoined them, putting an end to any further conversation on the subject. At the sight of her daughter, Megan's pensive expression was replaced with a smile. The change was swift, but he'd seen it in action.

"Hey, honey. What should we do tonight? There should be some Christmas specials on TV."

"Oh, yes. We have to watch *Frosty*, and *Rudolph*, and *Santa Claus is Comin' to Town*. Oh, and what's the name of the scary one with the old man?"

Megan laughed. "I don't remember any scary Christmas movies. Are you sure you don't have it confused with something else?"

"No. You know the one I mean. It has ghosts and the man is mean. And the little boy has a crutch."

"Do you mean *Scrooge?*" Sam asked.

"Yes," Becca cried out in excitement. "I want to see that one."

He hadn't seen it in years, but it wasn't one he'd likely forget. Laura had warned him over and over he was becoming like Scrooge, spending all his time at work making money. She'd been right, and he'd give anything to get back what he'd lost as a result. Repaying his father's debts meant nothing compared to losing his family.

"I should've guessed that one. We watch it every year. Several times." Megan grinned.

Agnes joined them. "Hmmm, this looks wonderful. Sorry I didn't help get dinner ready."

"You've got your hands full. Enjoy." Megan placed a big bowl of spaghetti in the center of the table. She scooped some out onto Becca's plate first.

"Dig in, everyone. Plenty to go around. I'll drop Frank's plate off and be right back."

"This is yummy, Mom."

"Thanks, honey. But you're easy to please when it comes to spaghetti." Megan laughed and headed down the hall. Becca twirled the spaghetti around her fork and hung it over her mouth, dropping it in, inch by inch. The spaghetti left orange marks around her mouth and on her cheek. When she looked at him and smiled, it was Lydia's face he saw.

Countless other times he'd corrected his daughter, telling her to cut it up first, to take smaller bites and not be so messy. Sam opened his mouth to say the words but then stopped. This wasn't Lydia. He'd give anything to have orange slop all over her face again, just to be given a chance to wash it off. He forced the image out of his head, trying to focus on Becca instead. "You look as if you have more on your face than you've gotten in your mouth."

"That's half the fun." She giggled.

"So, I've heard." Sam shook his head, enjoying the sound and her silliness.

Then there was Megan. Being around her made him feel better. Wanted. He sensed the attraction between them was mutual, but ironically, neither of them was happy about it.

Megan rejoined the group and sat in the chair next to Becca after filling her plate.

Everyone talked and laughed as if it were a normal family dinner. Sam looked around at the group of people who'd just met and yet interacted like old friends. People connecting with people.

Something he'd failed to do. He took a deep breath and exhaled, suddenly realizing the truth he'd been hiding from all along.

All the years he'd spent trying to prove he wasn't like his father had been for nothing. Instead, he'd become him. Working all the time—his eye always on the money. The reason had become irrelevant after his wife and daughter died. After all, family honor meant nothing when you had no family.

His father's debts were almost repaid, and then he'd be free to do whatever he wanted. What that was, he didn't have a clue. It had been so long since he thought about what he wanted, that he wasn't sure he knew where to find the answers, or that it even mattered anymore. The people he wanted to share his life with were gone.

"Let's go watch movies." Becca slid off her chair and headed for the kitchen, plate in hand. So much for waiting to be excused. But when the offset was a child willing to clear their own dishes, Sam was impressed.

In seconds, she was back in the room and eying the adults who had yet to move.

"Isn't anyone coming?" she asked, hope in her voice.

"Yes, honey. I'm coming. Let me finish and get cleaned up. Why don't you pick out what you want to watch first? I brought your case of Christmas DVDs. They are probably packed in the front pocket of your suitcase."

"Isn't anyone else coming to watch movies?" The crestfallen expression on her face was all it took for Sam to pull himself out of his funk.

"I am." Sam stood and took his plate to the sink.

"So will I. Hey, Sam, do you think you could get Frank into the living room again? It's good for his disposition and gives me a much-needed break as his entertainment committee." Agnes laughed.

"Sure thing. Becca, you put on a movie, and we'll all be here in a minute."

"Okay. Mr. Sam, will you sit next to me?"

"Of course." He ruffled the top of her head affectionately before following Agnes down the hall. The kid sure had a way of reaching deep inside of him and making him feel things he thought were long gone. Things like caring for another human being— really caring.

After bringing Frank into the fun, they all settled in to watch *Frosty* and then *Rudolph*. The movies brought back a flood of memories for Sam. True to his word, he sat next to Becca, and by the end of the second movie, she was leaning up against him.

Megan looked at her watch as the credits rolled and then at her daughter. "Becca, if you're going to watch *The Christmas Carol*, you need to start it now. Last one before bedtime."

"Aww, Mom. I'm being good, aren't I?" The never-ending battle between bedtime and children.

"Yes, you are, but it doesn't change bedtime. Remember, Santa's watching." Megan always seemed to know what to say, and this time was no different.

"I'm going to refill my water. Anyone need anything while I'm up?" Megan picked up her glass and waited a second.

"I'm okay, dear." Agnes picked up her drink and took a sip.

"Not many options available, so I guess I'll settle for water." Frank shifted to get more comfortable.

"It's not as if you could have anything stronger. Not with all the pain relievers you're taking." Megan laughed and picked up his glass.

"Can I have more hot chocolate?" Becky shot her mother a pleading look.

"Sorry. Too close to bedtime. I'll bring you water." Megan's gentle smile softened the rejection.

"Fine." Becca got up and flipped through the DVD case looking for the next movie.

"Sam?" Megan cast him a questioning look as she waited for his answer.

"I'll come help you. You've got your hands full

with orders already." He stood, picking up Becca's mug.

"Take your time." Agnes shot him a wink. The woman's matchmaking ideas were completely off base.

He followed Megan into the kitchen.

"Thanks for hanging out and watching movies with us. It means a lot to Becca. There haven't been any male role models around lately, and she seems quite attached to you."

"I have a way with the ladies, I guess." He chuckled, knowing the opposite was true.

"Just don't break her heart." The twinkle in Megan's eyes laughed back at him, but there was some truth to her words.

"Not a chance. I'll be gone before that can happen." He'd broken enough hearts and didn't relish adding any more to the list, and it's why he'd resigned himself to remain a loner.

"Here, can you carry this?" She spun around with a glass in her hand and crashed into him, spilling the water down his chest. "I'm so sorry," she squeaked.

Sam pulled the shirt from his jeans, unbuttoned it, and stripped it off his body. "Holy smokes, that's cold."

He had the shirt halfway off, but his arms got trapped in the sleeves. Megan started dabbing at his chest with a towel, her hand warm against his skin. He wasn't sure if getting stuck in his own shirt was a blessing or torture, because either way, he liked it. Too much.

Megan stopped as if suddenly realizing what she was doing, but her hand stayed pressed to his chest. He closed his eyes briefly, resisting the urge to kiss her sweet mouth that was just inches away.

"Sam... I..." Megan stumbled over what to say. "I should take these drinks to the others. I'm sorry." She tossed the towel on the counter, grabbed the drinks, and fled—all before he could respond. It would seem his brain had deserted him.

CHAPTER TWELVE

Sam looked out the window, the morning sun glinting off the snow practically blinded him. He was grateful there hadn't been any additional snowfall through the night, but the bigger issue was the emotion slowly seeping into his body, an emotion up until now he hadn't recognized. *Christmas joy.*

He'd come here looking for solitude to embrace his pain, and instead, merriment was on the menu. Megan and Becca were a powerful combination. He didn't stand a chance against them as they continued to make him feel more alive than he had in two years. Then there was the stirring of attraction that he felt toward Megan and couldn't deny. The sooner he left Hallbrook, the better. He wasn't sure how long he could hold out against her sweet appeal. Falling for her was not on his agenda. It couldn't be.

He made his way to the kitchen, started a pot of coffee, and then pulled out his phone and dialed the police station. "Good morning. This is Sam Wyatt. Just checking in to see if there are any updates on when the pass will reopen?"

"Good morning. And I'm sorry, I don't have better news. The side of the mountain is unstable, and it's slowing down the progress of reopening the pass. The latest projections are that it could take a few more days to clear Tinsel Pass."

"Days? That's crazy. Are you sure?"

"Yes, sir. Crews are only working daylight hours for their safety. I'm sure you understand. Also, if the next storm comes in and hits, it's going to slow the progress down more. We're hoping it skirts around us this time."

"You realize Christmas is Saturday?" Sam paced the floor, unsure how to feel about the news. It gave him more time with Megan, but the question was, did he want it? If he was honest with himself, he knew the answer was yes.

"I do, and I'm sorry. But I can't change the facts. Do you have any updates on Frank O'Malley? They're trying to figure out if we need to send in a Skidoo with a medic sled to get him out of there and to the hospital to make sure the prognosis is on the right track. We've got our hands full here, so if we can avoid taking those measures, it would be best."

"He's doing better. Megan is almost positive it's a sprained ACL, and between her and his wife, they're keeping ice on it, keeping it elevated, and keeping an eye on him."

"Sounds great. I'll pass the info along. I'm sure Captain James will be glad to hear it."

Sam brushed a hand through his hair and looked up, surprised to discover Megan watching him from the doorway. Her red sweater molded the soft curves of her body, the hem ending around her thighs. Faded jeans and fur-lined boots completed the fresh country-girl image.

"Thanks for the update." He let out a deep breath and hung up the phone.

"Who were you talking to?" She stayed by the kitchen doorway, keeping her distance from him.

He didn't know what to expect, but he was sure the news wouldn't be well received.

"I called down to the police station to get an update. It seems you're stuck with me until Christmas."

"Christmas? But Rachael? I can't have Christmas without my sister. There has to be a way to get her here." Hands on her hips, frustration dripped from every word she spoke.

"And me out of here, I'm sure." She'd wanted him gone since day one, and he'd done nothing to change her mind about him, so it shouldn't come as a surprise. "Try not to sound so miserable about it. It's not exactly what I planned either and it's out of my control. I would do anything I could to switch places with Rachael. Trust me. There's another storm in the area that they're worried about, and they need to work on the pass during daylight hours for safety reasons."

"It's not you." She shook her head. "It's the situation. This is supposed to be a fun Christmas. I heard about the possibility of an incoming storm when I checked the weather this morning. It seems strange because it's supposed to be nice today. The highs might even hit the low fifties, and everything will start to melt. Crazy weather this year."

"So true. The melting and refreezing on the roads will make road conditions worse. But don't worry, we'll make it work."

"Thanks. You really can be a nice man.'" Her smile made him feel warm inside, and even if it was temporary, he liked it.

"You keep saying that, but it's because you don't really know me. Best to keep it that way. I'm going to head to the neighbors and check in on everybody." Maybe if he found something to shovel, the hard work would tire him out, enough to put an end to his wayward thoughts about Megan.

"You don't have to leave because of me." She crossed the room to the coffee pot and picked up a mug.

"Who said anything about leaving because of you? I'm just giving you space to have your Christmas cheer, and I'm trying to help some of the others." And it was a way to escape the sudden urge he felt to kiss her. The soft violet scent he'd come to identify with her wafted around him, reminding him of all that was fresh and good—and alive.

It called to him in a way he hadn't expected and didn't want. Tomorrow was the anniversary of the day he lost Laura and Lydia, and it was wrong to be thinking of kissing someone. Filled with guilt, Sam hurried out of the room, unwilling to let Megan see his pain.

MEGAN WAS ATTRACTED TO HIM, pure and simple. And no amount of denial would make it go away. She'd have to keep it to herself because if her sister had any inkling of how she really felt, she wouldn't let the matter drop until she had Sam down on one knee and proposing. Something Megan knew would never happen.

Coffee in hand, Megan sat down at the table. Becca was sleeping in this morning, tired from yesterday's excitement. She gazed out the window, taking in the beauty of the woods behind the house.

Agnes joined her before long. "Good morning. Where's our little miss this morning?" She sat at the table after pouring a cup of coffee.

"Good morning. She's still sleeping, believe it or not. How's Frank? Should I check on him?"

"No, no. He's doing fine. Slept better. I'll take him more pain reliever in a few minutes. Just wish they had good-temper pills. He's bored stuck in bed and a tiny bit irritable."

"I'll see what we can do about getting him something to use as a crutch."

"That would be amazing. And heaven-sent." The older woman smiled.

Megan knew Agnes loved Frank and suspected the woman didn't mind the extra attention and the feeling of being needed.

Becca entered the dining area. "Morning, Mom, and Miss Agnes."

"Good morning," they answered in unison.

"I've got to take Frank his medicine. You can have my seat, honey."

"Thanks." Becca moved to the back door instead of sitting down and pressed her faced against the glass. She breathed hot air onto the pane and drew a snowman with her finger in the foggy spot.

"Mom, can I go outside and check on the dog? And can we build a snowman and our igloo today? Please?" Of course, the dog was the first thing on Becca's mind this morning.

"I don't see why not." She smiled at her daughter. Simple pleasures were the easiest and most rewarding gifts.

"Yay! Can I go now? I'll get dressed." Becca started toward the hall.

"Wait a minute. We need to eat breakfast. I'll make us some scrambled eggs and toast. Can you pour us some juice, please?"

They spent the next thirty minutes cooking and eating breakfast. Megan fixed a couple of plates to take to Agnes and Frank and left a plate for Sam in case he was hungry before he headed out this morning.

Sam stopped by the kitchen just as they finished cleaning up. "I'm taking off now unless there's anything you need while I'm here. When I get back, maybe we can search for the dog, Becca." He made his way to the coffee pot and poured a cup of coffee.

"Yay. I'd love to. We can try to follow his tracks." Becca was a bundle of energy this morning.

"I made breakfast and set aside a plate for you. You should eat before you go." It was all very family-like, something Megan hadn't experienced in years. It was oddly comforting.

"Thanks. Don't mind if I do." Sam grabbed the plate and sat down at the table.

"After we take care of the dog this morning, we're going to make a snowman. You should help us." Becca looked up at him hopefully.

"Sounds like fun, but I'm going to check on the neighbors again." He shot Becca a smile and then looked up at Megan. "How's Frank?"

Megan moved closer. "Better. Agnes mentioned he's becoming slightly less desirable as a patient. Any chance your woodworking skills are better than your coffee-making skills? I thought maybe you could find something to make into a crutch of sorts. Something simple that might help get him around better instead of needing help."

Sam shot her one of those warm and fuzzy, curl-up-your-toes smiles. "I'm pretty sure I can handle getting him some crutches."

"Perfect. And thanks. I'll give him the good news." Megan headed down the hall, leaving Sam to eat. That is if Becca let him. She laughed as she imagined her chatterbox daughter pitted against Sam. Megan would lay bets on Becca coming out the winner.

In short order, Megan was back and the three of them started to pull on their coats, bundling up as they prepared to head outside. Megan pulled on one boot, but the darn thing resisted her efforts. Off-balance, she fell into Sam.

His arm came up to steady her.

"Thanks." Caught in the moment, they simply stared at one another, neither one moving away. Megan resisted the urge to touch his face.

"Come on, Mom," Becca called to her from the back door, reminding her they had a witness to the interchange. A witness with a vivid imagination.

Sam suddenly stepped back. "Thanks for breakfast. I've got to go." He headed for the front door and was gone without explanation before Megan even finished getting her boot on. The gust of wind he let in chilled her from all the way across the room.

Becca's timing had saved Megan. What if she'd acted on the impulse she'd felt, only to be shut down and rejected in front of Becca? The pass had better be opened soon before Megan made a complete idiot of herself.

They went outside, Becca skipping across the back porch and around the side of the house. Stopping at the make-shift doghouse, Becca peered down. "Look, Mommy. He ate his food, and the blankets are all messed up. He stayed here last night. He liked it." Becca's grin reminded her of Christmas morning—filled with wonder and joy.

"Let me fill his bowl again, and then we can build a snowman. Sound like a plan?" Megan was worried about the little dog and hoped he'd come back during the day. "Can we take a walk and maybe look around for him? Please?"

The snowman would have to wait. "Sure thing, honey. A walk sounds wonderful. The birds should be active this time of the morning. Maybe we can count how many different kinds we see. Make it a game." On several occasions, she'd gone out to search for the dog already, not that she'd tell Becca, because that would get her daughter thinking about finders-keepers. Megan wasn't prepared to take on ownership of the mutt, but she wasn't averse to looking for him.

"Okay. I love games." Becca beamed and ran toward the wide-open backyard area. Surrounded by trees, it would make a wonderful bird-watching walk. She tossed some of the snow into the air, letting it fall over her rainbow-colored pom-pom beanie.

"With the snow melting, it'll be hard to see

tracks, but the birds will be easy enough to spot. Just don't get too far ahead of me."

"Okay, Mom." Becca rolled her eyes. Her daughter didn't understand it was just a reminder, not that she didn't trust her. Megan didn't know how to be anything other than protective. It was her job.

"We can pretend we're on an expedition to the North Pole. Won't that be fun, Mom?" Trudging through snow up to their knees made it difficult, but Becca didn't seem to mind.

"Absolutely." Becca had a terrific imagination, matched only by her joy to be outside and playing in their own personal winter wonderland.

Megan followed Becca, using her footprints to make it easier to keep up. Evergreen trees dotted the property to the right, their branches blanketed in white. Smaller branches drooped under the weight of the melting snow. The sun was up high and warm this morning, the warmth wonderful on her face after the past few days.

Birds darted from tree to tree, eagerly looking for food. "Look, Becca," she shouted, pointing at the beautiful red Cardinal that landed on the snow. Mrs. Cardinal flew in and landed next to him, her greenish-yellow feathers a giveaway to her identity.

Megan had read that Cardinals stayed with their

mates year after year, forever true. But what happened when one died? Did they find a new mate, or forever remain alone? An image of Sam flashed in her mind, his face and lips and their almost kiss. It hadn't been one-sided, not by a long shot.

Over the past couple of days, she'd come to appreciate him for the man she understood him to be, not the man he showed to the world. His smile warmed her heart, and the depth of his love for his family showed her a man capable of caring and deep love.

Megan looked over to where Becca was making snow angels, only to discover her gone. She made a sweeping glance of the area and soon spotted Becca off to the left in the distance, waving up at her.

"Mom! Mom! I saw him. I saw him. I saw the dog. He went that away," she hollered. She pointed toward another grove of evergreens off to the side. "Did you see him? He was white with brown ears, just like Mr. Sam told us. It was him. I just know it."

Her daughter took off running, or at least some semblance of running in the deep snow. She looked like a big bunny hopping through the snow. Megan cut across the field to join Becca, pulling out her phone to get a picture.

The sound of someone shouting caught Megan's

attention as she tried to focus on the picture. She turned back to see where the sound had come from.

Sam had returned and was waving at her.

Megan was too far away to hear him, but she lifted her hand to let him know she'd seen him. An eerie sound filled the air, much like the crack of a whip. It came from behind her, and Megan swung back around to check on Becca. She let out a sigh of relief when she spotted her daughter, and nothing looked out of the ordinary.

Another whip cracked, accompanied by a low moan, the sound sending a chill down her spine. Megan couldn't tell where the sound had come from, but it was unsettling. The recent avalanche at the pass made her nervous, but there were no mountains feeding into this area, eliminating the possibility. She heard the noise again.

Megan looked back at Sam to see him running in her direction, waving his arms. Something wasn't right, but she had no idea what.

Becca.

Megan took off running, her sixth sense kicking into high gear, her one thought to get to her daughter.

"Megan! Stop!" Sam called out from behind her. Her daughter needed her, and stopping wasn't an option, especially since she had yet to determine the danger.

"Megan! Stop! The pond!" Sam yelled.

Pond? She'd forgotten there was one somewhere behind the cabin. Sam was running by the trees toward where Becca stood, increasing her fear for her daughter's safety. She stopped a second to glance around, noticing water had begun to eat away at the snow. *Water? The pond.* Terror gripped her heart like a vice, squeezing until she felt or heard nothing.

It wasn't Becca in trouble—it was her.

"Megan, don't move," Sam ordered, the fear in his voice enough to make her stop.

"Mom!" Becca called out as she started toward Megan.

"Becca, stop!" Megan and Sam hollered in unison.

"You can't go out there. The extra weight will crack the ice, and you'll both fall in. Stay where you are, and I'm going to help your mom." Becca thankfully stopped, Sam's commanding voice having the desired result.

"Okay." Becca started crying.

Megan ached with fear as she thought of the danger she was in, especially as her daughter looked on. She tentatively took a step forward and then another. Her training in the military had prepared her for this type of rescue, but she'd never envisioned she'd be the one in danger. She tried to remember everything she knew.

Sam moved toward her, stopping fifty feet away. He couldn't go any farther, not unless he wanted to chance busting through the ice himself, a move that wouldn't do either of them any good.

Time slowed with each step she took.

"Keep coming. Nice and easy. You're doing great. One step at a time and try to step as light as you can." Sam's voice drew her to him, one foot after the other.

Becca's sobbing intensified, the sound tearing at Megan's heart.

"Mommy's going to be okay, honey. You'll see." She spoke the words as much for her sake as for her daughter's.

"She's right. I won't let anything happen to her. Trust me." His words sounded like a personal vow; a vow Megan had to believe.

"Okay. Is there anything I can do to help?" Becca might be scared, but her offer showed the inner strength her daughter possessed.

"There is. See the row of evergreen trees? That's the path back to the house. Follow them and head for the shed. There's an orange life ring hanging on the wall. Get it for me."

Becca looked torn with indecision.

"Please, Becca. If the ice breaks, the ring could save her. I'm not going anywhere, and I promise I won't let anything happen to your mother."

"Listen to Sam, honey. I'll be fine." Megan trusted him and whatever he thought was best, was exactly what needed to happen.

Another deep bellow sounded from the pond, spurring Becca into action, and she took off running down the path Sam had told her to use.

"Keep coming, Megan," Sam called out to her, reminding her to stay focused. She took another step forward, the water pooling around her feet.

"The water's coming up through the ice, and the snow is all slushy." She looked up at him, trying to draw from his strength. This was all her fault. With all the snow, she hadn't seen or even thought of the pond she'd seen in the brochure. She took three more steps.

"There's got to be a hole under the snow that we can't see. The ice is thin. Stay focused and keep coming. I'm right here." She was so close to him and would give anything for this to be over and to be held in his arms, safe from the danger surrounding her.

Another crack whipped through the air. Megan couldn't help the cry that slipped from her lips. "There's more water. What do I do?"

"Stop. Don't move another inch. Becca's coming with the life ring."

SAM SPOTTED Becca running in their direction. *Thank God.*

He couldn't fail. Not again. Today was the anniversary of Laura and Lydia's death, a time when he hadn't been there to save them, but there was no excuse this time. It was lucky he'd forgotten about the crutches and returned to get them. He'd immediately recognized the danger Megan was in when he stepped into the backyard and saw her taking a shortcut toward Becca. The pond was covered in a blanket of snow and unrecognizable as such, and this time of year, there was no telling how solid the ice would be.

Now he needed a miracle, not luck.

"Becca, come around from behind me and bring me the life ring. Quick," Sam demanded, trying to force her to focus and listen to his words and not her fear.

"Good girl," Sam said, taking the ring from Becca. "Go back and stand by the trees where it's safe." Becca followed his orders, but the fear in her eyes broke his heart.

Megan had closed the distance to about twenty feet, but there was too much water. He feared the area was unstable, the cracking and moaning sound becoming more frequent.

Sam prepared the life-ring rope, checking the line and wrapping it in coils. The ice moaned again, prompting him to move faster. He wanted the ring around her, just in case the ice gave way.

"Megan, listen to me. I'm going to toss you this ring. I don't want you to jump for it. If I don't make it the first time, I'll try again. Let me get it to you. No sudden moves, right?"

"Yes." That one word vibrated with fear. One word that ripped Sam's heart in two. A heart he didn't even know existed anymore, but one that clearly felt the desperation to save Megan.

He tossed the ring, letting the rope unfurl at his feet. The ring slid across the surface of the snow, coming to a halt six feet away from Megan. "Don't move. Remember what I said. I'm going to try again. I've got to get it closer."

"Okay. Hurry. The water has soaked through my boots and my feet are freezing."

They didn't have much time. Sam pulled the ring back, curling the rope as he went. He tossed the ring again, this time a tiny bit harder, careful not to overthrow. The last thing he wanted was to hit her and knock her down.

The ring slid to within inches of her feet. *Yes.*

"Thank you, Lord," Megan choked out.

Sam seconded the sentiment. "Okay, now reach down, grab the ring, and slide it over your head."

Megan did as he instructed, and Sam let out a deep breath once the ring was safely around her waist. "That a girl." He forced a smile, hoping to ease her fears.

He turned to Becca. "Can you run up to the house and tell Agnes what's going on and get us a blanket. Just in case. I've got her now, so there's no need to worry. I'm going to hold the rope and let her walk in toward me slowly. But as a backup, I want a blanket. Can you do this for me?"

"But I can't leave my mom." Becca was crying again.

"Do what he asks, Becca. Sam's got the rope, and I trust him." *Trust.* One little word that meant the world to Sam. A word he'd have to think about later. After Megan was safe.

Becca nodded, brushed away her tears with the back of her mitten, and took off running.

"Okay, Megan. Take a few more steps toward me, nice and easy. No matter what happens from here on out, I've got you. Understand?" He wrapped his end of the rope around his hand several times.

"Yes. And Sam, thanks for—" A thunderous roar filled the air as the ice suddenly gave way beneath Megan's feet, plunging her into the icy waters. "Sam!" The scream tore from her lips, chilling every fiber of his being.

"No!" he hollered, pulling hard against the rope to eliminate the slack. "Hang on, Megan. I've got you."

He had to get her out of the water as fast as possible. She was already chilled, and the icy water would suck the heat from her body all too quickly. He took another step forward, testing the ice with his weight, anything to close the remaining fifteen feet between them. Two more steps, and then he stopped. The water had turned the snow to slush. It wasn't safe for him continue.

Megan thrashed about, trying to get to the edge of the ice. "I'm so c-c-cold," she chattered.

The ring would keep her above the water's surface, but hypothermia was a real concern.

"Megan, try to put your arms on the ice that's still solid." He was close enough to see her lips trembling.

"Okay." He would have expected tears, but instead, she remained strong, fighting to stay brave. She moved her arms over the ice as he requested.

He'd read once that the arms would stick to the ice to help hold a person out of the water longer, keeping their upper body warmer.

"We need to get you out, and I'm going to need you to help me. Let your body go as limp as possible. Don't try to help me."

"Ok-k-kay." Her teeth chattered as she slurred the words, even as she tried to be funny.

Sam was running out of time. He pulled hard, the ring finally coming up over the edge of the ice, allowing the rest of her body to slide out of the water and on to the ice.

"So c-c-cold." Her entire body shook uncontrollably.

"I know. Blankets and heat are coming." Sam picked her up and ran a few steps back toward the trees, setting her on her feet only long enough to slide out of his coat and wrap it around her.

"Wh-where's B-Becca?"

"She's getting blankets, remember? She's fine." He picked her back up, and headed for the house, pulling her tight against his chest hoping some of his warmth would transfer to her body.

Megan's arms came around his neck, her face pressed against his shoulder, her body shaking. He looked toward the house, searching for Becca.

Agnes came running toward him, followed

closely by Becca. Sam stopped only long enough for Agnes to wrap the blanket around Megan.

"Is she okay?" Worry lined the older woman's face as she tried to tighten the blanket around Megan's head.

"Mom, are you okay?" Becca reached out to touch her mother, anxious and needing a connection.

"Y-y-yes, h-h-honey." Megan's purple lips uttering the halting words, spurred him back into action.

"She'll be fine. We need to get her to the house and out of these wet clothes." He moved as fast as he could, frustrated by the deep snow that kept him at a slower pace than he liked. "Agnes, can you run ahead and draw a lukewarm bath?"

"I'll see to it. Good thinking." Agnes might be older, but there was nothing slowing her down as she put distance between them.

By the time he got to the cabin, Agnes was at the back door, holding it open for him. "Oh, my goodness, the poor thing. Hurry, hurry. The bathwater is running, lukewarm like you asked."

He set off down the hall and entered her bedroom, setting her down on the bed. Sam removed the blanket and his coat from around Megan's body, and then started to work on her soaked and icy coat.

Agnes briskly rubbed at Megan's wet hair with a towel.

Becca stood by the door, tears in her eyes as she watched the action.

"Becca, come help your mother. She's going to be all right. Come see for yourself." It would do both mother and daughter a world of good to have each other for emotional support and healing.

Sam picked Megan up, clothes and all, and set her down gently in the tub. The lukewarm water would feel like fire against her icy skin, but he needed to get her warm. He held on tightly to her trembling body, praying for the warmth to seep through to her skin quickly.

"You doing okay, Megan?" Sam wanted to keep her talking and alert.

"I'm still c-c-cold." It was an excellent sign she was still shivering.

He lifted her wrist to check her pulse, satisfied when he felt her heartbeat steady and strong. "Becca's right here. She was a real trooper helping me out. You should be proud of her."

Megan managed a weak smile and reached for her daughter's hand. Becca leaned over the edge of the tub, practically climbing in.

Agnes pulled Sam's arm, propelling him toward the door. "I'll sit with her while you get out of your wet clothes. With Becca's help, I'm sure we can manage to take care of Megan."

"I don't know. I should stay and watch her progress."

"You won't be of much use if you end up with pneumonia. I don't know why you came back this morning, but we're all glad you did. You're a good man. First saving us, and now Megan. Seems you're handy to have around."

Agnes's gentle words and smile didn't reach his heart, her words a reminder of another time he wasn't so lucky.

"Not always."

CHAPTER THIRTEEN

Agnes rubbed her hands down Megan's forearms and throat, the pain of her touch almost unbearable, like concrete against raw skin.

"We need to add warm water and start to get you out of these clothes." The older woman's voice was soothing as she began to peel away Megan's shirt.

"Ok-kay." Her teeth chattered. The deep chill still invaded her body, but it was no longer numbing to the point she couldn't move, which also explained the excruciating pain of thawing. Megan tried to remember everything she knew about hypothermia, but her brain was running slow. If only she could get more heat.

"What can I do to help you, Mom?" Tear tracks were still visible down her daughter's face. Megan reached for her to offer comfort, but the effort was more than she could handle.

"You're doing it. I just want you near me." Megan attempted a smile and got half of one, but enough to mean something to Becca.

"I've got more towels and dry clothes. Can I get you some soup or hot chocolate? I'm old enough to heat those things up for you." Becca was a good girl. Megan's eyes drifted closed. She was so tired she was unable to answer.

"I think that sounds like a grand idea, young lady. And maybe you could ask Sam for help." Agnes answered for her.

"Okay, be right back, Mom." Megan sighed with relief after her daughter left the room. It was much easier to give in to the mind-numbing ache with Becca gone. She didn't want her daughter to see her having a tough time and cause her to worry any more than she already was.

Megan closed her eyes, and instantly she was back in the pond, clawing to get out of the icy water.

"Megan, honey, open your eyes. You're right here with me," Agnes's voice called her back to the present.

Megan forced her eyes open and found herself clinging to the tub in sheer terror. Her focus had been on Sam, his voice calling to her, telling her what to do. He'd saved her from the watery grave that would have robbed her from Becca's life. Her daughter had been through enough losing her father and then her grandmother. Megan couldn't bear the thought of the pain and suffering she would have caused her daughter if Sam hadn't been there.

Agnes's soothing tones lulled Megan back to a place of calm serenity, driving out the demons. It wasn't long before the heat of the warmed water began to seep deep into her body, and the shivering subsided. Megan tried to smile, but it fell short. A half-hearted attempt was all she could muster. "I'd really like to sleep now if that's okay. Maybe I can eat later."

"Sure thing. I'll let the young'un know. Let me help you out of the tub and out of the rest of your wet clothes. We need to get you in the bed and tucked in with lots of blankets to keep you warm."

Agnes wrapped her in fresh towels, never venturing more than an arm's length away.

"Becca laid out your pj's on the bed. Such a sweet child."

"Yes. Such a blessing."

Agnes finished helping her dress and pulled the comforter back, letting Megan climb into bed before covering her and tucking her in as if she were a child. Megan had never been more appreciative of the soft warmth. Sheer exhaustion caused her eyes to droop yet again.

The door opened, and her daughter walked in with a mug. "Here, Mom. We heated up some chicken noodle soup. Mr. Sam says you need to drink some before you fall asleep. Got to heat you up on the inside, too."

Megan forced herself to remain alert and sat up straighter to take the mug. "Sure thing, baby. I bet it's extra tasty since you made it." She wasn't hungry, but she'd make the extra effort for her daughter's sake.

"Don't be silly, I just heated it up. Mr. Sam uses the can kind of soup."

"Sounds perfect. Come crawl on the bed and lay down with me a minute."

Becca scooted in under the cover next to Megan, her little body giving off the much-needed extra heat.

Megan leaned over and kissed her daughter's forehead, hoping to reassure her. She took a few sips of the soup, but the effort was more than she could handle. "Thanks for the soup, sweetheart."

"Mr. Sam saved you. He was awesome!" The adoration in her daughter's voice bordered on reverence. Becca had grown attached, and now it was only normal she'd feel an unbreakable emotional connection to the man who'd saved her mother's life.

"Yes, darling, he was." Megan's eyes glassed over, but she fought back the tears, refusing to let them spill over and upset her Becca. "I'm so sorry, honey. I should have known about the pond and been more careful. I don't want you to worry, because everything is going to be okay. I promise."

"It's okay, Mom. Don't cry. I saw the dog and started chasing him. I know you've told me over and over not to go far away from you, and I feel as though this is all my fault. I'm sorry." Tears filled Becca's eyes, the sight enough to break Megan's heart.

Becca had been doing good until Megan opened her big mouth. "It's not your fault. I know you want to help the dog, and it's okay. I just didn't know when I cut across to reach you that it wasn't a field." Megan still couldn't believe the morning fun had turned into such a disaster. She had no idea why Sam had come back, but she would be forever grateful.

"No one's to blame, and it doesn't do anything to dwell on it now. It's over. Drink up, Megan. Becca and I are going to see what we can rustle up for supper." Agnes was right, but it didn't make Megan feel any better about letting her guard down around Becca.

Her daughter slid off the bed and took Agnes's

hand as the two of them crossed the room to leave. Becca paused and turned back. "Sweet dreams, Mommy."

Megan let out a deep breath when the door closed behind them. She couldn't smother the child in the future because of her own fears, no matter how much she might want to. Becca was being brave, and Megan needed to step up and match her daughter's efforts.

HE HAD to get out of the house and away from Becca. She was a living reminder of Lydia and combined with the traumatic events of this afternoon, the ability to control his emotions had been worn down. When she'd joined him in the kitchen and asked his help to fix her mother some soup and hot chocolate, Sam didn't have the heart to say no. They worked together as a team. Together. Like father and daughter—the reminder more than he could bear.

Agnes had thrown his jacket in the dryer, but it would still be soaked and useless at this point. Sam went out the back door, his gaze zeroing in on the dark patch where the ice and snow had collapsed.

The chilly winter air seeped through his sweater, but he didn't care. He retraced the well-worn path back to the pond and surveyed the scene closer. The fear in Megan's voice still echoed in his heart. All around him, the sound of silence broken only by the birds, seemed to intensify her scream in his head.

What if I hadn't come back?

But I did.

The voice came out of nowhere, answering his unspoken question. Sam looked around, the words all too real. The only thing he saw was the orange life ring, bright against the white snow. He picked it up and held it to his chest, images of Laura and Lydia surfacing yet again.

Their faces disappeared, a new one becoming clearer, more vivid. Megan. And then, Becca. *"We can be friends."* The little girl's words had been spoken with great trust.

He wasn't much of a friend. Leaving her alone was the last thing he should be doing after she'd witnessed her mother almost drown. Becca wasn't Lydia. She was a living and breathing young girl who deserved better from him and needed comfort, not cowardice. The last time he'd done this to her, he vowed to not let happen it again, and yet here he was. When would he learn?

Sam's heart melted a little more as he remembered when Becca had slid her small hand into his and looked up at him in earnest, trying to help him feel better. *"Marry my mom, and you can be my dad. We can be a family."*

Sam returned to the house in search of Becca. A card game or two would be the perfect thing to take her mind off her mother until she was up and about, and it would help Sam channel the emotions ripping him apart today. Megan's accident couldn't have come at a worse time—not that there ever would have been a good time, he amended.

A LIGHT TAP at the door woke Megan. Everything came rushing back to her. *Becca. The ice. Sam.* She shook off the image and rubbed the sleep from her eyes.

"Come in."

Sam entered the room. He looked wrung out emotionally, and her heart went out to him.

"How are you doing?" He sat down on the edge of the bed and took her hand in his.

She was warm and cozy under the comforter, but the extra heat could only be attributed to his touch. "Better. I can't thank you enough for what you did today. I will be forever grateful."

He felt her pulse, silently counting numbers in his head. "Pulse is steady and strong. And no thanks are necessary. I should have reminded you about the pond and made sure you steered clear of the area."

"Oh, come now. That wasn't your responsibility. One minute, she was close to me, and the next, she was gone. I'm such an idiot."

"You wouldn't have known unless you were familiar with the area. The snow has made it all look the same. It all ended well, which is what's important." He was trying to make her feel better, but it wasn't working.

"Yes, because of you. I'm supposed to be the in-control one, but I lost it out there. I thought she was the one in danger, not me."

He hated seeing her like this. "That's understandable. A good parent fears for their child's safety well ahead of their own. Accidents happen, and this one turned out okay." Sam touched her chin, tilting her face back toward him. "Think of the positives. You're both safe and warm. However, we should probably cancel the party tomorrow night. I'm not sure it's best to let you get worn out, and you probably shouldn't go back outside where you might get chilled."

"Nothing positive in that. Please, don't cancel it. I would hate to break Becca's heart."

"Mommy, are you—" Her daughter stopped in the doorway when she spotted Sam sitting on the bed. Her eyes grew big as saucers, her smile like the Cheshire Cat.

"What is it, honey?"

Sam stood and moved toward the doorway.

"Never mind. Miss Agnes is fixing dinner and I need to help." She was gone as fast as she arrived.

"Sorry about that. I'll have another talk with her. Wouldn't want her getting any ideas about us." Megan grimaced. Her daughter's fixation on making Sam a part of the family was embarrassing.

"Why would she get ideas? You mean the hero thing?"

"Well, there is that…but then she's an impressionable child. Never mind. I'll take care of it." The man was clueless, but his words served as a reminder to her own heart. *Don't get involved.*

CHAPTER FOURTEEN

Megan's body still ached from yesterday's traumatic experience. But after being pampered and cosseted throughout the day, she was ready to get out of bed and start the day fresh. She pulled her robe on and cinched the belt tightly, then slid on her slippers.

No one would have called Rachael and told her what happened. Luckily, all had ended well, and she could tell her sister the story herself. She checked her messages, but Rachael hadn't called. *Too busy having fun with her new friend.*

She headed for the kitchen and ran into Sam coming out of the bathroom. "I'm going to make a cup of hot chocolate and sit by the fire. Would you care to join me?"

"Of course. Should you be up and about?" Sam moved to stand next to her. His protectiveness was both endearing and frustrating. The ordeal was over and behind her. All she wanted to do was move forward.

"I'm fine." She hated the tremble of weakness in her voice.

"Want to talk about what's bothering you?" His gaze hadn't left her face, and she turned away.

"Talking won't change anything." She nuked two mugs filled with water, scooped in the chocolate, and stirred, all without another word.

Megan handed him a cup with only a cursory glance. She headed for the living room and sat down in the chair closest to the fireplace. Agnes was nowhere to be seen.

"Spill it, Megan." His insistence surprised her because talking meant getting closer, something he avoided most of the time.

"I just feel so guilty, and like a horrible mother." She leaned back, settling against the puffy cushions, and let out a deep breath of air. "I can't shake the awful feeling I failed."

"There was no way for you to know. In another couple of weeks, that pond will be frozen solid. With all the snow, it was impossible to tell the difference in terrain."

"What if it had been Becca?" She finally said the

words that had been bothering her the most out loud.

"It wasn't her, and you're still here. You can't live in the what-if world, and although this may not be the right thing to say, you should have some peace knowing your sister would always be there for Becca if something did happen. Not everyone has someone they can trust with the most important people in their lives."

"That is an awkward thing to say, but I know what you mean. It all happened so fast, and I've had all night to think about it. Experience it. I can't thank you enough for being there for me—saving me." She reached out to touch his arm, needing the connection.

Sam buried his face in his hands, but not before she saw the pain in his eyes.

"What is it, Sam? Talk to me."

"It's more than I gave my daughter or wife." The pain in his voice was almost too much to bear. She had no business trying to help someone through something so horrific. What if she said the wrong thing? Megan sensed he'd never talked to anyone about what was eating him up inside, and that somehow, at this moment, the words had spilled out.

Could she be strong for him and find a way to help him come to grips with his pain?

He must have sensed her gaze on him, because it wasn't long before he looked up at her, and the two of them were caught in time as it stood still. Sadness echoed in the depths of his eyes, making her want to fix things for him.

Megan came to a decision. "Tell me what happened. You need to move forward and you can't do that as long as you keep the memories on lockdown, afraid to expose them to the light of day." Megan spoke softly, trying to encourage him to share.

"You don't want to know, trust me. I'm not a good guy, Megan." He shook his head and started to rise as if to leave. She had to stop him.

"Sam?" She gripped his arm tighter, not letting him go.

His gaze drifted to her hand, and then he surprised her by sitting back down. Sam took a deep breath and exhaled.

"It was two years ago yesterday. Christmas time. Just like now. My wife and I rented this cabin to spend Christmas week together. I was in a meeting that ran over, and I didn't get here when I promised to meet them. They drove to town to pick up food, except they never made it back. It had been snowing, and an earlier freezing rain left the roads icy. Laura lost control of the car, and it slid off the icy roads into a ravine. Neither one survived."

A few tears slid down his face as she listened to his painful story.

"It sounds to me as though it were an accident. You told me accidents happen. And it's the same thing you told Becca when you tried to comfort her. You need to listen to yourself. You couldn't possibly be with them all the time."

Hearing his story made her realize how hard being here with her and Becca must be for him. No wonder he came across as withdrawn and grumpy at times. The man had every right to be. Life had dealt him a terrible blow.

"That's where you're wrong. I should've been here. She didn't like driving in the snow. I should've been the one driving the car. Maybe I could've saved them, but I'll never know because I wasn't here. I put work first, instead of my family, and as a result, they're dead." Sam drilled her with his gaze as if waiting for her condemnation. Something she had no intention of giving him because he had it all wrong.

"Oh, Sam. That's a heavy load to carry. You need to give yourself the freedom to let it go. They wouldn't want you to carry on this way. It could have happened anywhere, at any time. It's not your fault there was a storm. It's not your fault there were icy roads. It's not your fault they chose to head into town. Those are everyday decisions, and things happen that are out of our control."

"I don't agree. It was my decision to stay in town for one last meeting to close a deal. That affected her decision to go to town without me. So, yes, I am responsible they're gone."

Megan rose from her chair and stood behind him, wrapping her arms around his neck and shoulders in a hug. "I'm sorry, Sam. What a terrible burden to shoulder, but I hope you find a way to make peace with yourself and life. I know this might not make you feel any better, but do you realize that if you had been driving that night, you might have died with them, and then you wouldn't have been here to save me today? God brought you back to me this morning, knowing I needed you. And for that, I will be forever thankful. You owe it to their memories to live again. I have a feeling they loved you very much and wouldn't want you to carry this guilt around."

Sam shook his head and rose, breaking the contact between them.

"I don't expect you to understand. I've got to get those crutches for Frank."

"Running away won't change a thing, but I'm

sure Frank would appreciate them." It had been a start for Sam to open his inner emotions and talk to someone. She hoped it was just the beginning for him because eventually, something had to give. He deserved better than he was allowing himself.

"Wait right here." He tugged on his jacket and headed out the back door.

In less than five minutes, Sam was back with a pair of crutches in hand. "Here." He held them out to her.

"That was fast. You let me believe you had to make them." She stood hands on her hips, calling him to task.

"I didn't say anything about making them, you assumed. I forgot to get them for Frank yesterday. It's why I came back."

"I'm glad you have memory issues." She shook her head and grinned, the first hint of laughter surfacing after her ordeal.

"Me, too. I'm going to check on the neighbors since I didn't get a chance yesterday. See you later." Sam turned and left without a backward glance, but it didn't stop her from watching.

Megan headed down the hall and knocked on the spare bedroom door.

"Come in," Frank shouted.

"Good morning. Look what I have for you. Sam

found them in the shed." Megan held out the crutches and leaned them against the bed.

"This is perfect. I can get around without the wife now." Frank chuckled, teasing his wife.

"Hey, I was only trying to help, but you're a stubborn man and impossible to please." Agnes huffed.

"I know, and I love you dearly for your sweetness, but a man likes to take care of private business privately. As to being stubborn, it's a good thing, because I was stubborn enough to see through you turning me down twice before you agreed to marry me." He winked at Megan, a broad smile on his face.

"Yeah, yeah. You just want to make sure I keep making my strawberry-rhubarb pie, you old coot."

Frank chuckled. "And how are you doing today? Any issues from yesterday? I'm surprised to see you up and about, and you certainly need time off from taking care of an old geezer."

"I'm fine. Lucky for me, Sam forgot to get you these yesterday. He came back just in time to save the day. I wasn't in the water long enough to suffer anything more than mild hypothermia."

"'Tis a blessing indeed. Where's the young'un this morning?" Frank asked.

"Still asleep. She came to bed late. Thanks for watching her and for your help, Agnes."

"You're welcome, dearie. But I wasn't the one entertaining Becca, just so you know."

"What do you mean? Did someone come by?"

"Nope. Sam and Becca played games for quite a while. I think there were a few games of checkers in there at one point, and then a game of war that went on forever. I never did hear who won."

"Sam? That's unexpected."

"They say everything happens for a reason. Sam came back to get you the crutches he forgot, but they were needed because Frank got hurt. So, us coming here was all for good."

"I like the way you think. I'd go through this pain a hundred times over if it saved your life." Frank tested the crutches out, crossing the room.

"It stands to reason then, there's a reason you and Sam met." Agnes was still pushing for her and Sam to have a happily-ever-after fairytale romance.

"Yes. He had to save my life. Don't read anything more into it."

"I'm just calling it the way I see it." Agnes turned back to watch Frank. "Be careful, old man." She started his way every time he wavered slightly.

"Quit picking, woman. I got this." Megan could see the strain on his face as he fought back the pain. She wouldn't say a word in front of Agnes. Clearly, he was trying to be strong, and she wouldn't take that away from him.

"I've got to check on Becca and call my sister. I'll leave you two lovebirds alone." She laughed and headed for the door.

"Go on. I'll watch over him, even if he thinks he doesn't need it. Oh, and I'll fix breakfast and lunch to give you a break. I heard tonight's still on, so you need to rest until then. You look plumb worn out."

"Thanks. I feel worn out. I'll be in bed early tonight after the party, that's for sure."

Megan entered the darkened room and crossed to Becca's bedside. Her soft, even breaths indicated she was still sound asleep. Megan drew the blankets up and tucked them around her daughter, placing a kiss on her head.

She wasn't looking forward to calling her sister, but it had to be done. Reliving the experience would be difficult even though it had a happy ending. Rachael was sure to flip out, and it would make it harder that she couldn't be here with them.

"Hey, sis, what's up?" At least her sister was in an excellent mood.

"You got a few minutes?"

"Sure. Let me guess, you and the hunky man have fallen madly in love, and you're going to ride off into the sunset on a horse-drawn carriage. You need me to babysit, right?" Her sister's laughter and teasing were exactly what she needed to hear, even if it was totally ridiculous. Rachael was always the one with the outlandish imagination when they were growing up.

"Not even close. There was an accident. Everything is okay, but I thought you should know."

"Is anyone hurt? Becca? What happened?" Her sister's tone had grown serious, all laughter gone.

"Slow down. And, no, not Becca. Me. So clearly, I'm okay if I'm calling you. I fell through the ice while we were outside yesterday."

"What?" Rachael screeched.

"Calm down. I'm trying to tell you." She spent the next five minutes telling her sister everything.

"Like I said, I'm fine. Becca was scared, but I think she's okay now. Sam talked to her quite a bit. He's good with her. Me, on the other hand, I feel as though I dropped the parenting ball."

"You were both outside having fun. End of story. You can't control everything, no matter how hard you try. Some things are out of people's control. Ever since Andy died, you've been way too intense, and it needs to stop. You're one person, and you need to let go of the past and start living again. Taking chances." It wasn't the first time her sister had lectured her. Not to mention, the words sounded vaguely familiar—like the ones she'd said to Sam earlier.

"Pot, black. You don't let others in either, not since you moved to Portland. And I don't even know why, because you haven't told me. So, don't lecture me about living until you do it first."

"Maybe I have." Her sister's voice was barely above a whisper.

"What? The rescue guy?" Megan couldn't believe it. No wonder her sister hadn't been calling. She'd been busy making time with her new friend.

"He has a name. Brandon. And, yes. He's nice."

"Nice?"

"Okay, more than nice. I like him, but…"

"But what?"

"We live worlds apart. So, it's just for now, but when I return to work, it has to be over."

"Why? It can't be more than three hours from Portland to Hallbrook. It's not as if you're halfway across the country."

"Might as well be. Long-distance doesn't work. I know." Since when did her sister know enough about long-distance relationships to have been soured on them.

"How? I don't know of—"

"Because I was in one. When I first moved to Portland. You were right, something happened. I was in love. Then one day, I drove out to Concord, which I might add was just a couple of hours away. I went to his office, hoping to surprise him for a weekend visit. I waited for him to come back from lunch, so you can imagine my surprise when he showed up with a wife and two kids."

"Oh, Rachael. I'm so sorry." Her poor sister. And having to go through it all alone. It saddened Megan to realize her sister hadn't trusted her with the truth back when it happened.

"I'm over it. But I won't do long-distance ever again."

"The distance wasn't the problem. It was the slimeball and his lies." It was another reason why Megan wasn't willing to get back out into the dating pool. She'd never find another man like Andy, and he'd been far from perfect, so why try?

"Whatever. So now you know. And, yes, I'm starting to live again. So, to throw your words back in your face, you can do it, too. How is Mr. Grumpy? Seems to me, the man who saved you can't be all mean and rotten." She'd shared the nickname with her sister, and it had stuck.

"He's not. He's actually quite sweet when he chooses to be."

"Do I hear a hint of interest?"

"No. Yes. No."

"Well, which is it?"

"He's very deep and he's amazing with Becca, but he's been through a lot of pain. He's smart and ready to lend a helping hand to anyone. But neither one of us is interested in another relationship, so it doesn't matter." Aside from a few moments of weakness when she'd wanted him to kiss her. Then there was the one time she'd been positive he'd been about to kiss her.

"Take a chance, sis. Show him you're interested. I didn't miss the yes, so I know somethings going on in your brain. You're attracted whether you're ready to admit it or not."

"I've got to run. Becca needs breakfast."

"Run away, fine. Give her a hug for me when she wakes up and tell her I love her. I miss you guys, and I'm looking forward to seeing you. I'll keep checking on updates for the pass."

"Sounds to me as if you're too busy to miss us."

"Never too busy for family. Love you."

"Love you, too."

Megan hung up, surprised her sister hadn't freaked out the way she'd expected. Brandon must have really rocked her sister's world for her to be this calm. Her sister's past relationship explained a lot to Megan about her reticence to date and her commitment to work.

Maybe the right man could help heal Rachael's heart.

Could the right man work on my heart as well?

Megan entered the bedroom, a quick glance at Becca's side of the bed revealed her daughter was already up. The sound of running water clued her into her daughter's whereabouts.

The bathroom door opened, and an energetic Becca danced into the room. "Good morning, Mom." Becca raced across the room and flung her arms tightly around Megan in a hug.

"Good morning, sleepyhead. Do you remember what today is?"

"Yeppers. It's Christmas Eve, and the party is tonight." Becca's smile lit up Megan's world. The same smile that made Megan try so hard to make everything special for her daughter.

"That's right. We have lots of preparation to get ready, so I'm going to need your help."

"It's going to be so much fun, and I hope Aunt Rachael gets here. But at least Mr. Sam's here. I like him. It's too bad Mr. Frank can't join in, but maybe we could do something special for him to make him feel better."

"He's actually got crutches now and was able to get around a bit this morning. He's doing much better."

"Yay! And there will be kids here tonight, at least five of them. Of course, most of them are younger than me, but that's okay. It will be fun."

"Sounds great. I know you've been looking forward to this. I talked to Aunt Rachael, and she said to give you a big hug."

"Okay. Hurry, I'm hungry, and I want to check on Floppy."

"Floppy?" Meghan hated to ask, knowing the answer.

"The dog. His ears were long and floppy like a bunny rabbit."

"Becca, don't get attached. Don't forget, we're leaving Tuesday." Provided the Department of Transportation got the pass opened.

"I know. But he's got to have a name."

Megan laughed as Becca ran out of the room and then got dressed and went to help Agnes with breakfast. She was surprised to find her daughter and Sam sitting at the table together, cocoa and coffee in hand. They both looked up as she walked into the room.

"I thought you were leaving?"

"Eager for me to be gone?"

"You know better. Did you forget something again?"

"No. Look outside. It's started snowing. The

storm everyone hoped would stay away is officially here. I've already called the authorities this morning, and they've had to suspend work on the pass. The recent warmer temperature is making it dangerous, and now visibility is almost at zero."

"Does that mean Tinsel Pass won't open today?" She glanced at Becca to see how she was taking the news. If the pass didn't open, Rachael wouldn't arrive today, either. This was supposed to be a special Christmas with the three of them in her mother's favorite place, but it looked like Mother Nature had a different idea. Megan let out a heavy sigh.

"I don't think so. They said they'd update us later in the day, depending on what happens with the storm."

"But Aunt Rachael won't be able to come to the party." Her daughter's crestfallen face left an ache in Megan's heart. She wished she could make things perfect for Becca.

"I'm sorry, honey. We can't control the weather."

"Will she be here tomorrow? She can't miss Christmas."

"I can't promise anything, but we can say our prayers. I know she wants to be here, honey."

"Okay. Can I play outside after I check on Floppy?"

"We'll see. It depends on how much it's snowing. We may need to find things to do inside."

"But what about the party? We have to have the party." Becca's excitement had dwindled to disappointment. Her pout was a far cry from her earlier smiles.

"Your mother's right, everything depends on the storm. I tell you what, maybe we can go outside for just a few minutes while Agnes is cooking, and we'll let your mom sit and rest while she enjoys her coffee. If that's okay with your mother, that is. I need to grab some more wood and stack it up for the fire, and you can check on the dog, take him some food, and then give me a hand."

"Yes! Can I, Mom? Can I?"

Megan didn't fancy the idea of Becca going outside without her. Not after yesterday. She didn't want to be the one to disappoint her daughter, but she couldn't be in both places. Could she trust Sam to watch after Becca the way she would?

The way I would?

Anyone could do a better job than she had yesterday. Sam had proven he was much better in an emergency than she was, not to mention, he'd seen the problem long before it happened. He'd been on the run before Megan even realized the danger.

She wanted to trust Sam, to show him with

actions that she believed in him. Maybe it would help them both. "That would be fine. Just listen to what Sam tells you." Megan was tempted to give her daughter fifteen other instructions, but she bit back the words.

Sam shot her a look of gratitude.

Megan smiled, sending him a clear message. *I trust you.* "Run along. I'll call you in when breakfast is ready. Hopefully, it doesn't get nasty outside, and I can have fun in the snow with you both after breakfast." She was tired, but for her daughter's sake, she'd push through the weary haze that still hung over her.

"Goody. We can build a big snowman. Maybe I can find some stuff in the kitchen or around the house for his face. Oh, I know, there's some stuff in the craft bag. Wait for me, Mr. Sam. I'll be right back."

Becca ran down the hall, returning moments later with her craft bag. Megan watched as Becca and Sam bundled up before they left out the back door for their winter adventure. Sam and Becca seemed different, leaving Megan to wonder about the change. It was as though they'd struck up a true friendship, one that her daughter would miss when Sam left to go home.

Agnes joined her and started setting the table. "Frank's joining us for breakfast, thanks to the crutches. He's like a new man." Agnes's stress levels were considerably better, her cheerful attitude clearly related to Frank's mobility and disposition.

"That's wonderful. Becca's out back with Sam getting wood." She glanced out the back door.

"That's nice. Poor thing had a bit of a shake-up yesterday, so I'm glad to see her having fun."

"Sam's wonderful with her."

"And you. I keep telling you not to let him get away without at least trying to let him know you're interested."

"But, I'm not." Well, maybe a tiny bit, but it was pointless. Why risk rejection or getting hurt?

"You're a terrible liar." Agnes grinned. "I see the way you watch him, and, I might add, the way he watches you. I know you two keep telling me there's nothing between you, but I feel it every time I'm in the same room with both of you. You might want to think about not fighting the inevitable. I believe in fate. And I believe you two ended up in this cabin for a reason. You said it yourself, everything happens for a reason. Maybe your reason is outside building a snowman with your daughter."

Agnes had to be mistaken. However, the idea made Megan's toes curl, and she felt butterflies in her stomach for the first time in a long while. "The reason he's here is that his secretary didn't get his email to cancel his order to cancel. There's nothing more to it than that." She grinned. "Let me know when breakfast is ready, and I'll call in the troops."

Agnes shook her head and went back into the kitchen.

Frank hobbled into the room on his crutches. "Someone say breakfast?" He chuckled.

Megan pulled out a chair. "Sit here."

"I talked to the doctor again this morning, and they're convinced you were right about my ACL being sprained." They talked for a bit, Frank happy to be up and about under his own steam.

Megan went to the door and hollered for the other two to come inside when Agnes started carrying in a dish of scrambled eggs smothered in cheese and a plate of bacon and toast.

"This looks amazing. Thanks for cooking." It had been relaxing to let someone else take the lead, and it wasn't even her birthday.

The door burst open moments later. Sam and Becca came in from outside and stomped their boots on the mat. "Guess what? Floppy stayed here again last night, and he was still in his doghouse. He ran away toward the woods, but he's so cute. And he doesn't have a collar. Can we keep him, Mommy? Please?" Becca called her mommy when she really wanted something and was afraid she wouldn't get it. It was like pulling out the big guns. But there was no way she could say yes to a dog. And they still didn't know if Floppy belonged to anyone. Good heavens, Becca even had her calling the dog by his new name.

"You know we can't, honey. We're never home, and it wouldn't be fair to the dog."

"It's not fair that he doesn't have a home, either." Becca was sulking. Not something her daughter did often, and it broke Megan's heart not to give in.

Sam cleared his throat. "We've got plenty of wood stacked up out front by the fireplace ring. Later, I'll dig out a pit area. Should be more than enough for the party." Bless his heart for the change in subject.

"Mr. Sam let me help carry the wood. He said I was a good carrier. We even started our snowman, but we still need to finish. And after that, he promised we could build an igloo."

"He did, did he?" Megan eyed Sam with renewed interest. For a man having a hard time letting go of the past, he was fast becoming involved in a part of the present. But was he capable of a future? For the first time, Megan began to wonder if it was possible, and maybe even start to let herself hope.

"He did. But he said we had to eat breakfast first. I'm not even cold, but I am hungry. Let's eat!"

Megan laughed as she watched her daughter wash her hands and plop herself into the seat next to Frank, the subject of the dog forgotten—for the moment.

"Good morning, Mr. Frank. Is your leg feeling better?"

"It certainly is, thanks for asking. You look as though you're having a blast this morning."

"I am. Mr. Sam is fun."

Sam smiled at Becca. The look that passed between the two confirmed they'd connected on some deeper level. Megan felt left out, which was ridiculous, but it was the ugly truth. Agnes and Frank nodded in agreement, both listening intently as Becca told them about her morning outside. The conversation turned to the storm, the snow coming down heavier.

"Why don't I clean up the table and take care of the dishes since you ladies fixed breakfast?" Sam stood and picked up the first couple of bowls.

A man who offered to do the dishes was a rarity indeed, and Agnes didn't miss the opportunity to shoot her another don't-let-him-get-away look.

"Thanks. If you do that, it'll give me time to call Rachael again and see if there are any updates. She's having too much fun and might accidentally-on-purpose forget."

"What do you mean, Mom?" Becca's innocent face was a mask of confusion.

Megan grimaced. Not the best choice of words she could've made. "She's making friends and doing fun things since she can't be here."

"Just like us!" Her daughter's exuberance amazed her and was not to be second-guessed.

Megan picked up her bowl to carry it to the kitchen, unwilling to let anyone do it for her. She came face-to-face with Sam, almost dumping the remnants of her breakfast down his shirt.

"I've got this." He smiled, reaching for her bowl. Their gazes locked, and seconds passed.

Megan would give anything to know what he was thinking because she knew what she was thinking. Agnes's words were running through her head. If she just leaned in, would he get the message and kiss her? She swallowed hard. Letting the bowl go, she stepped back. "Thanks."

Chicken.

CHAPTER FIFTEEN

Megan had no way of knowing how much her trust meant to Sam. Combined with Becca's childlike adoration and trust, the ice around Sam's heart had melted. Something he never imagined possible. He might not deserve the ray of sunshine the two of them brought into his life, but for the first time since the accident, he wanted to bask in the warmth. Even if just for the short space of time they would be together.

He'd have to be blind to miss Megan's sweet smile, the soft freckles on her face, or the way her beautiful blue eyes darkened with interest each time they found themselves in close quarters. Every time it happened, it grew harder and harder to resist claiming her mouth in the kiss they both wanted.

He'd fully expected to see disgust in her eyes

yesterday after she learned the truth about him, but instead of condemnation, she'd shown him compassion and a healthy dose of understanding. The interest he'd seen in her eyes moments ago had been real. Proof her words meant something.

He admired the way she helped and cared for others, and the sentimentality toward her mother with all her Christmas traditions. It showed a deep love for people and family. An inner strength filled with determination to do anything she set her mind to. She was nothing short of remarkable.

It didn't look like Mother Nature was going to let him go anywhere today, which meant he had a Christmas Eve party to attend. At least one more day to escape the past and live in the present, something Sam was now all too willing to do with Megan and Becca.

Twenty minutes later, Megan returned to the dining room, Becca close on her heels.

"I talked to Rachael." The deep grooves in Megan's brow was a sure sign she didn't have good news. "She confirmed they've suspended all work on the pass. Her friend Brandon said they plan on starting back in the morning."

"But tomorrow's Christmas. Surely nobody's going to come out and work on Christmas." This wasn't even about him. He hated that Becca and

Megan's Christmas would be ruined if Rachael couldn't get here, but there were also the families of the rescue workers whose day would be interrupted. Sam couldn't help but feel awful for everyone involved. It was a no-win situation.

"Well, apparently, there are a few people who volunteered to start working on the pass at first light to finish it out."

"Hallbrook's way of showing Christmas cheer, I guess." He remembered all too well the town's good intentions. Two years ago, he hadn't appreciated the town's sympathy or willingness to help as he tried to deal with the accident, today he was grateful.

"I hate the idea of anyone having to work on Christmas, but I really want Rachael to be able to share Christmas with us. That sounds selfish, doesn't it?" Her thoughts echoed his own sentiment, but her look of disappointment made him wish there was something he could do to right her world.

"Not at all. Christmas is a time for family. The rescue team has volunteered to work on Christmas, it's nothing you're making anyone do, so you shouldn't feel guilty. It's natural for you to want to share Christmas with your sister. Until then, you need to have fun today and tonight at the party." He glanced at Becca, sending Megan a silent message.

"I hate that Aunt Rachael will miss the party. Mr.

Sam, I finished my breakfast. Can we go outside to search for Floppy again and then finish our snowman? We need to hurry so we can build the igloo out front so the other kids can play in it tonight." Becca stood next to him, one hand pulling on his arm.

"Well, I did promise." He winked, followed Becca into the laundry room, and came back out with his jacket and Becca all bundled up like a snow bunny.

Sam pulled open the front door and Becca raced outside; Sam close behind. She raced around in the snow, chasing snowflakes as they fell. It wasn't long before her hat and jacket were coated in white. She gathered up handfuls of snow and took several bites.

"Fresh and cold." Her innocent laughter filled the air.

"That reminds me, we need to make snow cream, especially with this fresh new snow."

"Snow cream?" It sounds like something you'd eat."

"It is silly. It's a tradition. You have to try it. Talk about *delish*." Becca laughed, grabbing his hand and swinging his arm back and forth as they tromped through the snow.

The past few days, he'd come to see Becca in a different light. She and Lydia may have the same outward features, but the two were as different as day and night, and he no longer saw Lydia every time he looked at Becca. Where Lydia was quiet, preferring to read and play with her dolls, Becca was outgoing and always on the lookout for the next exciting thing she could do.

Both unique children, and both loveable.

Hours later, he was exhausted from trying to keep up with Becca. Floppy was keeping his distance and nowhere to be seen. He and Becca turned their focus to a little snow fun and managed to do the impossible and finish the snowman and build the igloo. They stood back to enjoy their handiwork. Sam was impressed with both her willingness to work hard to accomplish both, but also her determination to finish.

Becca had her mind set on lunch in the igloo, but right now, he needed a break. "Becca, I think it's time we went back inside."

"Aww, really?" She stopped in her tracks, her low lip protruding as she resisted the change in plans.

"Yes, really. You've got a lot more energy, and you're staying warm, but I need to thaw some, so humor an old man."

"You're not old, silly. You're dad age." The words took him by surprise and wrapped around his heart.

"We should warm up by the fire, and then we can fix your famous lunch. Although it will have to be with chicken noodle soup because that's all we have.

But the good news is there's plenty of cheese for sandwiches."

"Goody. Now that sounds like a plan." Becca came to stand by his side, took his hand in hers, and led him into the cabin. Agnes and Frank were sitting by the fire, which looked like a pretty good idea to Sam.

Megan came out of the kitchen. "Did you both have fun?"

"Yup. We're all finished with the igloo and we need to make lunch." Becca's cheeks were rosy, her eyes lit with excitement.

"How about I fix the food while you two get warm?" Megan offered

"I was going to do that." Agnes started to rise.

"I feel good. Honest. Sit down and let me take care of this." Megan smiled and waved her hand to ward off Agnes from coming to help. She needed to entertain Frank more than Megan needed her help in the kitchen.

Sam shot her a look of gratitude. "Thanks, I think I'll take you up on the offer."

"There's only chicken soup, but that's okay cause we still can have grilled cheese sandwiches. Right, Mr. Sam?"

"Right, kiddo." He moved to stand next to the

fireplace and held out his hands, seeking the warmth.

"Are you going to eat outside with us, Mom?"

"Of course. Wouldn't want to miss an official igloo lunch after all your hard work to build it."

"Yay! Anyone else coming?" Becca turned to the others expectantly.

"Thanks for the invite, sweetheart, but I'll stay inside with Frank. You all will have a grand time, and then you can tell me all about the adventure."

"Okay, I can do that." Becca had moved over to stand by the fire with Sam.

Fifteen minutes later, he was hunkered down and inching his way into the igloo on his hands and knees, following Becca's lead. Megan handed him the feast and then crawled in behind him. Talk about tight quarters, there was barely room to move, much less eat.

Different but enjoyable.

"It's nice and warm in here, isn't it, Mr. Sam?"

"It certainly is. Thanks for inviting me."

Megan unwrapped the sandwiches, and handed them out on napkins, while Sam poured the soup from the thermos into bowls.

"Are you sure you're not getting chilled out here?" Sam was worried about Megan.

"I'm fine. I won't stay out long, I promise. I want to make sure I can enjoy the festivities tonight."

They ate fast, more because in the limited space there wasn't much else to do. Becca did most of the talking, but then she always did. Mostly about school and her friends, but occasionally, she'd slip in a comment or two that left Sam surprised at how perceptive a seven-year-old could be—and how persistent. Especially when it came to getting what she wanted. In this case, that meant getting Megan and Sam to see how perfect they were for each other, at least, based on her viewpoint.

Sam exchanged looks with Megan a couple of times, the two of them sharing some of the hidden humor in Becca's exuberance for just about everything. A happy child made for a happy life.

"I need to go to the bathroom. I'll be right back, so don't leave." She looked at them both, waiting for confirmation.

"We'll be right here. We promise," Megan answered for them both.

"Sorry." Megan grinned after Becca had crawled out. "She means well but doesn't understand grown-up relationships are more than two people living together and doing fun stuff."

"It's okay. Technically, that's a big part of it." Two people with common interests and future goals, with an added dose of attraction that went deeper than the surface. Something called love.

Once upon a time, he had three out of three with Laura. And now, well, there was no denying two out of three with Megan. As to the future, they'd never discussed it, something he knew was entirely his fault. Why discuss what he couldn't have? Not that it stopped him from wanting to know.

"True. But it's so much more. We've both had it and understand what it takes." Megan smiled.

"Are you looking to have it again? Do you even think it's possible?" *Talk about opening a can of self-torture.* What if she said yes? Then what?

"I never really thought about it until Becca said something. But, yes, I do think it's possible. And if I'm honest, yes, I would like it again. Not for Becca, but for me. I mean, don't get me wrong, it would be wonderful for my daughter, but I wouldn't get married for her. I would have to love someone and know that I was being given a second chance at a lifetime of love. Crazy, huh?" Megan confiding in him was something he hadn't expected.

"No, not at all. I admire your willingness to open yourself up like that and respect it would be for the right reasons. Some guy will be lucky to have you in his life." He meant every word, a part him of wishing he could be the one to share a life with her.

Megan shrugged. "Just as some woman would be lucky to have you in her life. If you give someone a chance, that is. Sam, you can't stay in the past forever."

"I hear you. I really do. And I'm sure you're right. I'm just not quite there yet." *Understatement.* "But if I was, I'd take you on a proper date and find out more about you." *Why on earth did I tell her that?*

"Well, this is like an unofficial date. What do you want to know?" She winked, her teasing hitting him square in the gut.

"Unofficial dates are good. Let's see, what do I want to know? Where do you see yourself in five years?" He wasn't sure what he wanted to hear—a match or no match. Which would make it harder? Because either way, he would leave alone when the pass opened.

"Hmmm. Five years. Maybe married. Living in the country. Working at a small hospital. I just want life to slow down a bit so I can enjoy it with Becca before she's all grown up and on her own."

"That should be easy to do now. The working part." He grinned. "Just do it." The slowing down part was a match. So was the small-town country living.

"It's not easy. The bills have to get paid, and I have to consider Becca's life and the impact on her."

"I think it's easy to see she'd love it in the country. So, what's really holding you back?" He didn't appreciate it when people pried into his private life, but for some reason, he couldn't keep from asking the question.

Megan looked away. "Maybe change. I don't know. So much has changed in the past few years, and all I have left are the memories of those of I love, most of which are tied to where I live now."

"I understand. It's not like I've moved, either. But maybe it's time I did. I think being here with you has helped me to understand I need to move forward. Maybe one step at a time, but forward. I'm going to sell my business when I get back to the city. Figure out what to do next. Maybe it's time you made changes and moved forward also." Putting the next steps of his future into words was uplifting and the more he thought about it, the more they sounded right.

"Maybe. Thanks for the vote of confidence."

"Anytime. I like you, and if there's anything I can ever do to help you in the future, just say the word." He meant every word.

"That's a sweet offer, but if I do this, I should do it on my own. For the record, I like you, too."

Sam felt an overpowering urge to lean in and kiss Megan. Their eyes met and held. What little space they had in the igloo seemed to grow smaller. Sam inhaled her fresh citrus and vanilla scent—one he'd come to recognize and enjoy over the past few days. He leaned forward, encouraged by the invitation in her eyes.

"I'm back. Miss me?" Becca announced from the entrance.

Sam drew back with only the taste of regret on his lips.

It had taken Megan a few seconds to recover, her disappointment a reflection of his own. "Of course. We need to finish up and head back inside." Megan started to gather up their stuff.

"Do we have to?" Becca was just finishing her sandwich and looked hopefully at her mother for a reprieve.

"We do if we're going to have time to start prepping for the party." Megan had smoothly turned that one around and Becca was all too happy to agree.

As soon as they were inside, Becca pulled on his hand, leading him toward the living room. "Do you know how to play crazy eights, Mr. Sam?" She was a nonstop ball of energy.

"No. That's not a game I've played before." Becca shot him one of those you-must-be-kidding looks. It wasn't something he was proud of, but he'd played very few games when Laura and Lydia were alive. It was always work for him. Work. Work. Work.

"I will teach you. It's easy, I promise."

"Deal." Once he'd committed to enjoying their company while he could, he was a changed man. There would be time enough later to retreat to his old self after he left.

"Anyone else going to play?" Becca addressed the O'Malleys, her excitement unmistakable.

"We're in," Frank answered for them both." Agnes pulled the coffee table closer to her husband to make it easy for him to reach and sat next to him on the couch.

"Mom, are you going to play?" Becca asked as her mother joined them in the living room.

"I really need to get started on the food prep for the party." Megan shook her head.

"I'll help and we can knock it out it no time. Everyone is bringing stuff, so we only need a few extra dishes and then decorations," Agnes volunteered.

"And I've already got the fire pit ready to go, so we're in good shape there." Sam added a few more logs to the fire.

"Okay, I'm in, but just a couple of rounds." Megan grabbed a pillow, tossed it on the floor, and plunked herself down on it, getting comfortable.

"Come on, Mr. Sam." Becca started shuffling the cards.

"We can get some chairs from the dining room." Agnes started to rise.

"No. No. I'll sit on the floor with Megan and Becca.

Becca flipped through the cards like an old pro, shuffling them repeatedly. Turned out, Becca was right. It *was* an easy game to learn. But he didn't win a single game in what turned out to be five rounds, something none of the others let him forget. Their teasing was merciless.

Sam looked around the room, enjoying the warmth of the family setting. "How about I fix a pot of coffee. Weak coffee," he grinned. "Becca, would you like another cup of hot chocolate?"

"Yes. Thank you. At least you won't have to suffer another loss." She giggled.

"There is that. Does anyone else want coffee?"

Everyone nodded in agreement, and Sam made his way to the kitchen, needing space. He could hear the laughter coming from the living room. He wanted to rejoin them, but his thoughts and emotions confused him.

When the coffee was finished, he took one of the trays down from the cupboard and loaded the four coffees and the hot cocoa. As he left the kitchen, he almost ran into Megan, raising his arms with the tray high in the air to prevent the collision.

"That was close. You're dangerous when someone's got drinks in their hands. First, you try to cool me off with cold water, now you want to burn me. Make up your mind, woman." He winked.

"Sorry, I came to see if you needed any help." He couldn't tell if Megan's flushed face was from the fire, or from the proximity they found themselves in again.

"Mom, Sam. You're standing in the doorway again. Look up." Becca had come up behind them quietly.

"Becca..." Megan looked at Sam for help, an apology in her eyes.

He glanced at Becca, ready to say something, but instead found three faces grinning back at him—Agnes and Frank having joined the group. At a loss for words, he contemplated the situation, unsure what to do.

"She's right. It's a Christmas tradition, and you two are standing under the mistletoe," Agnes chimed in.

"Go on, just kiss the girl. You won't get out of this with these two scheming against you." Frank chuckled.

Whether it was their encouragement or Megan's

uncertainty that pushed him forward, he'd never know, but in a moment of insanity, he wanted to give in.

He twisted the tray off to the side and lowered his head, dropping a light kiss on her mouth. Just for a second, he let himself feel the warmth and pressed for more, unable to stop himself. It was like coming home.

Home. He pulled away, confused by what he was feeling. Sam closed his eyes and swallowed hard, but not before he saw the hurt in Megan's eyes. With false bravado, he pressed forward. "The Christmas tradition has been satisfied." It had been so much more for Sam, but that wasn't something he was willing to share.

Agnes's grin hadn't faded, but Becca's face was just the opposite. Hers was the face of disappointment. Had she really expected magic between them? It was concerning to realize that perhaps she was still looking for him to be more than a friend. It was time to put things back into perspective.

"I should call the sheriff's office for updates. Hopefully, we get some better news." He pressed send on the auto-dialer for the dispatch center as he walked away. "This is Sam Wyatt," he replied when they answered. "The snow has stopped, and I wondered if there was any chance the road crews would start working again?"

"I'm sorry, sir. They've already shut down operations for the day. Some of the guys will be there first thing in the morning to resume working and finish clearing the pass. Rachael Milner is here, chomping at the bit to get to her family on Christmas. Trust me, with her cracking the whip on this side, we're doing all we can. Firecracker of a woman. If her sister is anything like her, I'm sure you've got your hands full." He laughed.

Even if he did, Sam wouldn't be telling him about it.

"Okay. I'll be ready and waiting to leave in the morning. And tell everyone how thankful we are for their offer to work Christmas morning. It's an unbelievably generous gift." It was past time he left, because his feelings for Megan had changed, and running away seemed like the best option for everyone concerned. He could never give them what they deserved—his whole heart.

"Gotcha. Small-town communities are like that— helping one another is just what we do."

It was true. He just hadn't been as receptive the last time he'd been a recipient of their generosity.

CHAPTER SIXTEEN

Becca helped Sam set up chairs in the front yard, while Agnes helped Megan in the kitchen, the two of them prepping food for the party. Time passed like a broken clock for Megan. She was anxious to join the others, or namely, one other. *Sam.*

In between measuring and cooking and answering Agnes's comments, she found herself thinking about the kiss. Sam might not have liked it, but Megan couldn't say the same. Her pulse had raced as if it were in the Indy 500, but the rejection in his eyes had been more like a crash and burn. She'd limped away to nurse her injured pride. And yet she still relived the moment over and over.

They left the kitchen, and Megan moved to stand in front of the living room window. Becca was helping Sam tend the fire from a safe distance. Megan's fingers went to her lips of their own accord.

"I told you there's something between the two of you." Agnes had come to stand next to her.

"It's not like that. It was...just a Christmas tradition."

"Not from where we were watching. Agnes knows about these kinds of things. You should listen to her." Frank hobbled over to watch out the window. "Wish I could be out there by the fire. Oh, well." He heaved a heavy sigh and returned to the couch.

It wouldn't do her any good to argue. The pair of them had become fixated on the idea of her and Sam as a couple, and it wasn't her place to explain that his past still controlled his life.

Becca came running in the house. "Do you see the fire? Mr. Sam is making it really big. I'm going to grab the sled from the shed."

"Let me grab my jacket and come with you." Megan wasn't ready to let her wander out back alone.

"I'm a big girl, and I know to stay away from the pond."

"Humor me." So what if she was over-the-top protective? It was her prerogative.

"Okay, but hurry. The others will be here soon, and I can't wait to play with the kids."

They went out back and headed left toward the shed. Megan glanced at the pond and shivered. The surface was now a clear-crystal color as the ice started to reform across the surface. Becca ran ahead, pulled open the shed door, and grabbed one of the sleds from the corner.

A horn tooted, the sound coming from the front of the house. "Got to go. Hopefully, the twins are here!" Her daughter vanished around the side of the cabin, eager to greet whoever had arrived.

Megan pulled her scarf around her neck tighter, then picked up the other sled and followed.

A blue SUV was parked in the driveway, and by the looks of things, Becca had gotten her wish. She was off playing with two identically bundled up abominable snow children, taking them down the slope one at a time for a ride on the sled. The twins' squeals of delight matched Becca's.

Megan joined the adults by the now-roaring fire. "Hi. I'm Megan Langley. We're so glad you came."

The Taylors introduced themselves, and handshakes were exchanged all the way around.

"A party was a fantastic idea." Tonia laughed and picked up the bag she'd put on one of the chairs. "Where should I put this? It's a casserole, and of course, some sugar cookies. The kids' favorite."

"I can take them in." Megan reached for the bag.

"That's okay. I want to pop inside and say hi to Frank and Agnes. How's he doing?"

"He's doing fine, but tired of being housebound, I suspect. Feel free to head inside. I'm sure he'd love to see you."

Tonia glanced at the twins.

"Megan and I will keep an eye on the kids, don't worry." Sam had seen them hesitate and jumped right in to make them feel comfortable.

"If you're sure. Thanks." Jack and Tonia headed toward the cabin.

When he wasn't lost in his own personal dark space, he was a caring, thoughtful man who put the needs of others far in front of his own. Agnes had him pegged right, but that's where her rightness ended. The attraction she insisted existed was one-sided. Hers. And even that, she was trying to fight. She hadn't come to the cabin to fall in love, not by a long shot.

"Nice fire." She tried to ease through the awkwardness.

"Thanks." He pushed a few logs around, stoking the flames. "Before the others get here, I just wanted to say I was sorry. About earlier."

"It's fine. Kids come up with the darnedest ideas. I'm sorry if it made you uncomfortable." She moved closer to the fire, not daring to turn his way. Megan didn't want him to see the truth in her eyes, as it would be a whole lot less embarrassing if he didn't guess the depth of her wayward feelings.

"She's cute." He chuckled. "Lydia would have done the same thing." It was the first time he'd spoken of his daughter without pain rippling through his voice. Becca was having a profound effect on him, but then who could resist the sweet innocence of a child? It was a huge step forward.

"Kids are kids, the whole world over. I'm sure she was special."

"Thanks. She was always trying to make me laugh or doing the silliest of things. Her imagination was quite creative." He grew quiet, his comfort level clearly at an end.

"That's a beautiful memory." Megan laid her hand on his arm.

He looked down at her hand and then at her. Neither one moved. Megan may not have wanted to fall in love, but that didn't mean she could stop it. And if she wasn't already, she was close. She couldn't tell what he was thinking, but it didn't stop her from hoping even an ounce of what she was feeling would be transmitted via heart-to-heart Morse code.

A sound from behind them broke the silence. Another SUV pulled into the driveway, and an older couple made their way to the fireside.

"Hi, we're the Ramseys. Steve and Patty. Great idea for the party. We can't thank you enough for hosting it." Steve and his wife shook hands with her.

"The more, the merrier. I'm Megan Langley."

"Good to see you again, Sam."

"You, too. I didn't expect to be here still, but sometimes things have a way of working out just right. Let me take your bag inside. We're leaving the food inside to keep it warm, and we thought if we ate inside, it would keep us warm at the same time." Sam took the bag and started across the snowy path he'd shoveled across the front yard.

Working out just right. His words were a shock, and she'd give anything to know what he meant, but there was no way she'd ask. She didn't want to give him a chance to say something that proved he was on a completely different page when it came to what he meant, or what she hoped he meant.

"Sam," she called after him. "Frank's feeling a little down because he can't join us out here. Is there any way we can make it safe for him to get to the fire?"

"Let me search around and see what's inside. The path I cleared might be too slick for a crutch." He disappeared into the house, and Megan turned back to face the newcomers.

Three more vehicles pulled up, and much to Becca's delight, the new additions came equipped with three more kids. One boy, a little older, had decidedly captured her attention. He could only be the video gamer, Devon. Becca had talked nonstop about him the first day they met at the Parker house. The other two kids were around three or four, and both appeared to fall in love with Becca as their new best friend.

Megan watched the kids play. Non-stop sledding, snow angels, and even an occasional snowball aimed at the parents. Becca's well-aimed shot managed to land a few bull's-eyes much to Megan's consternation.

Sam returned, and sure enough, he'd come up with a capital idea for getting Frank out to the fire safely. After rigging one of the sleds with a chair on it, Steve and Sam pushed Frank down the path and got him settled next to the others in front of the fire.

The adults relaxed, frequently going inside to help themselves to the food. It was an amazing way to connect with so many strangers. Even though the others all knew each other, they managed to make Megan feel warm and welcome in the little slice of heaven they called Christmas Cove.

Sam kept adding logs to the fire amid all the cheer, and Megan felt a peacefulness she hadn't felt in years wash over her. She looked up at the stars in the sky. *Thanks, Mom.*

In the hustle and bustle of life, this was exactly what she needed and had been missing. For years, her mother tried to get her up here on a vacation, and Megan now knew why. It was a place where country and community joined together, a place where people stopped and took time to appreciate the joys in life. A place one could call home.

"All right, everyone, it's time to have some more fun." Agnes laughed and looked around the group. "Hey, kids, come over here."

Frank was the only one who didn't look confused as his wife rounded up the troops.

"We need to sing. What's a Christmas party without Christmas carols?" Agnes formed the kids in a circle around the flagpole.

"What are we going to sing first?" Becca chimed in.

"Let's sing the Rudolph song," one of the kids called out.

"Sounds like a plan. Everyone should know it." The group all held hands and sang.

Including Sam. Megan was shocked to hear his rich baritone filter through the other voices. She couldn't quite figure him out. He'd made it clear to her and the others that he was leaving in the morning to wait for the pass to open. At least he'd promised to sit tight long enough for Becca to wake up and exchange Christmas cheer. It was yet another promise that her daughter had managed to drag out of him.

THE PARTY BROKE UP, and after everything was cleaned and put away, Becca and the O'Malleys headed for bed. Sam made his way down the hall toward the bathroom when it was his turn. Becca's voice drifted toward him through Megan's slightly ajar door.

"I can't wait for Santa. I made a special ornament for Mr. Sam, and I hope he likes it."

"I'm sure he's going to love it. But you need to get to sleep before Santa arrives and passes by the cabin. Remember, he sees you when you're sleeping and knows when you're awake."

"Okay, but you have to read me the story. It's tradition."

"Yes, of course, darling."

Sam stood poised in the hallway to listen, unable to break away from the moment shared between mother and daughter. The love in Megan's voice was entrancing.

It wasn't long before he knew what their traditional Christmas story was, the words bringing back memories of another time. A time when everything else in his life was put on hold, and he stopped to read the Christmas story to Lydia, a story he knew by heart. *Their Christmas tradition.*

Unable to resist, he stepped into their room and closed his eyes, letting the words pour into him, filling him with light. Sam began to speak the words with Megan as she read them. He opened his eyes when they finished, only to find them both staring at him.

He crossed the room to stand next to the bed.

"You came to hear my special story." Becca smiled.

"I did. It was beautiful." He leaned down and kissed the top of her head.

Megan leaned over and kissed her daughter on the forehead. She rose off the bed and headed for the door. "It's time for lights out, and for you to get some sleep. Tomorrow's going to be a big day."

"Goodnight, Mom. Goodnight, Mr. Sam." Becca rubbed her tired eyes.

"Goodnight," they answered in unison.

They walked down the hall and sat down at

opposite ends of the couch. The fire blazed in the fireplace, heat radiating from the flames as they cast a romantic glow of light across the room.

The kiss had made things awkward between them, but between the party and the Christmas story, the gap had been closed. If anything, Sam felt closer to Megan, the three feet between them on the couch doing nothing to stop the crazy urge he had to haul her into his arms and taste her sweet lips again.

Megan yawned.

"Tired?"

"Yes, but it doesn't matter. There's much to be done before I can turn in for the night."

"What's your Christmas routine?" Memories of sweet times with Laura and Lydia surfaced, but this time he didn't push them away, but instead, embraced them.

"We wait a bit for Becca to fall asleep. And then I play Santa as fast as I can so I can get to bed. She's an early riser on Christmas and morning comes way too quick."

"Do you need help? I could be Santa's elf." He chuckled.

"Will you dress up in a tiny red top and tight green pants? I'd love to see that." Megan smirked as she leaned back against the sofa to get comfortable.

"You'll have to settle for a plaid shirt and jeans."

There was no way he was playing dress-up. That was over the top for him.

"Fine. You're no fun. We can start by wrapping the gifts I have hidden in the trunk and filling the stockings. Gives her time to fall asleep without worry she'll catch us."

It reminded Sam of this afternoon when Becca did catch them. Well, almost. A timely intervention on her part. A few seconds later, and Becca would have been dreaming of a wedding tonight instead of Santa.

After getting out all the wrapping supplies, Megan checked on Becca. Sam filled the stockings with some of the fruit the neighbors had sent over, throwing in some of the candy canes and chocolate left from the party.

Megan came back into the room. "All clear. I knew it wouldn't take her long. Today was a busy day."

"Great. Here are the stockings." Sam held them out to her, not wanting to be responsible for the filling. Wrapping had to be a whole lot easier.

"But that's only three. You need more." She frowned.

"There's three of you last time I checked."

"There's always extra ones in the box for guests. You need three more, one for Agnes and Frank and you." She faced off with him, hands on her hips.

"Why do I need to make one for myself? I'm leaving."

"Because Santa wouldn't forget you." Megan shook her head, her brow furled in concern.

Sam laughed. "That's debatable. I'm sure I'm on the naughty list."

Megan pushed him back toward the kitchen. "Just do it."

"Bossy, aren't you? Elves can go on strike, you know."

"No self-respecting elf would strike on Christmas Eve."

"Fine. I'll fill them." Sam did as he was instructed and laid the new stockings out next to the others.

Megan was cutting wrapping paper and folding it around one of the gifts.

"Hey, can you get me a piece of tape while I hold this in place. I'm terrible at wrapping."

"I knew we had a lot in common. I was always terrible at it also, but I think I can handle tape." Sam chuckled.

"Good to know."

They worked together, laughing and teasing, wrapping and taping until they reached the last gift on the table. It was easy to get caught up in watching

Megan. He could feel the Christmas joy radiating from her. With all she'd been through, she still believed in the magic.

"Hey, watch what you're doing. You're supposed to be taping the paper, not my fingers." She grinned.

Sam looked down at the gift to discover he'd placed the tape over two of her fingers instead of directly on the wrapping paper. "Sorry. Maybe I should just finish wrapping you and put you under the tree." He laughed, bumping shoulders with her as he teased.

"But when you fill out the label, who gets me?" Her breathy voice immediately changed the seriousness of the conversation, taking it to a whole new level.

"That's a tough one. I could think of a couple people who would want to see their name on the tag." He knew what she was asking but owning up to what he meant would do no good. And giving her hope when there was none would be wrong.

"Would yours be one?" Megan looked at him, hope in her eyes. She cared, and he was playing with fire. The last thing he wanted to do was hurt her. She'd had enough of that in her life already.

He felt compelled to tell her the truth, the intimacy of the moment demanding it. "In a perfect world—perhaps. But life is never that simple. Is it?"

"No, I suppose not." The look of disappointment on her face was almost his undoing. He carried the gifts to the tree, arranging them underneath, while Megan arranged the stockings. The silence between them had made things awkward.

Maybe it would be better if he explained. "Megan, I'm—"

"Don't worry about it. I'm off to bed. Thanks for staying up and helping me tonight. Like I said, Christmas comes early with Becca around. Goodnight."

"Goodnight." Sam watched her walk out of the room, a piece of his heart going with her. Unfortunately, it didn't change his past or his future.

With all the goings-on, they'd forgotten to feed Floppy. Sam put on his coat, grabbed some food and water, and headed out the door. He switched on a flashlight to help guide him, not wanting to slip on the ice. With everyone in bed, it would be a long time before help arrived. He filled the dog's bowl with more water from the cannister and then added some of the meat leftovers to his other bowl. He stood, more than chilled and ready to get back inside. A small whimper caught his attention.

Sam froze. The whimpering reached his ears again. He took the flashlight, shining it into the darkness in the direction sound had come from. The beam landed on two glowing orbs glaring back at him. *Floppy*.

He crouched low to the ground, not wanting to scare the dog. "Here, boy," Sam called, reaching out his hand. "Come here. I won't hurt you." The dog didn't budge.

Grabbing the bowl of food, he held it out in front, hoping the dog would connect him and the food as one. It worked. The dog took a tentative step toward him, his head hung low.

"That's it, boy. Come on, no one's going to hurt you." The dog drew closer and closer. Sam set the bowl down and let him take a few bites before he reached out to let the dog sniff his hands and get familiar with him. It was a good sign when the dog didn't back away.

Floppy finished the food in record time, and Sam waited to see what he would do. When he didn't immediately retreat, Sam reached out to pet him. "Good boy. Nice and easy."

The dog was leery, but he stood his ground, not running away as Sam expected. After several minutes, the dog licked his hand as if in thanks. Progress.

Sam stood slowly, not making any sudden move-ments, and went toward the garage door. He opened it and stood half in, half out. "Come on, boy. Want to come inside? It's a lot warmer in here than it is outside." To his surprise, the dog walked toward him. Sam flipped on the light and stepped in the garage, the dog following him. Sam grinned. Earning the dog's trust was a big deal. After he closed the door, he led the dog inside the cabin. A snail's pace for sure, but slow and steady won the race as they made it to the fireplace.

If the dog stayed, Becca was going to have one heck of a Christmas present. Not that it was a permanent arrangement but spending her Christmas with the ghost dog she'd cared for all week would be a true gift. It was Megan who might not be thrilled. Her fear Becca would get too attached was justified. Sam would have to deal with it tomorrow because tonight, he'd made a new friend.

CHAPTER SEVENTEEN

"Mom, Mom! Wake up. It's Christmas. Hurry!" Becca bounced on the bed next to her, pushing her arm, trying to wake Megan up. She welcomed her daughter's enthusiasm and the morning with a renewed zest. Maybe the country air was beneficial for more than meeting wonderful neighbors.

She rubbed her eyes before opening them and grinning back at her daughter. Becca had always been an early riser on Christmas morning, and the glowing red digital 5:30 on the nightstand clock meant this year was no exception.

Megan stretched and yawned. "Merry Christmas, darling." She held her daughter's hand and smiled.

"Merry Christmas. Now get up. I want to see what Santa brought." Becca had slid off the bed and waited by the door.

"I'm coming." Last night, after Becca had gone to bed, Sam had surprised her when he lent a helping hand. She had to admit, her elf was kind of cute, and maybe not just a little responsible for the joy in her heart. It was becoming more and more difficult to deal with the idea of him leaving and walking out of their lives, but their time was almost at an end.

Megan brushed her hair and cinched her robe tight, slipping her feet into her warm and fuzzy slippers. "Let's go."

"Yay!" Becca ran ahead down the hall. There was no sign of Sam in the living room, but the smell of coffee wafted toward her, and she knew where she'd find him.

Becca danced around the tree, eyeing all the presents, picking up each one and shaking it, then putting it back down.

Megan glanced around the room and out the window. It was all so peaceful. Her mother would've loved the snow-covered ground. The house would have been filled with the scent of fresh-baked cookies by now, complementing the aromatherapy candles scenting the air with apples and cinnamon.

When she'd brought the cookie cutters, she'd planned on making a big event of the baking with her sister. But so far, the snowman, the Christmas tree, and the angel cookie-cutter forms had stayed in the box. Instead, they were eating the hordes of cookies the neighbors had brought for the party. She didn't have the heart to make the cookies without her sister, or have the ingredients for that matter, so it was all better the way it had worked out.

Not to mention, cooking had been her mother's specialty, something neither of her daughters had inherited. Becca, on the other hand, was a completely different story. She loved to cook and had spent many hours with her grandmother, learning the fine art of cooking with love. It was for her they would labor over the stove to make it a perfect Christmas once Rachael arrived.

That reminded her, she needed to make a grocery list and text it to her sister to make sure she brought everything needed for Christmas dinner. She was grateful for the neighbors' generosity, but baked chicken and canned green beans weren't exactly what she had in mind for the traditional holiday meal her mother always served. Ham with a cranberry orange glaze. Sweet potatoes. Green bean casserole. Apple pie. It was making her mouth water just thinking of the delicious food.

She prayed the pass would open early this morning for several reasons, except one. She wanted her sister to arrive and the workers to return to their families to enjoy the holiday spirit, but she didn't want Sam to leave. A far cry from when she'd first met him and had sent him out into the stormy night to get rid of him.

"Look, Mom. This one says to Rebecca from Santa." She picked up another package. "And this one does, too." She placed it back under the tree and grabbed the last one tucked up in the back. "And this one. I must've been a really good girl."

"I agree." Megan yawned, still trying to wake up.

"Can I open them?" Her daughter's eyes were big and round like saucers, a pleading look Megan couldn't resist.

With the O'Malleys still asleep, Megan was unsure whether to let Becca open presents, not wanting to be rude. She also knew how hard it was waiting all year, and the idea of making Becca wait any longer didn't seem right. The O'Malleys would understand, she was sure of it. "Yes, of course, sweetheart."

Megan glanced up as Sam walked into the room.

"Good morning. I thought we heard you in here." Sam smiled. Really smiled.

"We?" Megan asked, surprised either of the O'Malleys would be up this early.

Sam didn't answer, but his grin grew wider. *What was he up to?*

"Merry Christmas, Mr. Sam. Look at the presents I have. I was a good girl."

"I'm sure you were. Merry Christmas to both of you. Becca, before you get started on your tree presents, I've got one for you in the kitchen."

"You do?" Becca asked, her eyes wide with wonder.

"I do. But there's a condition that comes with it."

"A present with a condition. I don't like the sound of that." Becca's face scrunched up.

"The condition is you can only have this gift until you leave to go home, or until this gift chooses to leave, or until someone else wants this gift back."

"Now I really don't like the sound of this present. I can't keep it, it might leave, and someone else might take it away. Nope. Don't like the sound of that at all." Her lower lip jutted out.

Sam chuckled. "You might change your tune when you see what it is."

A yap sounded from the kitchen. Becca's face instantly lit up; her eyes wide with joy. "Floppy? Really?" She took off running for the kitchen.

"Don't scare him. Let him come to you. He's still skittish, but after a night of bonding, he's doing a lot better."

"A night of bonding? Do I dare ask?" Megan watched as Becca moved toward the dog slowly, talking to him as if he were her best friend in the whole world.

"He came to me last night, and I couldn't leave him outside. We talked and got to know each other, and eventually, he fell asleep in front of the fireplace. He's a good dog."

"I'm sure he is, but you realize how hard this is going to be to tell her we still can't take him home."

"I get it. That's why I gave her the conditions. And you wouldn't have left him out there, either."

"True. You're a wonderful man with a big heart. I keep telling you that. Now you just need to start believing it."

Sam shrugged and moved to help Becca. Floppy's tail wagged twice as fast as Sam approached. It looked to Megan as if Floppy had already chosen Sam as his new family. No one had stepped forward in town, but the question remained, would Sam accept the dog into his heart and his life?

Megan watched as they petted the dog and played with him. After a few pats herself, Megan fixed them coffee and hot chocolate. "Anyone ready to go back to the living room?"

"Me. Floppy is so sweet, but since I can't keep him, I want to open the presents from Santa that I can keep."

Sam and Megan laughed. They headed for the

living room, Floppy close on their heels. He curled up on the blanket Sam had laid on the floor in front of the fire. *The big softie.*

Becca opened the presents from Santa first. The pink ice skates with dark-pink laces should have been a big hit, but Megan understood her daughter's lack of enthusiasm. They could always find an ice rink, and perhaps it would be more than enough to overcome any fears she'd developed. The new doll that ate, drank, and wet her pants was a much bigger hit, as was the crib and highchair that came with her new baby. The tiny diapers were the cutest thing ever.

"Look, Mr. Sam. My new baby." She crossed the room and held up the doll for his inspection.

"Very nice. What will you name her?" Sam squatted next to Becca as she pondered his question.

"I don't know. What do you think?"

"It's your baby." He shrugged, giving Becca a lop-sided grin. "I'm not sure I'm the right person for suggesting names."

"What about Veronica, or Victoria, or Valerie?"

"I see you love the letter V. You should give it some serious thought because a name is important."

"Why did you pick Lydia when you named your daughter?" Megan saw Sam tense, the question catching him off guard.

"Well, we named her after my grandmother. It's a family name." A small smile settled on his face as if he were remembering the woman fondly.

"It's pretty. Hmmm...then Victoria it is." Becca rocked her baby, bouncing up and down.

"And why's that?"

"It was my grandmother's middle name. Maybe I won't miss her as much if I get to talk to Victoria every day." Becca's answer stunned Megan. And it brought tears to her eyes.

"I think that sounds like a very special name." Sam reached out to push the blanket back from the baby's face. "It's wonderful to meet you, Victoria."

Becca beamed up at Sam's approval. "I have something special for you, too."

"Really? You didn't have to do anything." After the initial surprise wore off, he looked touched.

"I made it. Wait right here." Becca rushed over to the tree, clutching Victoria.

Sam glanced at Megan; one eyebrow raised slightly in question.

She shrugged, unable to give him a heads-up because she didn't have a clue what Becca had secretly worked on and wrapped. Megan was just as curious as Sam.

Becca wanted a new dad, and there was no telling

what her daughter was up to. Megan couldn't put a new dad under the tree, but if she could, it would be a man like Sam. Her daughter had good taste. But it took two people to make a relationship to work, and Sam wasn't ready. He had much to offer, but he'd closed himself off from any future because of a past he couldn't control.

Becca reached into the tree and pulled out a tiny box hidden inside the depths of the branches. She went back to stand beside Sam and handed him the box wrapped in red paper with a gold bow tied around the outside.

"Go ahead, open it." Becca smiled, urging him on when he didn't start to unwrap it immediately.

Sam pulled back the paper gently and then opened the box. He held up a small angel, one Becca had made for him. She'd designed the angel's dress out of paper and sprinkled it with glitter. A blue ribbon was glued across the front, and a halo made of straw was attached to her head.

"She's pretty. Thank you for such a special gift." He looked up, his gaze locked on Megan's, his brow drawn tight. She wondered what he was thinking, but she was almost positive it had something to do with his daughter.

He crossed the room and hung the ornament on the tree. "I'm sorry I don't have anything for you. I can't claim Floppy since he's here by choice. But I didn't plan on being here this morning."

"That's okay. I already got my gift from you." Becca's smile was as radiant as the sun just starting to shine through the front window.

He looked at her in confusion. "What do you mean?"

"You're still here. That's what I wanted for Christmas. Remember?"

"I do. I'm glad your Christmas wish came true." Becca moved to stand beside him, her arms closing around Sam's waist. He pulled her close and hugged her, Megan breathing a sigh of relief.

Becca went back to the tree and pulled out another present, this one covered in red-and-white-striped paper with a blue bow stuck on the top. "Here's yours, Mommy. I made you something too."

"You little sneak. I didn't see you do this." Megan chuckled.

"That's because I made it when I was in school. I've kept it hidden for a long time."

Megan pulled back the jagged edges of the not-so-perfectly wrapped gift. Inside, there was a small upside-down canning jar painted on the outside with Christmas trees and stars. Inside, a tiny horse and sleigh had been glued to the lid, and the ground was covered in sparkling glitter. A snow globe. Simple, gorgeous, and perfect.

Tears sprang to Megan's eyes, and she shook the snow globe. Tiny pieces of glitter shimmered in the light as they floated through the water to the bottom. "Where did you find such a beautiful ornament?"

"Last year, after Christmas, Grandma took me shopping, and we found the tiny horse and sleigh. She was going to give it to you this year as your tree decoration like she does every year. When we were at her house, you know, after she went to heaven, and you were working cleaning up her stuff, I found it on her desk and took it. I knew she wanted you to have it. I was gonna wrap it and give it to you from her, but then the school wanted to do a special project, and I thought of this. So, this is really from Grandma and me."

She hugged her daughter, tears openly pouring down her face now. "I love this, sweetheart. I will treasure it forever." Megan couldn't think of any better proof her mother was here in spirit, making this Christmas special. They'd come here to honor her mother, and nothing would ever take away from her memories or joy of this moment.

Now all they needed was Rachael.

"Don't cry. Grandma knew you would love it."

"She's right. I do, and you did such a beautiful job. Wait until your Aunt Rachael sees this, she'll be so jealous."

Sam had moved toward the kitchen. "I should call the DOT and get an update on the roads and the pass. Maybe they'll have good news, and your sister can join you."

"You're welcome to stay even when it opens. It feels right to have you here." It was the closest Megan could go to expressing her feelings in front of Becca. She hoped he would understand the message.

"I'm sorry. I'm just not sure I'm ready for all this." He waved his hand at the tree and all the presents and then turned and went into the kitchen. Floppy got up to follow.

Without a doubt, the dog had decided. And Sam had too big a heart to walk away.

"Is he okay, Mom?"

"Yes, baby. He just misses his family."

CHAPTER EIGHTEEN

Sam knew he should have tried harder for Becca's sake, but it was all too confusing. How could something feel so right and so wrong at the same time? It's not that he didn't want to stay and be a part of the Christmas spirit they enjoyed. He did. A lot.

But the real problem lay in the fact he was beginning to want more than that. Just hanging out with them for today wasn't enough. It was unsettling to know he'd like nothing more than to explore his feelings with Megan and to realize Becca had wormed her way into his heart.

He wasn't sure that leaving would erase the memory of the time he'd been fortunate enough to spend with them, but Laura and Lydia would forever be a wall around his heart. He couldn't let them be forgotten. He didn't deserve to find the kind of happiness he was starting to envision.

And then there was Floppy. What was he supposed to do with the dog? He shook his head, staring at the furry friend who hadn't left his side since he'd brought him inside. Not even to go out and pee this morning.

Megan had made it clear they couldn't take him, and Sam didn't have the heart to leave him. Proof he had a heart, yes. But a dog? He wasn't willing to go that far just yet. He'd have to stop in town and talk with the sheriff. With any luck, someone would have stepped up to claim the little sweetheart.

Sam called the sheriff's office. "This is Sam Wyatt. Any updates on Tinsel Pass?"

"Merry Christmas, Mr. Wyatt. You'll be happy to know I just got a report in and they say it will be done within the next half hour." The dispatcher's excited voice didn't match his own reaction to the news. Everyone had worked hard to make it happen, but now, the idea of leaving left him colder than the freezing outside temperatures.

"Merry Christmas. Please be sure to tell everyone thank you for all their hard work." They talked another minute or so before Sam hung up the phone.

It was time to leave.

He headed down the hall to retrieve his duffel bag from the laundry room and then returned to the living room, followed by his sidekick. Standing off to the side, he drank in the image of Megan and Becca. The O'Malleys had joined them in the last few minutes, and the room was buzzing with laughter and music.

The sounds of Christmas joy.

He took a step forward to make his presence known. "I just talked to Captain James, and the pass will be open within the hour. Frank, they're sending in an ambulance to take you to the hospital to do an X-ray on the knee, just as a precaution. Rachael is already on the other side, waiting to come here." He smiled for everyone's benefit, a complete contrast to how he really felt. "The townspeople of Hallbrook really pulled together to make this happen."

Megan stood and crossed the room to his side and laid her arm on his. "But what about you?" Her voice was soft, almost a whisper.

"What about me?" He didn't want to think about himself. He'd done enough of that over the years.

"You don't have to leave. It's Christmas." Her invitation tugged at his heart, and it proved she cared at least a tiny bit. But even a tiny bit was too much because encouraging her any further would be wrong. Not when he had nothing to give Megan or at least nothing she deserved.

"I can't. I hope you understand. I care about you and Becca, but I'm not sure I can give you what you need."

"Hopefully, someday you realize life must go on. But I understand, everyone learns at their own pace. We will keep you in our thoughts and prayers." Megan's eyes glistened with tears that nearly undid his firm resolve to leave.

"Thanks." He meant it.

Becca jumped to her feet and came running to his side, tears in her eyes. Sam swallowed hard, the emptiness in him multiplying, the ache gut-wrenching.

"Goodbye, Mr. Sam. I'll miss you." Her bottom lip quivered. "Lydia's a lucky girl, even if she's in heaven. She had you." Becca clung to his waist; her face pressed against his chest.

Sam closed his eyes and took a deep breath, fighting the urge to stay. Becca didn't understand, and he didn't want to hurt her any more than necessary. She was just a little girl. Soon, she'd forget him, but the same couldn't be said for him.

He bent down on one knee and wrapped his arm around her, pulling her in for a hug.

"Thank you, sweetheart. I won't forget you. You're a special girl, too."

"Will you keep Floppy? And give him lots of love and hugs? I'm going to miss him." Becca hugged the dog and kissed him on the head.

He didn't want to make a promise he couldn't keep. "We don't know yet if anyone owns him, and it wouldn't be right for me to take him with me. I was hoping you and your mom could watch him until you leave. I'll make arrangements with Captain James for his care after you go home Tuesday, and if no one claims him, I'll come back and adopt him." So much for not making a promise. Sam realized it was an excellent decision. The right one for him and Floppy.

Sam reached out to pet the dog. Who would have thought he'd agree to keep a dog, especially one named Floppy? He really had changed since arriving here, and he owed it all to Megan and Becca.

Agnes crossed the room and hugged him. "Oh, good heavens, boy. You shouldn't be leaving on Christmas Day. What's the hurry? And it's not a day to be out on the roads."

"I'm sorry." Sam shook his head and shrugged. "It's just something I have to do. Trust me."

"Take care." Frank tried to get up. "Thanks for all you did for me and the others."

"Stay put. And you're welcome. It's been nice getting to know everyone." He meant every word. It just didn't change anything. Sam stood and walked toward the door.

Floppy tried to follow. "Stay, boy."

Megan bent down to hold the dog, but his whimper was enough to break Sam's heart. His gaze locked on Megan, and for a few seconds, nothing else existed. For a split second, he let himself feel the warmth of joy in his heart, a warmth she'd put there.

He turned and walked out the door and down the path to his SUV.

A red cardinal landed in the snow, not five feet away, drawing his attention and breaking the moment. Sam glanced at the flagpole, remembering Lydia.

Sam felt Megan's presence before he saw her as she came to stand by his side. With one hand on his arm, she stood there silently beside him, her head bowed in prayer. She always seemed to understand what he needed and when.

"This is the place the angel video was shot. Her last video. My little angel." His voice broke with emotion he couldn't hold back.

"I'm sorry, Sam. Truly."

"Thanks. Take care of yourself and Becca. She's a sweet girl."

Sam threw his bag across the front seat. It landed with a thud on the passenger side. He climbed into the vehicle, started the engine, and cast one last longing gaze at the cabin. He was surprised to see Becca coming out through the front door and running up to the car on the passenger side.

She climbed in on top of his suitcase. "You forgot your ornament!" Becca hung it from his rearview mirror. "You need your angel. It will help you to remember me."

"Thank you. You're right, I do need my angel watching over me."

"Just like I'll watch over Floppy while I can." Becca waved goodbye, climbed out of the SUV, and ran back to the front door to join Megan on the stoop.

Sam put the vehicle in reverse and started to back down the driveway, watching as they waved goodbye. Mother and daughter. His heart was heavy, torn with the guilt of the past and remorse for the future he could easily see happening between him and Megan. Life never promised it would be fair.

It was a brisk morning, the sunlight glinting off the packed snow on the road. Sam focused on maneuvering the vehicle, being extra careful as the tires slipped every now and then.

It was easier to sit by the pass and wait to pass

through when they gave the go ahead. Not too close, however. The memory of the thunderous roar as the avalanche wiped out everything as far as he could see into a blanket of white was not one he'd soon forget.

Sam drove around the bend that led toward the pass. The SUV started to slip and began picking up speed on the downhill slope. He tapped his brakes, holding the wheel firmly. The tires kept sliding on the ice. His stomach plummeted as the vehicle headed for the side of the road.

A sense of déjà vu hit him hard. He dropped into second gear to slow the engine as he fought to bring the vehicle to a stop in the center of the road, failing miserably. A sign on the side of the road loomed in front of him, growing larger and larger, as if in slow motion. The vehicle careened toward the edge, his attempts to regain control futile. Mother Nature was in complete command of his destiny.

The SUV slammed into a hard wall, and Sam was propelled forward, the crushingly hard blow to his chest excruciating, and then everything went black.

There was no way to know how long he'd been in the darkness, but a light glowing in the distance came closer. Maybe this was the light people spoke of when they died, only to reawaken and live to tell about it. Was his life over in the space of seconds?

He thought of Megan and Becca. They'd been through so much, and he hated to cause them more pain. The light in front of him grew stronger, calling him. He gave in and let it warm his face. Instead of the pearly gates of heaven, Laura and Lydia emerged from the haze, smiles on their faces.

They were singing around a Christmas tree, dancing and laughing. They held their hands out to him, beckoning him to join their happy circle. He was all too happy to join in their fun, his heart bursting with joy to see them again. It was like coming home. Their gazes were full of love and not the anger he deserved.

Moments later, Laura smiled at him again, this time dropping his hand. *Wait. What are you doing? Don't go.* Laura motioned from behind her, and two more people began to materialize into their snowy Christmas reunion.

Megan and Becca? What are they doing here? No. No. They can't be here. What had happened to them? Please, Lord, don't take them with me.

Laura took Megan and Becca's hands and joined them with his, one on each side. The circle closed, and they all began to sing. The chorus of 'Angels We Have Heard on High' reverberated all around him, the uplifting song filling him with peace.

Sam watched, unsure of what it all meant. Laura

and Lydia broke away from the circle, this time lifting their hands and waving as if they were leaving.

No. Don't go.

Their images grew distant, the snow coming down heavier to obscure his vision completely. Laura and Lydia had left him. *Again.* He turned to look at Megan and Becca, their smiling faces filling him with faith, hope, and love. Everything else around him turned back to darkness.

Tap. Tap. Tap. Sam rubbed his head, trying to fight back against the pounding of a headache that made his head feel like a log on a chopping block. He opened his eyes and looked around.

Tap. Tap. Tap. A man dressed in uniform stood at the window.

"Are you okay, mister?" The officer gestured for him to roll down the window.

Sam pressed the button. "I think so. I'm talking to you, which is a good sign. Just the pounding in my head and a crumpled front end to show for my efforts trying to control the vehicle when it went into a slide."

"I don't care who you are, Mother Nature has the ability to override any level of expertise. Accidents happen."

Accidents happen. It was the same thing he'd told

Becca and Megan. And the same thing Megan had tried to tell him, except he hadn't listened. Well, he was listening now.

"Well, Mother Nature certainly won this battle." Sam shook his head, trying to shake off the fog in his head.

"I can have the ambulance take you in if you need to go to the hospital and get checked out."

"I'm not sure why the airbags didn't deploy, but all things considered, I'm doing okay. Thanks anyway, but I'll be all right."

"If you're sure, then I'll let the ambulance go through. They're going to pick up Mr. O'Malley. I'll call a tow truck to help pull you out of the bank."

"That would be great. Thanks." As Sam waited, he thought about the vision. Had it been a message? Had Laura and Lydia come to say goodbye? Had they been his angels protecting him in the accident? The only thing he knew for certain was the clear message they'd given him.

It was time for him to move on.

Laura was guiding and directing him to move forward with his life—to live it. With Megan. He'd been wrong to think if he'd been driving, he could've prevented them from sliding off the side of the mountain. Talk about a lofty impression of his abilities to think he could control Mother Nature and freak accidents. Even if he'd been there, everything might have happened the same.

And Megan was right, if he'd been in the accident and died, he wouldn't have been there to save her. Becca and Megan were a reason to live. And he'd left them standing on the porch waving goodbye, knowing he was breaking their hearts.

Sam had walked away from the love in his heart and he needed to go back. He needed to make it right. The gift he'd been given a second time in life was nothing short of a miracle, and it filled him with warmth and joy. He hoped her offer for him to stay was genuine because he wanted to take her up on it. Forever.

But for now, he'd start with today and tomorrow and the next day.

Somehow, he needed to prove what was in his heart to Megan. The angel hanging from the rearview mirror rocked back and forth, catching his eye. Sam reached up to touch the ornament. *His angel.* Becca had been surrounding him with angels ever since they met, for which he was grateful.

You could never have too many angels watching over you.

CHAPTER NINETEEN

A knock at the door alerted Megan they had a visitor. She jumped to her feet and rushed to the door, hoping it was Rachael. "Oh my gosh, I'm so glad you're here!" Megan flung her arms around her sister's neck and let out a sigh of relief.

"Me, too. Merry Christmas, sis." Rachael laughed.

"Merry Christmas. Here, let me take your stuff." Megan removed the shoulder bag and took control of the roller suitcase.

"Thanks. Now, where's that niece of mine. I'm dying to see her again."

Floppy barked, eying Rachael with interest but using caution as he approached. "What a cutie pie." Her sister bent down to give the dog a playful rub. "I can't believe no one has claimed him yet. Are you going to keep him? I know Becca's been wanting a dog."

"You know I can barely manage everything now. A dog would make it even harder. Besides, Sam is going to take him if no one can find his owner."

"That's wonderful. I'm glad to hear he'll have a new home." Floppy was enjoying the attention, his tail wagging. She was relieved when he stopped moping for Sam.

"Becca!" Megan hollered. "Last I saw her, she was headed for the bathroom to give Victoria a bath."

"Victoria?"

"Her new baby doll."

"*Awww*. How cute." Rachael looked up as Becca entered the living room. "There you are." She held her arms open wide.

"Aunt Rachael! You made it. Yay!" Becca ran to Rachael's side and was engulfed in a bear hug.

"I did. Merry Christmas, munchkin. No way I was going to miss all the fun."

"Meet Victoria." Becca held the doll up for Rachael's inspection.

"What a sweet baby, just like her mommy."

"I have to feed her, change her diaper, change her clothes, and put her to bed. It's a lot of work. Right now, I need to give her a bath. You want to help me?"

"I don't know much about bathing babies, but

after I get settled in, I'll check in on you both. How's that sound?"

"Great. Isn't Floppy adorable? I wish we could keep him, but Sam's going to instead. And he really needs a friend, so it's all good. I'll be in the bathroom." Becca took off running down the hall. She was like an energized bunny, hopping from one thing to the next, full of excitement.

"I remember those days. You played with the army men, and I played with dolls. Go figure. And of course, you ended up getting to act out both our childhood fantasies, and me, nothing." Rachael's voice held a touch of resentment.

"Whatever. Nothing stopping you from finding a husband and having your own baby doll."

Rachael shrugged. "True."

Wait. What? The adamant, never-going-to-happen Rachael, was nowhere to be found. She'd have to ask her for more information later, but not now in front of the O'Malleys.

"Rachael, this is Frank and Agnes O'Malley. Frank was injured when he fell in his driveway, and their power is out, so they've been staying with us."

"It's a pleasure to meet you, my dear. We've heard lots of wonderful things." Agnes had joined them in the foyer.

"Nice to meet you." Frank waved hello from the couch.

"It's nice to meet you also. It's been a crazy few days, and not much has gone as planned. But at least we are all together for Christmas." Her sister's cheery attitude was the facelift the group needed after Sam's departure.

"Thanks for picking up all the food for Christmas dinner. My cooking won't be as good as Mom's, but it's the effort that counts. Right?"

"Absolutely. I hope you don't mind, but I invited Brandon to come to dinner tonight."

Megan shot her sister a wide-eyed look of wonder. Things between Rachael and her new friend had progressed far more than expected if she was inviting him to a family Christmas dinner.

"This is a surprise." The soft-pink blush on her sister's cheeks was all the answer she needed for confirmation.

"Yes, and not another word. We're just friends. He's alone this Christmas because his parents are out of town, and I thought it would be a lovely gesture."

"*Ha.* If you say so." Megan's thoughts turned to another man who would be spending Christmas alone. By choice. When he'd driven away, he'd taken a piece of her heart. A piece she hadn't even known existed anymore, but there was no denying it, she'd fallen in love with Sam.

"Lovely tree, by the way." Rachael glanced around the room, determined to change the subject. "You did a beautiful job decorating. It's warm and welcoming with all of Mom's special decorations and tree ornaments."

"We agree. In fact, Becca and I were thinking of doing this every year. The only problem is, we have to beat Sam to it." Megan smiled and shook her head.

"So, where is this Mr. Grumpy, who also happens to be the handsome hero who saved the day?"

"I didn't say handsome." She couldn't remember all the things she'd said, but the last thing she needed was her sister joining forces with the O'Malleys. Agnes thought she was crazy for letting Sam leave without telling him the truth.

"He is," Agnes interjected. "Very. And there's nothing grumpy about the guy. He's just hurting. Men aren't so hot with emotional stuff."

"Agnes, you need to stay out of it. He's gone, and your matchmaking attempts have fallen short this time, so let it go." Frank chimed in from the couch in a typical male tone of voice to end the sappy lovey-dovey conversation.

"But—"

"Let it go." Frank and Megan spoke at the same time and then laughed.

"You both might be able to tell her what to do, but I just got here. Someone needs to fill me in." Rachael was using her bulldog voice.

"With the pass opened, Agnes and I should be packing. They'll be sending someone to get me, and we should be ready. We'll let the two of you catch up." Frank hobbled toward the hallway.

"He's a good man, and your sister needs to step up and let him know how she feels. That's all I'm going to say." Agnes was determined to get in the last word.

"Wife, let it be and come on," Frank grumbled.

"I'm coming, I'm coming, old man." Agnes followed him down the hall.

"So, where is he? I'm really curious about him now," Rachael persisted.

"He left right after Becca opened her gifts."

"But why? It's Christmas Day. And when was that?" Rachael's brow drew tight, and all sense of excitement vanished.

"He needed to get back to New York City and left about an hour ago. Sam wanted to wait by the pass for when it opened." Which translated to, he couldn't get out of here fast enough. But it wasn't a thought she was ready to share with her sister.

"What does he drive?" The question was totally unexpected; the intensity of her sister's tone alarming.

"A black Navigator. Why?" A shiver of fear slid down her spine. These weren't normal questions.

"Oh, Megan, I'm so sorry. I don't know how to tell you this, but when I came through the pass, there was a black SUV that had crashed into the side of the ditch. The police cruiser's blue lights were flashing, and there was a uniformed officer directing traffic to steer clear. I don't know anything else, but it sounds as if it could've been him."

Megan stilled, closing her eyes to fight back the image. "Sam?" His name came out a strangled cry. She bent down and pulled Floppy close, needing the connection.

Impossible. It can't be him. Please, Lord, don't let it be him.

"I need to call the station to see what I can find out. The O'Malleys are packing their stuff and getting ready to leave. Can you stay with Becca? Just don't say anything about Sam. She really likes him and is already upset he left. This would break her heart."

"Sure. Everything will be fine. You'll see. Stay strong."

A sound from outside caught Megan's attention,

and she went to the front window to see what was going on. It felt as though her heart had stopped.

Red and white lights flashing, an ambulance sat in the driveway. *Sam?*

Breathe. Why would they come here? She raced to the front door to meet the paramedic. "What's going on?"

"Merry Christmas. Sorry it took us so long, but we're here for Frank O'Malley. They want to run him into the hospital for X-rays as a precaution. I thought someone would have told you."

His words started to sink in. *Frank O'Malley.* He was here for Frank. It wasn't Sam.

"Yes. Yes. I remember. Come in. They are almost ready. I'll let them know you're here."

"Thanks." The man removed his hat and stepped inside.

"My sister mentioned an accident on this side of the pass. You wouldn't happen to know anything about it, would you?"

"No, ma'am. Only that we were advised to continue on course to pick up Mr. O'Malley."

Megan was numb with fear. She needed answers, and she needed them now.

After sending Rachael to tell the O'Malleys the paramedics were here, Megan escaped to the kitchen to make a phone call to the authorities. As she waited for someone to answer, she poured a cup of coffee, hoping the warm liquid would soothe her nerves. Liquid sloshed over the side of the cup, forcing her to set the cup down. She grabbed a towel and started to wipe it up just as someone came on the line.

"Hi, this is Megan Langley. I'm staying at the rental cabin on Christmas Tree Lane, and I understand the pass just opened. I also heard there's a black Navigator in the ditch. Can you tell me anything about it? My friend just left here not long ago, and I'm trying to find out if it was him."

"What's his name and are you family?" the dispatcher asked kindly.

"Sam Wyatt. And, no, we're just friends. He's been staying with me the past few days while the pass was closed."

"I see. Let me check my records."

Megan hugged herself tightly, rocking back and forth.

"Ma'am?"

"Yes?" She closed her eyes and waited to hear the verdict.

"I'm sorry; I don't have any information. I've heard about the same thing you already know. There's been no report filed yet, so I have no way of knowing what's happening. I wish I had more to tell you, but I simply don't have the information." The woman sounded sincere.

Megan knew what she needed to do. "Okay. Thank you." She needed to get to him and make sure he was okay. She needed to be there for him, offering help in any way possible. He'd saved her life, and she loved him. What more reason did she need to go after him? Agnes was right. Given the chance, she needed to tell him how she felt. This time, if he left town, it would be with the truth.

Five minutes later, goodbyes and hugs were exchanged, and the ambulance pulled out of the driveway, leaving Megan time to gather her emotions and come up with a game plan.

"Becca, I've got to check on something, why don't you and Aunt Rachael play with Victoria, and you can show her how to change a diaper." She was trying to keep things upbeat for her daughter, but inside, she was frozen with fear for Sam.

"You can't go anywhere. Aunt Rachael just got here, and it's Christmas."

"I'll just be a few minutes, honey. I promise." At least she hoped she wouldn't be gone long.

"Okay. Come on, Aunt Rachael. I'll let you change Victoria this time."

Megan pulled on her winter jacket and headed for the garage door.

"Here." Rachael tossed her the keys. "Take my truck. It's quicker this way since I'm parked behind you."

"Thanks." Megan turned back and headed out the front door. A black SUV pulled into the driveway.

Sam. Thank you, Lord.

She let out a deep sigh of relief. The SUV had a dented front end, but the man himself opened the door and stepped out of the vehicle as if nothing had happened. *He looks okay. And he's come back.*

Tears threaten to escape, but Megan held them in check, not wanting to miss any part of his return. She had to know everything.

"I hope it's okay that I'm here. There was an accident." He closed the distance between them, not taking his eyes off her face.

"I heard. I was just leaving to find out what was going on because no one could tell me anything." Her voice was much steadier than it had been a few short moments ago.

"You were coming to check on me?" The incredulous tone of his voice was a true indicator he really didn't know how she felt about him, but it was past time she let him know.

"Of course. I care about you, whether you want me to or not." There, she'd said it. It was like lifting a weight off her shoulders to say the words.

"Caring is good." His voice was different, but she couldn't put a finger on what had changed.

Megan looked at him with renewed interest. This wasn't the same Sam who'd walked out of their lives nearly an hour ago.

"Look, Megan, I shouldn't have left. I was afraid." He reached for her hands and pulled them up to his chest, drawing her in close.

"Afraid? Of me?" Why would he be afraid? She wouldn't hurt him. They'd both had more than their share of pain to deal with in the past.

"Of us. Of what was happening between us." There was a new light in his eyes, one filled with peace.

"Keep talking, I'm trying to understand."

"Can we go inside? I promise I'll explain, but I'd kind of like to sit down, my head is killing me."

"I'm so sorry. I should have thought of that. Did they call an ambulance?"

"No. I told them I was fine. I just wanted to come back here. To you."

"I need to examine you."

"And I'll be more than happy to let you nurse me after I get to sit down." He grinned.

Megan pushed open the door, waiting for Sam to follow her inside. Floppy met them at the door, barking and jumping excitedly.

Sam bent down to pat his head with one hand while pressing the palm of his hand to his temple. The dog licked his hand, happy to see his best friend. Megan could relate but forced herself not to be as exuberant in her joy.

"Mr. Sam!" Becca came running down the hall, making a beeline for him. "You're back!"

"Easy does it, honey. He's been in an accident and I need to examine his head and clean the cut on his forehead."

Sam bent down and gave Becca a bear hug. "I'm back. And if your mom lets me stay, I'd be more than happy to join you for Christmas dinner." Sam looked up at Megan, hope in his eyes.

"Of course, you can stay." She laughed, shaking her head. As if she'd send him away. Both the sisters would have a Christmas date. Things were starting to look up for their family.

"Rachael, this is Sam. Sam, Rachael." They shook hands, and then her sister pulled him into a hug. Leave it to her sister to make sure he felt warm and welcome and a part of the family.

"Thanks for saving my sister and for taking care of my family when I couldn't. I'll be forever grateful you were here. Keeping them out of trouble is a full-time job." Rachael winked.

"Don't I know it." He grinned again. It was a sight

Megan could get used to frequently. "I'm thankful neither one of us was in the avalanche."

"Becca, can you get me a wet washcloth and my first aid kit? Rachael, will you grab Sam a cup of coffee to help warm him up? And a blanket out of the hall closet. Thanks."

"We're on it." The two of them took off, all too willing to help.

"So, what happened?" Megan gestured for Sam to sit at the table. It would give her the best light to check his wound.

Floppy followed, settling in at his feet after he sat.

"I slid into the ditch and hit my head on the steering wall. I was knocked out cold as best I can tell. And while I was unconscious, I had a vision. I know this is going to sound crazy, but Laura and Lydia came to me. We were singing around the Christmas tree, and the next thing I knew, she was welcoming you and Becca into the circle. We all sang, and then before I knew it, they waved goodbye and disappeared into the darkness." Sam shook his head and ran a hand through his hair.

"Wow. That's incredible. It must have been wonderful to see them again, even if just for a moment. You know, they will never be far away because they will always be in your heart."

"I would have never believed it if it hadn't happened to me, but now I'm a believer. In lots of things. Faith, hope, and love. All-consuming and all-powerful—but real."

Megan would never have believed it either, but she believed Sam. "Do you think it meant anything—like a message?"

"I feel as though they came back to let me know it was okay to move on. With you. My angels were showing me the future I was walking away from. I want to be here to take care of you and Becca, even though you don't need me to. I want to share a future with you. I don't want to walk away anymore."

The tears that had threatened to escape previously now ran down her face unchecked. "I don't want us to be your replacement for Laura and Lydia. Maybe you feel you need to protect us and have a new family, but I need more than that from a relationship." She had to know the truth, even if it hurt.

"You're wrong. You and Laura are nothing alike. I'm not substituting anything. Laura was a city girl through and through, whereas you seem to be the most country-city girl I've ever met. My company is in the city, which is how I met Laura, but my heart will always be in the mountains. I didn't know it was possible to love again, but Laura showed me it was okay. I've never felt better, other than the headache threatening to explode." His smile reached his eyes, the truth reflected in the depths.

She believed him. Shivers of joy rippled through every inch of her body. He wanted her. "I feel the same way about you." Megan reached up to brush a lock of hair away from the cut on his forehead. "What can I do to make it better? I'm sure I've got some more pain relievers in my purse, which would probably help if there's any swelling." Megan walked to the end of the dining room table to pick up her purse.

"I've got a better idea." Sam pushed back his chair and stood. He took a few steps toward the kitchen.

"What's that?" Megan frowned.

He looked first at Rachael, who stood a few feet away with two cups of steaming hot coffee in hand and grinned. And then he turned a mischievous grin on Megan, causing her heart to skip a beat.

"You can kiss me." He glanced up at the mistletoe hanging in the doorway.

Megan hesitated, glancing at Rachael, who stood smiling but not saying a word.

"What's going—" Becca asked, joining them in the dining room.

"Christmas tradition." Sam and Rachael answered in unison.

"I thought I had to be standing under the mistletoe with you?" Megan couldn't help but tease. The idea of kissing him thrilled her. The idea of kissing him in front of Becca and her sister was way more serious. She still didn't want to give her daughter the wrong impression.

"Well, there is that. But if you managed to get over here before I pass out, I might be able to get it right this time."

Megan immediately crossed the room to his side, not wanting to be responsible if he fainted on her watch.

Sam wrapped his arms around her and lowered his head, claiming her mouth in a kiss that spoke of feelings and a future. A kiss that made her feel as though they belonged together. Forever.

"Yes! Now that's more like it. I knew my mistletoe would do the trick. Does this mean Mr. Sam gets to stay for more than dinner?"

"Becca!" Megan choked out. Her daughter's boldness knew no bounds and Rachael's laughter didn't help the situation. Floppy repeatedly barked, joining in the fun.

"It's up to Sam. Christmas is a time of joy and peace. And a time to be with those you care about."

Becca looked up at him with hope in her eyes and held out her hand.

"Of course, I'll stay. And if your mom gets me those pain relievers, maybe we can find out if Victoria needs her diaper changed or to be fed. I think I hear her crying for her mommy."

Becca went flying toward the crib and picked up her new baby doll, leaving the grown-ups laughing.

Hours later, with lunch over and the dishes finished, Megan marveled at how the day had changed completely from what she expected when she woke up this morning. It was, indeed, nothing short of a miracle.

The sun had come out, warming up the outside temperature. Becca was more than ready to play outside, and everyone bundled up to join in her fun.

Becca ran around the front yard, dropping to the ground to make a fresh snow angel.

"Since we have four people, can we have a snow-ball fight?" Becca called out.

"Fine by me." Megan was all in. Her arm and her aim meant she wouldn't come out on the losing end.

"Of course, you want to have a snowball fight. Miss, I used to play softball in high school." Rachael shook her head as she stood there, hands on hips, positive she would be on the losing end of the bargain.

"I want Sam on my team," Becca hollered. "Please. Please."

"Well, let me think." He grinned as he looked at each one of them. "Rachael, no offense, but you're the first one I have to rule out in the situation."

"None taken. We all know who the winner will be. You haven't taken your eyes off her for more than a few minutes at a time unless she's out of the room." Rachael laughed.

"You have a point there. The truth is, I choose them both." *Cute.* But Sam's diplomatic answer wouldn't cut it. Not in a snowball fight.

"But—" Becca and Rachael chimed in. Megan was all too happy to let the others settle the problem and kept quiet.

Sam held up his hand. "But...for the snowball fight—" he tapped his chin with his forefinger, enjoying the suspense, "—I choose Becca." Sam winked at Megan. Her heart did a flip-flop, knowing how much he cared about her daughter. He was trying to show her how he felt about them both.

"Sounds fair to me," Rachael grinned. "For once, I get the ace-rocket arm on my team."

The fight picked up in intensity as the four of them played in the front yard, Floppy joining in the fun, doing his best not to get hit, but running around trying to catch snowballs midair.

Darting and dashing around the two vehicles and the flagpole, everyone used whatever they could as a shield to protect themselves from being pounded with a snowball. Megan picked up a bunch of snow and rolled it into a ball, took aim, and released. A direct hit landed on the front of Sam's chest, the ball bursting into pieces and blasting him in the face with snow.

"Score!" Megan laughed, reaching to pick up more snow, but only enough to make a Becca-sized snowball.

"Watch out!" Rachael hollered.

Megan ducked down to avoid getting hit. As she straightened, she noticed Sam headed her way. The look in his eyes meant she wouldn't get away with the hit without retribution and judging by the size of the snowball in his hand, he meant business. She twisted out of his reach, making a dash for the evergreen tree. A game of cat and mouse ensued, Megan hoping he'd soon lose interest. Either that, or she was a goner.

Megan miscalculated her escape, the packed snow from the party last night more slippery than she expected. The minute she fell, she knew she was doomed. Crossing her arms in front of her chest, she tried to ward off the worst of the snowball attack.

Sam landed on top of her, his snowball held high over her head.

"You better not dump it on me!" It was worth a

shot, not that she believed for a minute he would show her any mercy.

He lowered the snowball, closer and closer, the icy white ball destined to shower her in a cold blast of chips. "After your last shot, you leave me no choice."

"Please, don't do it. For me. I'll do anything." She wasn't above begging.

Sam brought the snowball within inches of her chest, grabbing hold of her collar and peeling it back, his intention clear. "Anything?" The gleam in Sam's eyes meant trouble, but the idea of an ice-cold snowball down her shirt was enough of a reason to give him the answer he wanted.

"Yes."

"Interesting. Does anything include dating me?" He was grinning like a fool in love, and she had a feeling he was entirely serious.

Not at all what she expected. He'd gone from leaving to staying forever in the breath of hours. But if nothing else, in those last few hours, he'd more than proven he wasn't looking for a replacement.

She swallowed hard and looked around to discover Becca and Rachael had stopped the fight and drawn close to watch the main attraction. Their smiles meant they heard every word he'd said.

Megan couldn't help but tease Sam, the love in

her heart overflowing. "Give me one good reason that I should date you?"

"I'll give you four. One. My snowball. Two. Becca's snowball. Three. Rachael's snowball. Four. I love you and might even want to marry you someday soon. And as a bonus, I'll take all the snowballs aimed at you right now, if you say yes."

"*Hmmm.* Since you're willing to take the hits, then I guess you leave me with no choice. I'll date you. And as to the marrying part someday…It depends on how much of a snowball blocker you are."

His grin faded slightly in direct contrast to her ever-widening grin that made her cheeks ache. "And that's the only reason?" She needed to put him out of his misery.

"Well, that, and because I love you, too."

Sam tossed his snowball off to the side, instead targeting her mouth with his lips. It was a kiss of love. A kiss of hope. A kiss of life.

Seconds later, Rachael and Becca started pummeling Sam with snowballs, some of the crystals falling into her hair and across her face.

"Knock it off, you two," Rachael called. "This is a snowball fight, and there are children present."

"Yeah, Mom, knock it off. I'm here, and we should be playing." Becca and Rachael did a high five right before they erupted into a fit of laughter. Her daughter had been right all along. They were meant to be a family.

Sam rolled off her, grabbed a handful of snow, and tossed it at Rachael, and then some at Becca. The fight turned into a free-for-all until Megan called it quits. Cold and wet, it was time everyone went inside. Dry clothes and a warm fire held appeal, although not as much as the man next to her. It had turned out to be a great Christmas.

EPILOGUE

"I'm so happy we could rent the cabin again for Christmas. What a perfect way to spend our holiday." Megan glanced into the backseat of the Navigator, her gaze landing on their newborn daughter. Angel.

Long-distance relationships were hard, but it had still come as a surprise when Sam sold off his company and moved the outskirts of Boston to be closer to her. It hadn't taken him long to propose, and it had taken her even less time to plan a wedding. The three of them had been anxious to start their journey together, with Floppy happily by their side.

Angel, on the other hand, had been a joyful surprise, a gift from their honeymoon. Becca had chosen the name, and somehow, it stuck. A beautiful name for a beautiful girl, born of love. A true blessing. Becca was an amazing big sister, although, at times, she preferred Victoria when it came time to help change diapers or feeding time. Real poopy diapers didn't sit high on her list of things she liked to do.

"Look, Mom. I can see the cabin. I can see it." Becca had been excited for months after she found out they were going to rent the Hallbrook cabin again. She was anxious to meet up with all her friends from last year.

At first, when Megan pulled up the realtor's site and discovered the listing had gone off the market, her heart had been filled with disappointment. That night, after telling Sam and Becca the disappointing news, she had reassured them with more positivity than she'd felt that she would find something else just as wonderful.

It had been a complete surprise when two days later, Sam announced he'd spoken with the realtor and had it all fixed. It didn't matter how he'd pulled it off, Megan was thrilled to be going there again. Rachael and Brandon were coming to stay, and she couldn't wait to see them again, even though she'd seen them over the Thanksgiving holiday. Her sister had been gaga over the new baby. It wouldn't surprise her if she and Brandon announced they were getting married, with a baby not far behind in the planning.

The drive through Hallbrook flooded her with wonderful memories. She'd kept in touch with the O'Malleys over the past year, the bond they shared last winter, one of a never-ending friendship.

Megan turned to watch her husband as he pulled into the driveway. The word husband still sent tingles down her spine. The wedding had been magical. She wished her mom could've been there, knowing she would've loved Sam, but Megan had come to a place of peace. A place where her world was filled with the renewal of life. With her family.

She hadn't expected to get pregnant as fast as she had, but they'd discussed it and had decided whenever it happened, it would be the right time. She wasn't sure Sam had meant within weeks, but that's exactly what they'd gotten.

The flagpole had been decorated and lit, the same as the previous year. It was like coming home. Even the evergreen tree in the front yard had been decorated. Sam shut off the engine and grabbed her hand before she could slide out of the SUV. He leaned over to kiss her on the cheek.

"Welcome home, honey." His voice had dropped a notch as if it meant something to him as well, making her wish it was true.

"Home. It has a lovely ring to it, and it's our home for the next week. I'm so happy you worked it out for us to come back."

Sam got out and unbuckled the baby from her car seat. Becca got out on the passenger side and ran around the side of the vehicle toward the house, Floppy running around the front yard, taking in all the new smells.

"Leave the bags. I'll get them after I get you three inside and settled. It's cold out here."

"Our hero. You won't have to tell me twice." She laughed as they started to walk up the sidewalk. "It looks as though they've done some work on the place. It's the same, but look at the addition that's been built on the side. Did the realtor say anything to you about them changing it?"

"No, I don't believe he did. Let's go see." Sam pulled a keyring out of his pocket, the code entry pad missing. He opened the door and stepped back to let them enter. "Here, boy," he called to the dog, who came running.

The house was warm and welcoming, a fire already going in the fireplace. "What a sweet touch. You'll have to thank Mr. Harper."

"I'm glad you appreciate it." Sam smiled but didn't say much else.

"Look, honey. They've got new furniture. I love

the rustic touches. They've really turned this into a beautiful home. What are they trying to do, make sure we never want to leave?" She chuckled.

"Maybe." Sam's smile widened into a grin.

"I want to see what they did to the bedrooms." Becca took off down the hall and disappeared into the first door. A squeal sounded from her room, causing Megan a moment of panic.

"Sam?"

"I've got this." Except he didn't move. He just stood there, grinning. It was the same grin he wore when she agreed to marry him. The same grin he wore when they were married. The same grin he wore when Angel was born.

Whatever it was, something good was about to happen. Megan trusted that grin.

Seconds later, Becca came out of the room, a strange expression on her face. "Mom, um, you need to come see this. This is just too weird."

"What do you mean, *weird*?" Megan was confused. "What's wrong?"

"You know how I wanted to paint my room in shades of purple and have white unicorns dancing across a rainbow?"

Megan walked down the hall, not understanding what any of this had to do with anything here at the cabin. Or why now, of all times, Becca was bringing it up.

"Yes. We discussed it, and I told you that we needed to find a new home first. It wouldn't make any sense to redecorate your room right before we move."

"I know." Becca looked back and forth between Sam and her. "Look." Becca pushed the door wide open.

Megan glanced around the room, her confusion now a mirror of Becca's own expression. The room was painted in shades of purple, and white unicorns danced across a rainbow. *No way.* She looked at Sam for an explanation.

"Merry Christmas to all the leading ladies in my life." He leaned down to kiss Megan.

"You mean?" Megan tried to say more, but the words wouldn't come.

"I do. I did. I hope you love what I've done because it's our new home. I got the idea to buy the place after you once said you wished you could live here forever."

"*Yes!*" Becca danced around the room in circles, twirling like a fairy princess.

"I love it! But what about my job and your consulting work? Can we make this work?"

"I built an office here, and I'm going to work remotely from home. I know you love it here in Hallbrook, and I spoke to the medical center administrator on your behalf. They'd love to have you come work for them, especially after all you did for Mr. O'Malley. But if it's not what you want, you can always commute to Lancaster. There's a decent-sized hospital there. And of course, the other option is to stay home and take care of the girls. The choice is yours."

"As long as I'm with you and the girls, I'll make it work. What a perfect Christmas present." More time with her family was exactly what she'd wished for.

Becca came up, and Sam met her partway, bending over to receive a bear hug. "I love my room, and I love you, Dad."

"I love you, too." Sam's eyes glazed over as he turned toward the door.

"I have one more room to show you." He took Megan's hand and led her down the hall. He opened the door to reveal a nursery. Paper angels dressed in white gowns with gold ribbon and glitter hung from the ceiling everywhere. He'd copied Becca's angels from last year.

The pink and white of the nursery was simply beautiful, the birds, clouds, and small furry animals all sweet and welcoming. Angel had her own nursery, and it was more than perfect. Sam had poured love into fixing up the house for them, and it showed in every detail.

"It's wonderful. Just like you." Megan smiled. She'd always known Sam was amazing, but this was over the top.

As they walked back through the house, Megan noticed mistletoe hanging over every doorway. "What's with the added greenery?" She was pleased he remembered. After a year, she still loved nothing more than when her husband stopped everything just to steal a kiss. It had a way of making a woman feel loved and cherished.

"I always want this house filled with mistletoe and angels. One, so I have an excuse to kiss you anytime I want, and two, to honor all the angels who brought us together."

WHAT'S NEXT?

**Read the first chapter of LOVE & ORDER, book 1
of HOLIDAYS IN HALLBROOK...**

Garrett clicked the buckle of his harness into place and pulled tightly on the ends of the straps. "Ready for takeoff." He gave the helicopter pilot a thumbs-up in case he couldn't hear him over the low hum of the spinning blades and the motor propelling them. Normally, he would just take his own plane for such a short flight, but he wasn't in the right frame of mind to be piloting anything, making this chartered flight an easy decision.

The pilot went through a series of checks with the control tower, and it wasn't long before the whirring sound increased and the helicopter began to vibrate with the increased power, blocking out any chance of regular conversation. The huge metal bird lifted off from a private section of the airfield. The ground below faded away until New York City became an aerial view of rooftops and skyscrapers all blended together. Garrett let out a deep breath.

The flight from La Guardia to Glen Haven, New Hampshire, the closest private airport with a helipad to Hallbrook, was ninety minutes by helicopter and then a fifteen-minute drive north to the town where he'd spent most of his childhood. It was a trip he would always regret not making more often. The news of his mother's death had come as a shock, and now, days later, the ache he felt had deepened, spurred on by guilt. He hadn't even known she was having heart troubles, but then according to Charlie, her friend and solicitor, she hadn't either. Her heart attack had taken everyone by surprise. It was hard to believe she was gone.

He tamped down on the emotions trying to emerge, finding it easier to focus on what needed to be done. Once he settled his mother's estate, there would be no reason to return to his hometown, a place he'd left long ago and only manage to visit once or twice a year, much to his mother's consternation. Work had been his priority for as long as he could remember, and the corporate law offices of Bradley & West were proof of the success he and his best friend and partner, Jim, had achieved as a result of their dedication.

But being rated as the top law firm in Manhattan and in the top twenty nationwide didn't do a thing to ease the pain of knowing his mother was gone forever, especially since he'd disappointed her by canceling his visit this past summer. The Baden-Hamilton merger had derailed, and the multi-million-dollar deal was his baby, and therefore his responsibility to save. And then one thing after another had popped up, and before he knew it, September was fast rolling in. But for his mother, there would be no September.

Angelica, his sister, had been notified of their mother's passing through official Naval communication, but as a U.S. Naval officer on a submarine somewhere in the Pacific, there was no telling when she'd be home. Charlie was taking care of their mother's arrangements per her wishes, and a woman by the name of April St. James was taking care of the house. Charlie had insisted Garrett arrive as soon as possible to deal with some legal issues. Garrett had cleared his schedule, making sure he could be at the celebration of life to honor his mother on Saturday and could stick around for the reading of her will on Monday.

Luckily, his partner would be able to help Garrett

with his caseload while he was out of town. Garrett wasn't sure where to begin with his mother's estate. Until he talked to the solicitor and his sister, his hands were tied. He'd have to close up the house until he could sell it. Neither he nor his sister were in a position to live in or manage a country estate. Finding a buyer would be the easy part, selling it… not so much.

The place was filled with mixed memories for him and his sister, mostly because it had been the start of their new life without their father after a bitter divorce. His mother had poured her heart into the place after purchasing it, her love of the land filling her with the determination to make a success of the place. Garrett's love, however, was for the city. His sister's love of the sea drove her career in the Navy. They'd been three completely different people on different courses in life.

In no time at all, the pilot landed the chopper in Glen Haven, the closest town to Hallbrook that had a private airstrip. Garrett removed his seatbelt, pushed open the heavy door, and waved his thanks to the pilot. He crouched low as he jogged out from under the air current of the blades and made his way to the waiting limousine.

"Good afternoon, Mr. Bradley. Sorry to hear about your mother. Sarah was a fine lady." George

Bowman owned the limousine service, and he still operated some of the bookings for select customers. He was used to Garrett coming and going, although the visits had been few and far between the past few years.

"Thank you. It came as quite a shock." His mother had been an integral part of putting Hallbrook on the map. She'd not only managed to raise him and Angelica on her own, but she'd found the time to create a niche for the small town by attracting tourists to the area in search of artisan crafts made by the locals. She'd given up everything for him and his sister, including her marriage and home. And in return, he'd been a horrible son, making business more important than visiting her more often.

"If you'll drop me at the house, that would be great. It sounds as though I've got a lot to do." Garrett's guilt factor ramped up another notch.

"Ain't that the truth." The man shook his head, putting the car in drive and raising the privacy window. But not before Garrett caught the odd expression peering back at him through the rearview mirror.

Garrett made a mental note of their progress as they got closer to the house.

They passed by several farms, including the

largest dairy farm in the state. Old man Peterson's place. His mother used to treat him to the delicious hand-made ice cream for excellent grades as a reward. His reward, of course, had been getting into Yale and eventually out of Hallbrook.

It wasn't that he hadn't appreciated the town, but he'd loved the action of the city. It was the land of opportunity, a place where you could make your mark, other than by winning first prize for the fattest cow at the 4-H fair.

He spotted his old high school, Turlington High. The place where he'd gotten into his first fight with a bully, protecting a girl. They'd dated on and off the first couple of years of high school, but then her interest had turned more toward the high school quarterback and less on the geeky guy who'd preferred to study.

George turned right onto East Main Street as he made his way through town. The closer they got to the center of Hallbrook, the bigger the houses got. Many of the stately Victorian and Colonial homes had been restored to their former glory by the families who'd inherited them. The place hadn't changed much in the twenty-five years since they'd first moved there, other than the slow growth and addition of businesses and a few more homes. He spotted Sally's Diner and smiled, remembering the place fondly. For Garrett, the diner was where he had his first date, his first kiss, and the best peach pie in the county.

When they'd moved here, he'd been bored out of his eight-year-old mind and hated the hard-labor and dirty chores that had come with living in the country and his mother owning farmland. He'd dreamed of escaping back to the city. It had driven him to study harder to make that happen. His success as an attorney was proof of the determination, but each time he returned to Hallbrook, he felt a tug in the region of the heart.

They reached the outskirts of town, passing Angie's corner grocery and gas that had long since closed the gas pumps, the place now a convenience store for many of the locals. Fresh fruits and vegetables were readily available from farms nearby, but the store was filled with a hodgepodge of other endless items crammed into the place.

George slowed, turning right at his mother's driveway, passing under the stone archway and through the wrought iron gates. The dirt road had been recently recoated with a fresh load of gravel. He spotted the two-story white house seconds before he noticed an unfamiliar dark-blue sedan parked out front. It was an older car that had seen better days, and one Garrett assumed belonged to the woman staying here and taking care of things until he arrived.

George slid the dividing window down. "Here you are, sir. Hope things go well for you."

"Thanks. Don't bother to get out. I can handle everything." He grabbed his travel bag off the seat in front of him, looped his briefcase over his shoulder, and slid out of the car. He stopped to glance around and took a deep breath, inhaling the fresh country air and the scent of blossoming roses. There was no shortage of rose bushes strategically placed all around the house, another of his mother's passions.

The sun would be setting soon, and the front porch looked inviting as a viewing place for a glorious sunset. His mother had loved the orange-red colors that illuminated the sky with the setting sun, and she'd tried to capture the elusive perfect picture on her favorite camera so many times he'd lost count. Tonight, in honor of his mother, he'd do the same. Sunsets like this didn't happen in New York City, at least not with rolling farmland as far as the eye could see. His sunsets came complete with skyscrapers, and he'd be back to those in four days. Four short days to take care of business. It was all the time he could afford to be away from the office.

Garrett approached the house, climbing the three wooden steps that led to the front door. He wasn't sure whether to knock to announce his presence or to simply use his house key. The last thing he wanted to do was scare the poor girl watching over the place. Maybe a combination of both was in order.

Knock. Knock. Knock.

He tried the door handle and discovered it unlocked. Garrett started to push the door open, but it slammed shut, a loud bark coming from inside. He took a step back, unsure of what to do. He wasn't a fan of dogs, not by any means. The dog's bark was deep. Big-dog deep. Garrett swallowed hard, his hand automatically going to the scars on his arm, a reminder of a run-in with a not-so-nice canine.

He heard voices on the other side of the door but couldn't make out what the words over the barking dog. The decision was made for him when the door started to open, and he came face-to-face with three young kids. The boy, who appeared to be the oldest of the three, had a hold on the dog's collar, keeping the huge brown and white Saint Bernard barely in check as danced, trying to break free from the restraint, slobber dripping to the ground.

"Hi, I'm Garrett Bradley. This is my mother's house. Are you all here with April St. James?" He addressed the boy, thinking he was the best option for reasonable answers.

"Yup. She's cooking dinner. Do you need to talk

to her?" The young boy stood straight and tall, answering his question as if he were in charge.

"Yes, that would be perfect." It would be a whole lot better than trying to talk to three kids, something he had zero experience doing as an adult. He was quite surprised Ms. St. James had brought her children and an oversized beast of a dog with her while she watched the house. It was a little unorthodox.

"Melanie, go get her. I've got to hold the dog 'cause you're too puny to handle him." The boy spoke to the oldest of the two girls who couldn't be much more than seven or eight.

"Am not. You get her." Garrett couldn't believe this. He shook his head, trying to figure out what to do.

"Hey there, kids. Why are you hanging half in and half out the front door? This isn't a barn. Shut the door and come back inside." A feminine voice called out from somewhere behind the children.

"There's a man here to see you." The older girl spoke up.

"A man? Oh, good heavens, let him in. It must be Mr. Bradley." The woman's voice was soft and yet persuasive.

"That's what he said. But the dog won't budge," the boy spoke up, trying to pull the dog back.

"Come on, Rufus." The brunette came to his

rescue, all barely-over-five feet of her. She wasn't much of match for the hairy beast, but she did manage to wrestle him back from the door enough for Garrett to step into the foyer.

"Sorry about that." She beamed at him, her eyes a striking shade of sapphire. She kept hold of the dog, much to his relief.

He nodded. "Thanks. I'm Garrett—"

"Bradley. Yes, we've been expecting you. I'm so sorry about your mother." She glanced at the kids and winced. "Kids, why don't you head into the kitchen, and I'll be right in. I need to talk to Mr. Bradley alone for a second."

The older boy shrugged and left; the others close on his heels. Apparently, they didn't care who Garrett was.

"Sorry, I don't like to talk about your mother in front of them. They loved her like a grandmother, and it's been so upsetting to them. I'm sure you understand."

"I do. It's been a shock for everyone, I imagine. I appreciate you stepping in to help keep the house in order and taking care of her horses." April shot him an odd look, one that disappeared just as quickly as it happened. It was the same look he'd seen on George's face.

She extended her hand, "April St. James. It's nice

to meet you, although the circumstances could have been better."

He shook hands with her, holding on a tiny bit longer than necessary. The strength of her grip took him by surprise. So did the warmth. "Garrett Bradley."

"I know you just got here, and I hate to do this, but I've gotten behind at work and need to head to the office. I need to run."

"I'll be fine. I'll make arrangements for everything before I leave so you won't need to worry about a thing." Garrett hoped it would be as easy as he made it sound.

April shrugged as she bit her lower lip, her head tilted to one side. "I hope you enjoy spaghetti because I made a huge pot of it. I thought it would be easier than you needing to find something to cook soon as you got here tonight."

She pulled the dog toward the front room. "Stay, boy." April closed the door behind her, locking him in the room. "If he isn't put up, he thinks he's one of the family and should be able to eat at the table accordingly." She laughed. "I don't usually him let back out until after dinner."

"Sounds like a handful. Looks like a handful. Must be a handful." Garrett forced a smile. April was insane to add a giant dog to her already chaotic mix of responsibility. He followed her down the hall and into the kitchen, the aroma of tomatoes and garlic greeting him. His stomach rumbled. He hadn't had a thing to eat since this morning on his way to the office.

"You have no idea." She grinned. "But you'll get a chance to find out." Her soft laughter was like music.

Garrett frowned, unsure of what she meant. He was almost afraid to ask, but he sure hoped his mother hadn't taken in a dog—especially not one the size of Godzilla. He wouldn't have a clue what to do with it, especially considering his dislike of dogs. He may not have visited his mother often, but they talked at least once every two weeks, and not once had she mentioned getting a dog.

"Let me introduce you to the kids properly. This is Bryan, and he's nine." She tapped the top of his head and then moved on down the row of children, almost like a game of duck-duck-goose. "This is Melanie, and she's seven. And this is Sandy, and she's three. Sandy doesn't talk much, but the doctors say she'll be fine in no time. They've all had a lot to deal with over the past few months, and her way of dealing with the emotions has been silence."

"I'll take your word for it." It sounded as though the kids had gone through more trauma than a child should have to deal with, and it made him wonder about their story. When he was Bryan's age, the trauma of his parents splitting up had been monumental, especially given the divorce was his fault.

April lifted the lid off the first pot. "Just stir this occasionally until you're ready to eat. The noodles get dropped in the sauce, stir them frequently, and they'll be ready in ten minutes if you prefer them al dente, otherwise, let them cook a minute or two longer. Easy enough, right?" April looked at him with confidence in her eyes, a confidence he didn't deserve.

"Smells awesome. Looks as though you made enough to feed an army."

"That'll last you a day, tops, but I'm sure your mother's friends will be stopping by with lots of food to help out. Here's my card if you need anything. You can call, and I'll help any way I can. I know this is going to be a tough transition for you —" she reached out to touch his arm, "—but you'll be fine. I'm sure of it."

"Thanks. I appreciate that. And don't worry, I'll be okay. I've handled this sort of thing before."

"If you say so." April crossed the kitchen to where a wheeled suitcase was parked in the corner. She pulled up the handle and started toward the front door. Garrett and the kids followed, Melanie stopping to let the dog out.

"Here, let me get this for you." He picked it up and hauled it to her car. He would have expected a much bigger suitcase considering the kids.

"Thanks. Don't forget, call me if you need me." She leaned down and hugged each of the kids. "I'll see you three soon, I promise. Be good for Mr. Bradley."

April wasn't making any sense. And why weren't the kids getting in the car with her? And for that matter, why wasn't she getting the dog? Something was seriously wrong with this picture.

She slid in the driver's seat and started the car before manually rolling down her window. "Take care." April waved, put the car in reverse and started to back up.

The motion of the vehicle snapped him out of his trance. "Wait. Where are you going? You can't leave your kids here." Normally calm under fire, Garrett couldn't keep the panic out of his voice.

She stopped the car and leaned toward the window. "They're not my kids, they're yours." April seemed confused. Which was far better than stupefied, and exactly how he felt. She had this all wrong.

"I don't have any kids." The children looked as though they were about to cry, and he felt awful, but he couldn't let April drive off without them *and* the dog.

"Should have known he wouldn't want us." The boy grumbled in a low voice, grabbing his younger sister's hand and taking off for the house. Melanie glanced at April and then glared at him before running to catch up with her brother and sister.

"What's the meaning of this?" Garrett demanded an answer, his patience running out. He could handle a lot of things, but this wasn't in his wheelhouse.

April got back out of the car and faced off with him. "Your mother adopted these children three months ago. Haven't you talked to her solicitor yet? I would have thought—"

Garrett wince. *Adopted.* As in legally hers. Why would his mother adopt kids at this stage of her life? She hadn't even consulted him about such an important issue. And she'd had three months to tell him.

You haven't been home in over six months.

"You thought wrong. What am I supposed to do with them? I don't know the first thing about children. I have a job. An apartment in the city. What am I supposed to do?"

"Step up." Her answer was short and to the point, the thin set of her lips driving the point home. She was serious

He swallowed hard and turned back to the house

where three kids and the dog were waiting and watching.

"I'm sure Charlie will explain everything." The compassion in her voice was genuine, making him feel slightly better.

"Our meeting isn't until Monday, and the celebration of life is tomorrow. Don't you think you could provide me with a few more details? You seem to know a thing or two about the situation." He was desperate, and he couldn't let her leave without a better understanding.

"The children lost their parents three months ago, and your mother didn't want them to end up in the foster care system, so she adopted them with a promise to always do what was best for them. Their mother was a friend of hers from church. I was the assistant caseworker assigned to them, which is why I volunteered to stay with them until you arrived. They know me. They are sweet kids, and it's been hard for them to lose their parents and now their grams."

"Grams?" There was so much he needed to ask her, the meaning of Grams the least of them, but that's what came out.

"It's the name they called your mother, short for grandma."

April got back in her car. "I'm a sucker for these

kids and will do anything I can to help, but right now, I've got to make sure I can keep my job. I've missed a lot of work and need to catch up on my caseload."

"Fine. I'll figure a way through this situation for the next few days until my sister can get leave and decide what she wants to do. Clearly, she's the better option to handle this unexpected situation." He didn't feel as confident as he tried to sound. There were two problems. He didn't know when his sister would be home, and he didn't know a thing about taking care of kids, not even temporarily.

What happens next?
Don't wait to find out...

Head to Amazon to purchase or borrow your copy of LOVE & ORDER so that you can keep reading this contemporary romance series today!

Holidays in Hallbrook – Sweet Promise Press

Welcome to Hallbrook, New Hampshire. A small-town filled with the unexpected, lots of love, and of course, a beloved dog to ramp up the excitement. Home is where love leads you.

Love & Order

A powerful attorney, a woman with a heart too big for her own good, and an instant family neither was prepared for...

Garrett Bradley commands the attention of some of the most influential clients in the country as one of the leading corporate attorneys in New York City, but one phone call changes everything. He must return home to Hallbrook, NH, where he soon discovers he's responsible for three young kids and one monster-size Saint Bernard.

April St. James, the social worker assistant assigned to the children's case before Garrett's mother adopted them, was staying with the children until Sarah Bradley's prodigal son returns home to take up his responsibilities. Unfortunately, it puts her own job in jeopardy.

A powerhouse in the business world but clueless when it comes to children, Garrett turns to April with an offer she can't refuse, enticing her to come to the city as a temporary nanny. The deal will allow her to finally pursue her dreams once the job is done. But three kids, a dog, a nanny, and an uptight attorney don't mix well in a fancy NYC penthouse. And when Garrett makes a mistake at work, he realizes somethings got to give before the situation destroys his reputation, the company, and most importantly—his new family.

Find out if Rufus can help this mismatched pair realize their love is the perfect glue to hold their newfound family together! This sweet tale of family, trust, and total chaos is one you won't want to miss. Order your copy and start reading today!

http://bit.ly/2NGfHgrLOAmazon

Love & Family

A small-town doctor, a woman determined to find answers, and the power of family. Will the truth finally bring peace to these troubled hearts?

Dr. Jake Duncan is a busy man—what with being the local doctor, a member of the rescue squad, a volunteer with the GiddyUp Kids program, and most importantly, raising his young hearing-impaired son, there's not much time for anything else. Especially not an event planner who comes to town looking to stir up trouble for one of the few men he considers a close friend, retired pro bull rider, Chad Andrews.

Hard-charging Gemma Watson is shocked to discover the identity of her biological father on accident. She's determined to pay Chad Andrews a visit but it's not a social call, more of a piece-of-her-mind call. But when Brody, her excitable golden retriever, gets into a bit of trouble and it's 911 to the rescue, her plans change.

To get closer to Chad, and smooth ruffled feathers of the handsome Dr. Jake, Gemma offers to organize a fundraiser event for the rescue squad, and he can't say no. In fact, when it comes to Gemma, Jake is finding it impossible to stop her from getting her way. And he might just love her all the more for it...

http://bit.ly/2lQiVC0LFAmazon

Love & Peace

Sam wanted to be alone and miserable for the holidays, but Megan and her daughter are determined to show him the Christmas spirit. Because sometimes love and peace find you when you least expect it.

Sam Wyatt goes to a cabin in Hallbrook each year at Christmas looking for solitude with the memories of his wife and daughter, who he lost in a car accident a few years ago. Except not long after he arrives, Megan Langley and her daughter take up residence and refuse to leave. A quick call to the rental agent and Sam finds out the cabin has been double booked and he's kicked out to the snowy cold. But when an avalanche closes Tinsel Pass, he's forced to return to the cabin.

Megan was supposed to spend this Christmas celebrating and honoring her mother at her favorite place this year.

When one night housing Sam turns into more, Megan and Becca are resolved to get their Christmas spirit back. They keep Sam busy, giving him zero chance of finding the solitude he craves, especially when a stray dog comes around and Becca's determined to help the mutt.

When the pass reopens, Sam is torn emotionally between the past and present. Can a little Christmas magic save him from making the wrong decision?

http://bit.ly/2mdNPo0LPAmazon

Love & Chocolate - Coming Soon

Love & Hope - Coming Soon

Love & Liberty - Coming Soon

Gold Coast Retrievers – Sweet Promise Press

Special Golden Retrievers help their humans solve mysteries, save lives, and even find love...

Fun, stand-along stories from different authors.

Defending Dakota

The picture of a man she vaguely knew splashed across the front of a tabloid shook Dakota Mitchell to the core. It might be thirteen years after she suffered the double trauma of having her home burglarized the same night her parents died in a car accident, but the man's tattoo reawakened memories locked hidden away. Pressed to discover the truth of what happened that fateful night, she finds out the man has her mother's favorite locket. She teams up with her therapy canine, Halo, to take back what belongs to her—even if it means stealing it.

Colt Jackson is furious when a woman and her golden retriever land in the middle of his stakeout. He can't afford to have her rat them out to his mark and blow the Wingate investigation and he can't trust her not to return and try again. So instead he makes a deal with her, one that will get her what she wants and put the bad guy behind bars.

But when the bad guy gets out on a technicality, it's up to Colt and Halo to save Dakota.

This sweet tale of suspense, danger, and righting wrongs is one you won't want to miss. Order your copy and start reading today!

http://bit.ly/2UeVqQlDDAmazon

Catching Carol – coming soon

When she was a teenager, a Golden Retriever/Lifeguard duo on duty rescued Carol Graves from drowning in the Pacific Ocean. As an adult, she returned to Redwood Cove and has devoted her life to breeding these special dogs for service. Unfortunately, her doctor has ordered that this year's litter be her last. But what will Carol do and who will she be without her dogs?

Isaac Turner still remembers the beautiful woman he and his dog saved from drowning more than thirty years ago. What he doesn't know is where she went or how he can find her now.

Even though their romance was short lived back in the summer of '78, he's never forgotten her. He's an empty nester now and determined to find Carol, curious how her life turned out and if her heart still belonged to him. And the best place to start looking is where they met—Redwood Cove. But will the memories of what tore them apart all those years ago be too much for either of them to put aside?

Join Carol and Isaac—and a very special group of golden retrievers—as they venture into their pasts to discover their futures. This sweet tale of suspense, secrets, and second chances is one you won't want to miss.

The Celebrity Corgi Series – Sweet Promise Press

Loveable corgi's and their celebrity owners in fun stand-alone stories from different authors.

Digging the Driver

As a professional race car driver, Lissa Walker is used to dealing with all sorts of threats. But when a dognapper starts targeting her hometown, she'll do anything to protect her corgi Bella— refusing to take chances. Even if that means hiring Damien Trent, an arrogant, too-smart-for-his-own-good know-it-all. Who also happens to be the one who broke her heart so many years ago.

Damien isn't too thrilled about taking a job that would require him to work in close quarters with Lissa, let alone one that would require him to be a doggy bodyguard. Unfortunately, for the sake of his company's reputation, he has no choice but to stick it out.

The history between the two provides much more friction than any racetrack ever could, but they'll have to put their past differences aside to keep little Bella safe. Everything else-- including the new feelings surging between them--will just have to wait. Can they take it slow and steady when both are so tempted to zoom full-speed ahead?

http://bit.ly/2yV7hJyDTDAmazon

Trinity River Cowboys – Sweet Romance

Ranchers and farmers depend on the Trinity River for water, but when a secret conglomerate starts buying up property by fair means or foul, it's time for the landowners of Tumble County to fight back—Texas style. But what they don't count on, is finding love in the process.

Back in the Rancher's Arms

Dylan Hunter has always loved the girl next door. Part of loving her meant making sure she left their small town to study to become a veterinarian. He just never expected it to take this long for her to come home. His hands are full raising his younger brother and bringing his ranch through the drought, but one look at Kayla and his feelings are back full force.

Kayla Anderson's not prepared to see the guy who broke her heart in high school again, but she can't get out of returning home to be maid of honor at her cousin's wedding. She's determined to have fun and celebrate the special day, despite the fact Dylan is her family's closest neighbor and the best man, and then get the heck out of Dodge.

But Dylan already lost the woman he loved once. This time, he's determined to win her back...

http://bit.ly/2uVHuBRBitRAAmazon

ROMANTIC SUSPENSE

The Gold Coast Retrievers

Six special Golden Retrievers help their humans solve mysteries, save lives, and even find love...

CONTEMPORARY ROMANCE

The No Brides Club

When six friends make a pact not to let love get in the way of their careers, the No Brides Club is born. But could the right man at the wrong time cause them to break their vows to each other?

The Celebrity Corgi Romances

Meet six Corgis who live the high life as celebrity BFFs. One thing's for sure: When their people fall in love, it better be with someone who loves dogs as much as they do!

The Sweethearts of Country Music

Six musicians come together to form an all-girl country band. But when love comes calling, will the ladies be able to balance their musical worlds with their romantic lives?

Holidays in Hallbrook

Welcome to Hallbrook, New Hampshire. A small-town filled with the unexpected, lots of love, and of course, a beloved dog to ramp up the excitement. Home is where love leads you.

<u>Mommy's Little Matchmakers</u>

For these moms, a second chance at love may need a "little" extra help.

First Street Church Romances

These sweet and wholesome small town love stories with the community church at their center make for the perfect feel-good reads!

HISTORICAL ROMANCE

The Pioneer Brides of Rattlesnake Creek

Their fortunes lie out west...and so do their hearts.

Sweet Grove Historical

Go back in time to follow the lives and loves of Sweet Grove's founding families in this historical romance series.

COZY MYSTERY

Pet Whisperer P.I.

Glendale is home to Blueberry Bay's first ever talking cat detective. Along with his ragtag gang of human and animal helpers, Octo-Cat is determined to save the day... so long as it doesn't interfere with his schedule.

Little Dog Diner

Misty Harbor boasts the best lobster rolls in all of Blueberry Bay. There's another thing that's always on the menu, too. Murder! Dani and her little terrier, Pip, have a knack for being in the wrong place at the wrong time... which often lands them smack in the middle of a fresh, new murder mystery and in the crosshairs of one cunning criminal after the next.

The Funeral Fakers

Professional Mourning can be a deadly business. Luckily, these 6 out-of-work actresses are on the job!

Texas Sized Mysteries

The stars at night are big and bright, deep in the heart of Texas... but so is the trouble. These cozy mysteries feature characters who are larger than life and cases just begging to be solved by any reader clever enough to rise to the challenge.

ABOUT THE AUTHOR

Elsie Davis discovered the world of Happily-Ever-After romance at the age of twelve when she began avidly reading Barbara Cartland, the Queen of Romance, and has been hooked ever since. After building her dream log home on top of a small mountain, she turned her attention to do what she loves most, writing. A #1 Amazon category list best-selling author, Elsie writes sweet contemporary romances and romantic suspense from her heart, hoping to share a little love in a big world.

When she's not writing, she can be found birding, kayaking, camping, fishing, playing disc golf, and taking nature walks—hoping to spot wildlife. Basically, she loves all things outdoors, EXCEPT cold weather. She and her husband are avid Caribbean cruisers, but Elsie's favorite vacation was their cruise to Alaska. (In spite of the cold!) Indoors, she enjoys a toasty fire, a glass of red wine, and of course, a great romance with a guaranteed Happily-Ever-After.

https://elsiedavishea.wordpress.com/

Made in the USA
Coppell, TX
05 November 2019

10980351R00222